Revealed
BY YOU

BY

J.M. WALKER

Revealed by You
Copyright 2014, J.M. Walker

ISBN-13: 978-1500352028
ISBN-10: 1500352020

Dedication

I'm dedicating the second part of this trilogy to someone that I miss dearly. I know that she would be so proud of Brett for his strength and growth. Her love for my characters have kept me going even though she's no longer with us.

Brenda Smith Travis, you will always be in my heart and thoughts and this book is dedicated to you. Always and forever. You inspire me. You live on in my words that flow from my fingertips.

Miss you Mama Hen. xx

Revealed by You

Love hard. Love deep.

Acknowledgements

First off, I would like to thank You. When I had no faith, You nudged me. While I was doubting myself, You whispered that I could do better. I could be better. At times when I felt like giving up, you pushed someone or something in my path to help me. Guided me along with a helping hand.

I may not write what everyone approves of but I don't hide who I am. As soon as the first words flowed from my fingertips, I knew it was my calling. I live to tell a story.

As this story grows, the spirituality and love strengthens. You need to fall before you can be picked up.

Without my husband, none of this would be possible. He's my rock. My one. My only.

Thank you to my family and friends for constantly supporting me in my journey of writing. I wouldn't be where I am without each and every one of you.

My PA. Angie Stanton-Johnson. My FS (inside joke). Your faith in me and my writing is astounding and although I know your heart belongs to Garrith, thank you for allowing a little bit of Brett in there as well. ;)

To my book club, you all are amazing and special to me. I'm so thankful to have gotten to know you throughout the years.

Chrissy (C.A. Szarek), thank you for the fantastic blurbs and for the constant support, bestie. I love you!

My team of awesomeness:

My girls. My Jems. You know who you are and your constant support is appreciated and I have no words to describe how much you mean to me.

My beta readers: I can't thank you girls enough for your critique, encouragement, your constant support. Thank you for helping me make Brett's second book much better than the first.

Brenda Wright, my very patient editor. Thank you for everything!! Your patience is awe-inspiring and I will never be able to repay you for all that you do and more.

To all the blogs out there. There are just too many to name but I love each and every one of you. You all have helped me in your own way and for that, I thank you.

Angie Stanton-Johnson, Melinda Huff Bones, Brenda Wright, Jennifer Duncan Robbins with Twinsie Talk Book Reviews. You girls are my sisters and I couldn't do this or the pimpage without you. Thank you for everything, for always hosting my tours and for just being you.

Once Upon a Time Covers: Thank you again for the beautiful and sexy cover!

And last but surely not least, my readers. I wouldn't be where I am today without the support from all of you. You're my rock, my light, my constant encouragement to keep going and trudging on. Thank you to everyone for your support and never ending encouragement. Words cannot describe how much you all mean to me.

Revealed by You Playlist

Here is a list of songs that reminded me of Brett and Evvie, either together or apart. I hope you enjoy them as much as I do. Even if you don't like the music, the words are what captured me and brought me into their world. Now as I listen to them, I think how far Brett and Evvie have become but still have so much to go through before they will finally be happy

.

A deep and powerful love is never quiet, never dormant but loud and fierce. ~ J.M. Walker

Bound to You – Christina Aguilera, Burlesque Soundtrack
Radioactive – Imagine Dragons
Unconditionally – Katy Perry
This is the Best – USS
Stay – Rihanna ft. Mikky Ekko
What Now – Rihanna
Adore You – Miley Cyrus
Wrecking Ball – Miley Cyrus
Loving Me 4 Me – Christina Aguilera
Give Me a Reason – Pink ft. Nate Ruess
Try – Pink
I Am – Christina Aguilera
Mirrors – Justin Timberlake
Demons – Imagine Dragons
Say Something – A Great Big World ft. Christina Aguilera
I'll Be There For You – Bon Jovi
Better Than Me – Hinder
Bad Things – Jace Everett
Haunted – Taylor Swift
What Do You Got? – Bon Jovi
I've Just Seen A Face – Beatles

Revealed by You

Warning
Due to the graphic and adult content, this book is
not suitable for a younger reading audience

ONE

PEOPLE MAY not believe in love at first sight. The first pull. The first thing that tugs at your heart, leading you to that person. Hell, I definitely didn't. Not until I met *him*. My best friend. My lover. Four weeks, three days and eight hours had passed since I've seen Brett MacLean.

The day he left for New York felt like a lifetime ago and I couldn't wait to see him again. For him to come home. We weren't living together yet but I spent every day at his apartment, needing to be close to him in some way. Needing his scent.

Although video chats were a new thing for us, it wasn't the same. I missed his touch, his hot breath against my skin, him telling me what he wanted and how he wanted it, the dark possessive air about him as he claimed me. Even though he was dark and brooding, demanding and controlling, I gave in willingly.

Working with Mathis Verlinden, a powerful billionaire that had his hand in everyone's pocket whether it be legal or not, was good for him. He gave him free rein of his club, *Club Rouge*, and as long as money was made, everyone was happy.

My phone rang, interrupting my thoughts as I leaned against the black town car and waited. The airport was bustling with people, heading to or from places but there was no sign of Brett anywhere.

I frowned when I saw that my oldest brother was calling me. "Hello Evan."

He chuckled. "Always so happy to hear from me."

"I am. Just not when I know a lecture is coming on." He was worse than our father. Having three brothers and a dad and being the baby of the family, being myself was not always easy growing up.

"Now why would you ever think that I would lecture you?"

I rolled my eyes. "Seriously?"

"Have you talked to dad?"

My back stiffened. "No. Why?"

"He's going through some changes. Really odd stuff. Like he's going through man-o-pause or some shit."

I frowned. "He's been through a lot, Ev. A change in life is bound to happen sooner than later."

"Just call him or even better, go see him. I know he would love to spend some time with you."

"You still staying at his place?" I asked, my stomach clenched at the guilt I felt for not seeing our father in a while.

"No but I visit often."

"Thanks for making me feel way better, jackass."

Evan laughed. "Anytime, sis."

I shook my head as he hung up and made a mental note to go visit our dad. After his heart attack a couple of weeks ago, I should really have been over more often.

I sighed. I wasn't going to let it bother me. Today was a happy day. Brett was coming home.

Butterflies flew around in my belly and I had to wipe my sweaty palms every so often on my thighs. God, I couldn't keep still. We talked every night and video chatted as much as we could but I needed more. I always needed more. His touch, his kisses, him telling and showing me how much he loved me.

The sun glowed in the distance on the unusually warm afternoon. I looked down at myself. Was I dressed okay? The white spring dress was long enough to leave something to the imagination but hugged my curves perfectly. Only having the cotton fabric on me and nothing else, sent a thrill down my spine knowing Brett would approve.

A heavy sigh escaped my lips and I bent over, putting my blonde curly hair up in a messy bun. The hairs on the back of my neck tingled making my stomach flip.

I slowly rose to my full height and found Brett standing a few feet away from me. His suitcase in hand, aviator sunglasses on his handsome face and four buttons on his white dress shirt unbuttoned. My stomach flipped, my heart thumping hard against my rib cage at the mere sight of him. God, he was beautiful. Possessive and dominating, dark and sensual. Sex rolled off of him like a cool morning fog.

He pulled off his glasses, his blue eyes locking with mine. A smug smile formed on his hard chiseled face. A dark line of scruff covered his jaw and I couldn't wait to lick every inch of him.

My body bloomed, needing his hands on me after so long but I was frozen. Captivated by his deep blue stare as he stalked towards me.

He handed the driver his bags and closed the distance between us. He cupped the back of my neck, brushing his thumb over my bottom lip. "Hi, *my* Evvie."

Hearing him claim me by just his words, made my insides quiver. "Hi," I breathed. My heart gave a thump. I swore my insides just turned to mush.

He smirked and leaned down to my ear. "I missed you." His lips brushed down the length of my jaw. "I've missed your smell. Lavender. Vanilla. Me."

My heart thumped hard, pounding in my ears as he held me restrained just by his hand and mouth. I couldn't move even if I wanted to.

His fingers brushed down my cheek before capturing my mouth in a hard demanding kiss.

My lips instantly parted, taking his tongue deep inside me. The feel of his warm lips against mine after all of these weeks ignited something I hadn't felt in a while. A wanton need spread through me. I gripped his shirt, pulling him against me. *More.*

A soft groan erupted from the back of his throat as the kiss deepened. Pushing me up against the side of the town car, his hold on the back of my neck tightened.

I moaned, sucking and pulling at his tongue.

He chuckled and released my mouth, trailing kisses down to my ear. "I've missed you so much, lover," he whispered.

"Hmm…I've missed you," I said, leaning my head to the side.

"I can't wait to do nasty dirty things to that hot little body of yours," he growled in my ear, inhaling deep.

I bit my lower lip to keep from panting and brushed a hand down his hard chiseled chest.

His teeth grazed up the side of my neck. "I can't wait to get you alone."

I frowned. We were alo—

"Brett!"

I bristled at a feminine voice coming up behind us and looked past him to see a tall slender woman heading our way. She was dressed in black Capri sweatpants and a tight pink t-shirt and although it was casual, she was gorgeous. She looked like one of those women who could wear a burlap sack and still walk down a runway.

I bit back a snarl and inched closer to Brett. God, what was wrong with me?

She smiled and waved when Brett looked over his shoulder.

The woman placed a hand on his arm and kissed his cheek.

Much to my amazement, Brett only grinned. What the hell? My mouth fell open. Who the fu—

"Evvie, this is Anna Brinson. Anna, this is Evvie Neal," he said, motioning between the two of us.

I didn't care who she was. Why was she all over *my* man and why didn't he introduce me as his girlfriend?

"Brett, darlin', you didn't tell me she was so beautiful." The dark haired woman grabbed my shoulders and kissed both of my cheeks. Sweet vanilla perfume wafted into my nostrils. A slight British accent coated her words and although I instantly found myself not liking the woman, it was still sexy as hell.

My stomach clenched. So he did tell her about me. But why the hell didn't he tell *me* about her?

"How do you know each other?" I asked, grabbing Brett's hand in a firm grip.

He kissed my forehead and pulled away before walking around the other side of the car.

I frowned.

"Oh we go way back. Met in high school, actually," Anna explained, handing the driver her bags.

"Were you friends with his sister?" I asked, opening the door.

Anna blushed. "No."

16

I looked back at Brett.

He shoved a hand through his short brown hair, his jaw clenching as he opened the door. "Get in," he demanded.

Something told me that there was more to their relationship then just friendship. Much more. Realization slapped me in the face. Did he sleep with her?

I got in the car, Anna following in behind me. Sitting across from them, I stewed over what was happening. I had all of these special surprises planned for him. First one being in this car but since we weren't alone, that idea flew out the window.

"You just visiting, Anna?" As much as I wanted to claw her face off, I was trying to be the better person.

She smiled, her green eyes twinkling. "No. I live here."

Of course you do. Why Brett never mentioned her before was beyond me. "How did you guys meet up?"

"Anna works for Mathis," Brett said, not removing his gaze from mine.

"Such a small world when I saw this handsome guy walking into *Club Rouge* the first day," she laughed.

Brett chuckled.

My gaze danced between them, watching them interact with each other.

Brett looked my way every so often and as the minutes went by, I became more and more pissed off.

The two of them talked about work, about Mathis and other shit that I didn't care to listen to. It may have been childish of me but I wanted him all to myself.

"Anna's going to stay at my apartment for a couple of days while hers gets renovated."

My head whipped around. What the hell?

"Is that fine, Evvie?" he asked, his gaze darkening, challenging me to argue with him. Oh I would argue, just not with company around. I was a lady.

I pasted on a smile. "Oh sure. That's quite alright. She can stay there forever if she wants to. See if I care."

Anna looked between us both. "Okay, well thank you. I promise I won't be an inconvenience."

I ignored her and looked out the window. She already was.

***

AS SOON as the town car pulled up in front of Brett's large apartment building, I escaped the confines of the small space. Needing to get away from the beautiful British woman and my boyfriend.

The way they chatted about anything and everything, made me wonder if they haven't kept in contact all of these years. Yes I was jealous. I would be the first one to admit it but who wouldn't be? If it was the other way around, Brett would pound the guys face in.

Brett loves you. I scoffed. I never once questioned his love for me but now, seeing the two of them together when it was supposed to be just him and I, had me wondering what Anna's motives truly were.

We reached the elevator across the large lobby and I punched the button leading to the top floor where Brett's apartment was. I couldn't believe that he would be living with another woman. *They are just friends, Evvie. Just friends.* I repeated the mantra over and over in my head and took a deep breath, easing the racing of my heart.

Laughter boomed behind me and I rolled my eyes and stabbed the button again. The large door opened as Anna and Brett came up behind me and I stepped into the open space. Leaning against the wall, I crossed my arms under my chest.

"Brett, remember when you told Mathis…" Anna giggled and shook her head.

Brett laughed along with her. "If the fucker would have given me full control like he said he would in the first place."

She placed her hand on his arm. "I am Mathis Verlinden. I know all and see all. I am God's gift to everyone," she said, in a fake European accent.

Now they had inside jokes? Really? My blood boiled. I couldn't get away quick enough.

Brett's smile faltered when he caught my stare. His gaze heated, taking me in.

Get over yourself buddy. I'm pissed at you.

The doors opened a moment later and I shoved past them both, stomping down the hall. My head reeled. Did they spend time together in New York? Did she have a boyfriend? Was she after mine? Never experiencing this kind of jealousy before, I didn't like how it made me feel. I was ashamed of myself. My daddy raised me better.

I sighed and unlocked the door to Brett's apartment and headed to his bedroom. Needing to get away, I shut myself in his bathroom. Yes, I ran. Again. But I needed to collect myself. I needed to figure out what the hell just happened.

Squeezing my eyes shut, I gripped the white counter top until my knuckles ached. After all that we've been through, you'd think that this would be nothing but why did I feel like my heart was being ripped from my chest?

The sound of the door shutting made me startle. I looked up and met Brett's stare in the mirror.

"Do you know what I had planned for our drive home?" I bit out.

"No," he said, leaning against the door.

I shook my head. "Of course you don't." I wanted to tell him about the odd phone conversation with Evan but I couldn't concentrate on anything other than the man standing a few feet away from me.

"You're pissed." Brett rolled his sleeves up to his elbows, the veins in his thick forearms protruding at the movements.

My mouth watered as memories of those strong arms holding me, flooded my mind.

Maybe I was overreacting. Anna could be a nice person. I bit back a scoff. No woman could be friends with Brett or even just work for the guy and not want to fuck him. It wasn't possible. I was living proof of it. "Where's your friend?"

"She went back to her place to grab some things," he responded, watching me.

"Did you sleep with her?" The words left my lips before I could even think twice about what I was asking.

His gaze snapped to mine, his jaw clenching. "Why?"

I didn't move from my spot at the counter as he stood behind me. "Did you?" I demanded.

Brett's fingers grazed the back of my neck before trailing down my arm.

The light touch sent goose bumps raising over my skin. My body hummed. It had been way too long. Self-satisfaction wasn't enough when you had this man to take care of your every waking desire.

"Are you jealous?" he asked, placing a soft kiss on my bare shoulder.

"Should I be?" I watched him in the mirror as his lips parted, reining soft feathery touches on my skin.

He fisted a hand in my hair and pulled my head back.

I gasped, my core throbbing at the rough but delicious movement while I gripped the counter tight.

"The answer to your question, my little vixen, is no, I did not fuck her." His other hand wrapped around my throat, squeezing my jaw in a firm hold.

I swallowed. "Ever?"

Brett tugged my head back further. "We're old friends. I've never fucked her."

"Okay," I whispered. As jealous as I was of the beautiful British woman, I believed him. I had to.

Our gazes collided in the mirror.

"Do you believe me?" he asked, his voice lowering.

I nodded.

"Tell me," he demanded.

"Yes, I believe you." But I still had a feeling that Anna wanted more from him than just friendship.

"Good because you are it for me," he whispered, nipping the soft skin just under my ear. "My one."

I smiled. "My only."

A cheesy grin spread on his rugged handsome face.

My body vibrated at my head being restrained by him and I reveled in it. Needed it on a level I hadn't felt in weeks.

"Did you miss me?" he asked, grazing his teeth up the side of my neck.

Yes. "Hmm…no," I teased.

He paused and looked at me in the mirror, momentarily stunned by my lie. His eyes darkened. "It makes me hard knowing how jealous you are."

I licked my lips and smiled. "Not as bad as when you get jealous."

"Keep your hands on the counter," he snarled.

A hot shiver ran down my spine at the hard command but even if I wanted to move, I couldn't. I was frozen in place, needing the control from him that I always so willingly gave in to.

"You didn't miss me? At all?" he asked, smoothing a hand up the back of my leg under my dress. "I think you're lying."

I jumped when his finger brushed over my soaked opening.

A deep growl erupted from his chest as he pushed two fingers into me.

I whimpered as he pumped into me and spread my legs, taking him deeper.

"Your body deceives you, lover," he purred. He released the hold on my hair and lowered to his knees.

Cool air coated my skin when my dress was lifted to my waist.

"Do you know how hard I am, knowing that you weren't wearing any panties all this time?" he husked.

My body bucked when his thumbs spread my folds and his tongue entered my pussy. "Brett," I cried out.

He moaned. "Fuck me, I've missed the sweet taste of you."

Brett lapped at my center, licking all the way up between my ass cheeks, lubricating me.

A hot shiver ran down my spine at the unexpected pleasure in an area no man had ever been before. A rush ran through my body at him taking me to new heights. New amounts of ecstasy that I would only travel to with him.

21

His tongue brushed back down to my core. It thrust into me at the same as his finger brushed over the puckered area at my rear.

God, I missed him. The way he knew everything about my body, what I liked and didn't like, left me breathless. He controlled me, owned me in a way I never thought was possible.

His arm wrapped around my middle as he dove at my core, devouring me to the point of breaking. He held me tight, making love to me with his tongue when his finger entered the tight hole in my rear.

I moaned, clenching around him, embracing the burning of the tight sensation. "*More.*"

He snarled and pushed his finger all the way, pumping into me at a frantic speed.

My body shook as I gasped for breath, feeling an onslaught of pleasure erupting from deep within me. An undeniable amount of bliss exploded from inside of me and I screamed, the powerful release shaking through my body.

After my muscles calmed down, he released me and rose to his full height. He wiped his chin, a smug smile spreading on his face as he unbuckled his belt.

I bent over the counter and waited in baited anticipation.

Brett fisted my hair and turned my head, covering my mouth in a hard bruising kiss. His tongue invaded my lips, taking control as he ran the tip of his cock over my sensitive clit.

I always loved tasting myself on him. The sweet acidic juices from my body, swirling through my senses, making my core pulse.

I jumped, a shiver running down my back while he continued to tease me.

His hips moved, thrusting his cock between the folds of my pussy. The velvet softness of his length rubbed over the hardened nub. New sensations traveled through me at how good it felt.

"Brett, please," I moaned.

His breathing picked up. "Tell me."

"Fuck me. Now," I demanded.

He thrust into me so hard, my waist lifted off of the counter. He didn't wait for me to get used the size of him. He was as desperate for me as I was for him. His hard frantic movements turned rough as he gripped my hips, plowing into me with a fervor I hadn't felt from him in a long time.

"Shit, Evvie." His length swelled inside of me, pouring his semen into my center but his thrusts didn't stop. "Come for me. I need you with me."

I pushed back against him, our bodies slapping as I felt his long cock hitting a bundle of nerves that were meant just for him. A tremor of ecstasy roared through me and I broke, crashing over waves of bliss as his name left my lips.

"Don't move," he said, pulling out of me.

His warmth trickled down my thighs and just when I was about to question him, he thrust between my folds.

A hot shiver ran down my spine as he covered my sex with his release.

"Feel me all over you," he husked.

"I do." I reached between my legs and wrapped a hand around his thick cock. I moved my hips, rubbing myself over the length of him, the fluids from our bodies coating my hand, my thighs, my core.

"Faster," he growled and fisted my hair, pulling me to an upright position.

I leaned my head against his shoulder and squeezed him.

He grunted. "Come on my dick, Evvie."

My body burned as I circled my hips up and down his length. Gasping for breath, I shook, a tremor of a pleasurable high erupting through me as he rubbed over my aching clit. His name left my lips, bouncing off the walls of the bathroom.

His cock swelled and before I could even process what he was doing, he thrust back into my waiting heat, lifting me into the air. "Lean against me."

I did as he said when he grabbed under my knees, spreading me open to take him deeper. I swallowed a gasp.

"Fuck, I've missed your greedy cunt," he growled and pushed into me as deep as he could go.

A whimper escaped my lips, my muscles burning from the added force. I craved the pain, embraced it even as he pumped into me hard.

He held me suspended, pulled out and slammed back into me.

I could feel the liquid from his previous release running down my inner thighs. It was messy, hot and sexy as hell.

His sharp teeth grazed up the side of my neck making my core pulse. He grunted and bit down.

An explosion set off inside of me and I whimpered his name.

Brett thrust into me one last time before shaking through his own release. He kissed my neck, holding me in the air.

Our breathing labored, I sighed in peaceful bliss. "Don't leave. Ever again."

He placed me back on my feet and turned me in his arms. "Next time, you're coming with me."

I smiled and pulled off my dress.

Brett wrapped an arm around my middle and brushed his knuckles over the top of my mound before pushing a finger through my folds.

A moan escaped my lips and I gripped his shoulders tight, digging my nails into the hard contours of his muscles.

He leaned down, his hot breath scorching my neck as he inhaled. "I've missed smelling me on you." His finger entered me, pushing his semen deep inside of me.

A shudder tore through me and I threw my head back, slowly moving my hips against his hand.

"Do you like that, my little vixen?"

I nodded and chewed my bottom lip. "I've missed you being inside of me."

His blue eyes darkened, filling with hunger knowing that I wasn't just talking about his cock.

Him in general, I've missed. I never wanted to be away from him again. I didn't care how long it was for.

His thumb pushed against my clit, setting off a quick explosion.

I shook, trembling in his arms as I came hard and fast.

A smug smile formed on his lips as he brought his hand to my mouth. "Open. Taste our orgasms, lover."

My lips parted, the sweet scent of my arousal mixed with his previous salty release rushed into my head, making my mind spin.

I took his fingers in, sucking them as hard as I could.

His nostrils flared. "*Swallow*," he growled.

I did as I was told, my pussy pulsing at him being inside of me in more ways than one.

He replaced his fingers with his mouth. Biting, nipping, sucking my tongue in hard rough pulls. "I've missed you. So fucking much."

My heart swelled to the point of exploding but I needed to taste more of him. I gently pushed him back and with shaky legs I turned on the bath before looking back at him. "Video chats aren't as satisfying, lover boy?"

He grinned and unbuttoned his shirt before kicking off his pants.

My mouth watered at the glorious sight standing before me. His tanned hard body, chiseled and strong from hours of working out, his length growing, begging for my touch again. God, I couldn't get enough of this man.

"See something you like?" he asked, taking a step towards me.

I met his gaze and licked my lips, waiting.

"*Kneel.*"

That one hard demand always did me in. Lowering to the floor, my skin hummed as I knelt before him.

His nostrils flared as he wrapped a hand around his growing erection. He leaned down and gripped my jaw, pushing my head back. Placing a hard kiss on my mouth, he sucked my bottom lip before releasing me.

I moaned, swaying towards him at the delicious impact.

He smirked. "It's been over a month since I've fucked that pretty mouth of yours."

A breath left me on a whoosh. I would never get used to the way he spoke so casually about sex.

He licked back into my mouth. "You're going to swallow my dick and then I'm going to fuck that tasty pussy over and over again for the rest of the night. You want that?"

I panted and nodded.

"You want me inside of you, filling you with my come?" he purred.

"Oh God, yes."

"Good. It's been too long." He leaned his head from side to side, cracking the tendons in his thick neck. His gaze met mine, his hold on my jaw tightening. A wicked glint flashed in his heated stare. "You have no idea how much I want to come all over that hot little body, making you smell like me. Marking you as mine."

My core pulsed at the image he put in my head.

"Hmm...maybe my little vixen would like that."

The way he dominated and took control, always left me aching and panting for more. I craved him. He was my drug and I was like a junkie that needed my fix. I wouldn't be satisfied until I got my fill of him. A dark part of me knew that I would *never* be satisfied and that sent a thrill down my spine.

Two

THE BLACK satin dress hugged my pale curves, the hemline stopping just above my knee. The built in bra enhanced my already full bust giving me a look of sex appeal that I normally didn't embrace.

I pinned my curly hair up on my head as Brett entered the bedroom. Since he had been away, I couldn't leave his place, needing to be as close to him as possible, so I moved some of my clothes in.

Warm arms wrapped around my middle followed by a light peck on the side of my neck. "Hmm…I enjoy seeing your stuff in my home."

"Really? It doesn't freak you out?" I asked, turning in his embrace.

Brett frowned. "Why would it freak me out?"

I poked him in the chest. "Because you are Brett MacLean. Budding super star in the nightclub world," I teased.

He rolled his eyes and cupped my ass, pulling me flush against him. "Knowing that a piece of you is always here, does not freak me out, Evvie."

My heart thumped.

Since he came home from New York a week before, something switched in our relationship. I didn't realize it until I was lying in his arms every night, staring up at the ceiling wide awake. I more than loved him. It was an all-consuming powerful need that I felt. I had to have him. Those same words he told me weeks before, reined in my mind. We were hungry, desperate for each other and we couldn't get enough.

I cleared my throat and pushed out of his grasp. "We have to go."

"We have time," he growled in my ear and pulled me back in his arms.

I smiled. Even if we didn't, he didn't care. He had shown me every day since he got back how much he had missed me. He cooked for me, showered with me, and spent every waking

27

moment with me. Even when we were at work we were always together.

And tonight, he would make time again to show me how much he missed me. How much he needed my touch. You'd think that he was gone for years but being gone for just a month, almost did us in.

He released me and stepped back. "Bend over the bed and lift your dress. And, lover?"

I did as he said and looked up at him over my shoulder.

A wicked glint flashed in his gaze. "I'll try not to be too messy."

***

MY MUSCLES ached, burned and twitched with every movement. Every step I took, I could feel him deep inside of me. Marking me. Owning me. He took possession of me from the very beginning. With one look, one touch, I was his.

As we walked hand in hand into Brett's club, *Club Red*, I couldn't help thinking about the last week. And to think, I would have him all to myself in two weeks. In Mexico. No cares, no worries, just him and I. To enjoy each other's company, to get to know one another more. We may have been in love but our relationship happened so quickly, we really needed to take a breather. I didn't know his favorite color. I didn't know what movies he liked to watch, if any at all. My stomach clenched. I hardly knew anything about him.

The hairs on the back of my neck tingled.

I looked up and met his gaze.

He kissed my head. "Thinking about me?"

I smiled. "I always think about you."

A smug grin spread on his handsome face as he wrapped a hand around my neck. "Were you thinking how just a half an hour ago, my cock was buried deep inside your pussy?"

My core pulsed. "God, even your words turn me on."

He chuckled and kissed my nose. "I love you," he whispered in my ear.

My heart swelled and I linked our fingers as we walked down the dim narrow hallway. "I—"

"Surprise!"

We stopped in our tracks as the lights flashed on and a group of people surrounded us. I gaped at the multi-colored balloons and streamers hanging on the ceiling.

Anna greeted us, wearing a short black satin dress much like the one that I was wearing. She squealed and threw her arms around Brett, forcing him to let go of me. "Happy Birthday, gorgeous."

My mouth fell open. *Birthday?*

Brett's cheeks flushed and he looked away. "My birthday isn't until Sunday, Anna."

"Why the hell didn't I know this?" I asked, grabbing his arm and turning him towards me.

He met my stare, his mouth grim.

"Uh…I'll be mingling. Come find me when you're done." She turned on her heel and headed in Kane Stohl's direction. My roommate and Brett's bouncer flashed a toothy grin when he saw the British bombshell approaching him.

"Evvie."

I looked up at Brett. "Why didn't you tell me?"

He shrugged.

The movement was so casual yet it still sent a flutter through my belly.

"It's just another day," he mumbled and nodded at people as they walked by us.

"Brett," I said, my voice firm.

He raised an eye brow and wrapped an arm around my waist. "I didn't think you would make a big deal of it."

I pushed him but his hold only tightened. "Of course it's a big deal. It's your birthday."

"So?" he said, kissing my forehead.

I huffed and pried out of his grip. The fact that Anna knew about his birthday and that I didn't, pissed me off. "How come she knew about it then and not me?" I winced at the whine in my voice. What the hell was wrong with me?

His eyes searched my face. "Is that what the problem is, Evvie?" he asked, pinching my chin.

I tried shoving my head out of his grip but he held me firm in his hand.

"Are you jealous that she knew it was my birthday and you didn't?" he asked with a teasing lilt to his voice.

He wouldn't be teasing me if the situation was reversed. I pulled my head from his grip and glared. "I know we're both knew at this relationship thing but *I'm* your girlfriend. I'm supposed to know these things about you."

"I'm sorry. I didn't realize my birthday was that important to you," he said, trying to fight back a smile.

"That's not the issue and you know it. I'm the one that you're in love with." I pointed at myself. "I'm the one that you're fucking and I hardly know anything about you."

Throats cleared around us, reminding me that we weren't alone.

My cheeks heated. "I'm so—"

His eyes narrowed and he grabbed my hand, dragging me behind him.

Once reaching the hallway to his office, I pulled out of his hold. "Brett, stop. I just—"

He spun on me, slamming me up against the wall and placed a hard kiss on my lips. His hands roamed down my body before cupping my ass.

A moan escaped my lips as his kiss deepened.

All too soon he released me and wrapped his arms around my shoulders. "I love you. Don't fucking forget that, Evvie."

I sighed, snuggling into his chest. "I just realized that I hardly know anything about you."

He leaned back and cupped my face. "What are you talking about? You know more about me than anyone. I let you in. *You,* Evvie. No one else. Ever."

"I know but—"

"But what?"

"Never mind. It's stupid," I grumbled.

His eyes warmed. "Nothing you say is stupid. Tell me."

30

"I just…" I chewed my bottom lip. "I don't know your favorite color. I don't know what movies you like to watch. I don't even know you're favorite food."

The corners of his mouth tugged. "Horror movies and anything I can eat off of you."

My cheeks burned. "That's—"

"And you seriously don't know my favorite color?" He laughed. "Hasn't it been obvious?"

"I…" *Red, you moron.* My neck heated. "Okay. That one's dumb but I still don't know a lot of other things about you."

He smiled and placed a soft kiss on my mouth. "Those are things that we'll find out in time. We don't need to know them right away, Evvie."

I huffed. I was never a patient person. Needing to know everything about him now, I had to force myself to be patient and wait. *Ugh.*

"And we will have two weeks to ourselves to learn more about each other," he purred against my lips.

Our trip to Mexico couldn't come quick enough. I realized this when I found Anna standing at the end of the hall, watching us. Her eyes were cold as she sneered my way.

A chill ran down my spine and I held Brett closer.

Her gaze landed on him and she licked her lips.

Here I thought I was the only one that was jealous. Anna was in love with my boyfriend and he had no idea.

Bile rose in my throat. Now I had two women to worry about.

I cupped the back of his neck and brought his mouth down to mine, shoving my tongue between his lips. Needing to claim him, to show Anna that he belonged to me. *Mine.*

When I looked back down the hallway, she was gone.

***

AS PISSED off as I was that I wasn't the one who planned the birthday party for Brett, I did enjoy myself.

Anna went all out. Invited everyone that Brett knew. His sister and her boyfriend. I even saw my brothers, Evan and Ethan. Everett of course, was nowhere to be found, as usual. A sad sigh escaped my lips. He was the one that I worried about the most.

I watched as Brett's face lit up when his gaze landed on his sister. The small petite woman laughed and wrapped her arms around his neck as he swung her around.

The larger man that she was with, was Hollywood beautiful. Blond hair, blue eyes. He looked like he just walked out of a magazine.

Brett looked my way, his smile widening. He nodded at me and the three of them headed in my direction when Anna stepped in front of him.

Heat flushed through my body as he looked down at her.

She looked at me over her shoulder and winked before turning back to him. Placing her hands on his chest, she let them graze down his torso.

I bit back a snarl as I watched the action before me. How could he—

He frowned and gripped her wrists, stopping her from going any further.

A breath left me on a whoosh and I turned away.

The hairs on the back of my neck stood on end as I felt him approach the booth I was sitting in. It was the same booth we had had some fun in after too many drinks a couple of weeks ago. Memories reined in of that night. Tequila, rum, me bent over the bench...desire curled in my belly and I let out a sigh. I liked to think of it as our booth.

"Evvie."

I jumped at the deep smooth voice in my ear and I looked up at Brett before noticing that his sister and her boyfriend stood beside him.

His eyes warmed. "I want you to meet my sister."

The small woman smiled and held out her hand. "We've met once before, but I'm Keisha. It's so nice to see my brother finally settle down with a good woman," she laughed.

32

As opposed to a non-good woman? "Thank you." I returned her hand shake. "I think."

The larger man with her chuckled. "All he does is talk about you." He held out his hand. "I'm Garrith."

I nodded. I remembered him as well, drinking his life away a couple of months ago. The couple looked happy, whole. Complete.

I watched as Keisha fingered a small black collar around her neck when Garrith placed his arm around her shoulders.

"We have to go. Just wanted to say hi and meet the woman who finally captured my brother's heart," Keisha explained.

We said our goodbyes and they left, hand in hand out of the club.

"What's wrong?" Brett asked, sliding into the booth beside me.

"What did Anna want?" I asked. Every so often she would look our way, her gaze filling with a longing for the man that was with me.

"Wanted me to mingle," Brett said, brushing his finger down my arm.

"She's in love with you." As soon as the words left my lips, I believed them myself. I tried convincing myself that she didn't have feelings for my boyfriend. I just met the woman but the look I had seen on her face every time she looked at him, reminded me that I gave him that look also.

He stiffened beside me. "She is not."

I scoffed and turned to him. "No? How come she touches you every time she can or looks at you with a longing like she needs to have you?"

He shook his head. "That's not tr—"

"Don't say it's not true because it's the same look that *I* give you."

He sighed and scrubbed a hand down his face. "She was in love with me in high school but I thought she got over it. It's been years since I've seen her. I expected her to move on."

A laugh escaped my lips.

He frowned. "What?"

"As much as I don't like the way she looks at you, I get it. If it was me, I would never be able to get over you, Brett."

His mouth inched closer to mine. "I don't want you to get over me."

I smiled. "She just better remember that you're mine."

"Even if she doesn't, she won't get what she wants," he said, brushing his lips across mine.

"You don't know the power of a woman," I whispered.

He lifted his head, his eyes narrowing before he pinched my chin. "Do you trust me?"

I swallowed at the harsh tone of his voice. "Yes, but I don't trust her."

His hand wrapped around my throat, holding my head in place as he stared intently into my eyes. "I don't expect you to. But you better trust me. I love you. You are it for me. I don't want anyone else. How many times do I have to tell you that?"

I huffed. "I'm not questioning that. I just worry that she'll try to dig her claws into you."

His mouth pressed against mine, hard and demanding. "Don't. I am *yours*."

I kissed him back, pouring everything into the touch. He just came home a week ago and already issues had begun, thanks to other people. We needed to get away. To be alone. Our trip couldn't come fast enough.

He placed small pecks on my lips before wrapping his arms around me, whispering that he loved me over and over again in my ear. I didn't doubt his love. Never have. But when I saw a person that had previously threatened to destroy our relationship come into the club, I questioned whether we were strong enough to deal with *her* again.

Three

CLAIRE FUCKING Morgan. After her claiming that Brett had gotten her pregnant and then to accuse him of beating her, if I never saw her again, it would be too soon.

The vibrant red haired woman headed our way, her full glossy lips turning up into a sneer as she caught sight of me.

"Shit," Brett snarled.

The bitch from hell slid into the booth across from us, her grin widening. "Well, it's nice to know that you got home safe, Brett."

Brett tensed beside me. "Why the hell do you care?"

She crossed her arms under her full chest and sat back, her gaze landing on me. "Keeping him satisfied, Evvie?"

My jaw clenched. "More than I can say for you."

Her green eyes turned cold. "Why don't you go do your job and get us some drinks?"

I scoffed. "Please. I'm no one's bitch, especially not yours."

"Claire, you need to leave," Brett stated, his voice firm.

Claire smiled. "Now where's that brother of yours? I heard he was coming tonight." Her voice dripped with lust at the sexual innuendo.

My blood boiled. After the first time they had slept together, he promised he wouldn't again, but knowing him, it wouldn't surprise me if he had. As much as it would piss me off, I couldn't control what my brother did. Just the thought of Claire digging her claws into another person I loved made me sick to my stomach.

"Hey Ev."

I looked up as Ethan approached our table.

"Ask and you shall receive." Claire grinned. "Hey, gorgeous. I was just asking where you were."

Ethan's big body tensed, his gaze landing on the woman sitting across from us. A woman he had been with before he knew what kind of person she really was. "I...what...shit."

I frowned. "Ethan?"

He scrubbed a hand over his shaved head and shook himself. "I gotta go." With that, he turned on his heel and left.

Claire moved to get up but I grabbed her wrist, stopping her. Her eyes narrowed, looking at my hand on her before she met my gaze.

"You leave my brother alone," I snarled.

She pulled out of my grip. "Tell your brother that."

I watched her get up and leave, following Ethan. Once she caught up to him, she pushed him against the wall, grinding her hips against his. His hands automatically fell to her waist, gripping her in no doubt a tight hold.

Bile rose in my throat and I turned away before I could see anything else.

"He can take care of himself, Evvie."

I huffed and met Brett's stare. I was worried for my brother. He had been in and out of jail most of his young life so the first chance he had with a woman, he took it. She would destroy him. Eat him up and spit him out before he even knew what was happening.

I was the youngest of my siblings but why was I always doing the protecting?

***

MY SKIN hummed, adrenaline pumping through me as I walked by Brett. I could feel his gaze on my body as he followed behind me.

I needed to get away. To get away from his guests. From the women that were in love with him. From reality in general. I wanted him and only him. The feel of his skin against mine. Him deep inside of me. Just *feel*.

In a quick jaunt, I went up the steps to the second floor of his club. No one went up there. Ever. It was mostly storage rooms, two bathrooms and empty tables and chairs.

Knowing he was still following me, I stopped once I found the perfect spot. It over looked the edge so you could see the whole vast expanse of the main floor of the club but it was dark.

The music boomed. People danced as the regulars and customers filed in, mingling with the guests from Brett's birthday party.

I didn't want to be rude in stealing him from his friends but we were both distracted. After Claire started practically fucking my brother in front of everyone, I had to get out of there. I could have just left but I didn't want to give her that satisfaction.

Hot breath scorched my neck and I smiled, licking my lips. He knew me well. One heated look and he was on me, taking what he wanted and giving me what I needed.

Brett ran his hands up under my dress, squeezing my hips.

I pushed my ass against him, the hard erection in his pants twitching under my touch.

The deep base of the music pumped through me as the desire I felt for this man heightened, giving me that extra edge. It worked better than alcohol. The lust filled courage poured into me, seeping into my bones as I rubbed my ass over the bulge between his legs.

He growled in my ear and lifted my dress to my hips before landing a sharp swat on my ass.

I whimpered.

He rubbed the spot of my flesh in a smooth circle before slapping it again.

My core pulsed, liquid seeping between my thighs. I gripped the edge of the railing, my gaze travelling over the crowd below us.

I bent at the waist, giving him the angle that he needed when he thrust into me so hard, I was lifted onto the balls of my feet. I gasped, my eyes rolling into the back of my head as he forced the pleasure from my body.

No words were said, no kissing required. Just pure raw animalistic fucking.

I loved it and I loved the man doing it. Giving us both the satisfaction that we craved. He appeased my hunger for him but always left me wanting. Needing more.

His long length pushed deep, spreading me open as he pounded into my pussy. He grunted, filling me.

A tingle spread through my body. The thought of losing control in a room full of people, sent a thrill down my spine.

He hit the bundle of nerves, setting me off.

I screamed, coming around him, my cries of ecstasy swallowed by the loud music.

His cock swelled and just when I thought he was about to come, he pulled out and ran the tip of his length over the tight area between my ass cheeks.

A hot shiver ran down my spine.

He pushed against me but not enough to enter me. Just enough to leave me curious, panting with need. He repeated his movements, rubbing the liquid from my core up to the tight hole at my rear.

A moan escaped my lips and I gripped the railing tight.

Brett fisted my hair, pulling me up right and spun me in his arms. In a quick move, he lifted me, wrapping my legs around his hips. He slammed me against the wall and gripped my throat, staring intently into my gaze.

His eyes heated, darkening with desire as he drove into me with a fervor I craved.

I watched him lose it. His brow crinkled, his jaw tensing, small bursts of air left his full lips.

He powered into me, stretching me to meet his size. He thrust into me one last time before quaking around me, shaking through his release. He came so hard, I could feel him spurting his warmth into me.

At that point I kissed him, swallowing his moans and grunts of pleasure. My heels dug into his ass, taking him as deep as possible and not letting go. I didn't ever want to let go.

Running my fingers through his hair, I pulled him against me, deepening the kiss. His hips stopped moving and we just felt. Him inside of me, my core clenching around him. It felt like home. Pure and utter mind blowing bliss.

His tongue pushed against mine as he devoured my mouth. He swallowed my moans and whimpers of pleasure and ran his hands over my body.

A chill ran down my spine and I opened my eyes to find Anna watching us. Again.

Even though it was dark, I could see the coldness in her gaze that was also mixed with lust. At that point, I wasn't jealous when I was the one that Brett was fucking at that very moment. But I had a feeling that in time, just like Claire, Anna would do anything to get a grip on my boyfriend. It was only a matter of when.

"What's wrong?" Brett whispered, cupping my face in his hands.

I smiled up at him, reveling in the feel of him still inside me. "Nothing. At all." I kissed him again, staking claim on what was mine.

My core clenched around him making him jump. I grinned and did it again.

He sucked on my bottom lip before a wicked glint flashed in his eyes. He nipped up the side of my neck, inhaling deep. Smelling me.

God, I loved it when he did that.

"I could live in you, lover," he breathed against my neck.

My heart swelled and I wrapped my arms around his neck bringing his mouth back down to mine. My gaze travelled back to the corner where Anna once was but she was gone.

"I could spend the rest of my life buried deep inside of you, giving you the pleasure I know you crave," he purred against my lips.

"Hmmm…tell me more," I panted.

He smirked and started moving his hips.

I looked down, watching his cock thrusting in and out of me. Glistening by the juices of our bodies, a shiver ran through me at the sight.

"My dick fits perfectly inside of you, spreading you open, splitting your pussy wide as I fuck you," he husked.

The veins of his length protruded around his thick cock. I could feel every ridge, every inch of him as he moved inside of me at a slow tortuous pace.

"What do you want?"

I looked up and met his dark heated gaze. "More," I moaned. "Make me feel you for the rest of my life. I want to break."

His thrusts sped up as he gripped under my knees, pushing them to my chest. "For the rest of our lives, I promise you, Evvie, I will make it so you dream and think of only me. I am the food for that hunger that lives deep inside of you."

I whimpered as his thrusts deepened, mixing with his erotic words, sending me over the edge of pure ecstasy.

"And you are mine. My addiction. My lover. My Evvie. *Mine*."

Four

AFTER OUR rendezvous on the second floor, I couldn't help but feel as though we were being watched. Yes, Anna had caught us but Brett was the owner and I was his girlfriend. So we had sex in public? It wasn't like it was in the middle of the crowd or anything.

I was never into exhibitionism until I met Brett. He brought out this urge in me. This deep seeded need to be owned, controlled. *Marked.*

It's like I was getting used to his possessive ways or even wanted them for that matter. I couldn't explain it but whenever a man looked at me and Brett didn't do anything like he did in the beginning, it bothered me. But then I felt like a tool when I realized that the only reason Brett didn't notice was because he was paying attention to me.

When he looked at me, nothing else mattered. It was all about me and that's it. He saw *me* and I loved him more and more each day because of it.

I watched him mingle but his gaze kept glancing my way. I smiled and waved and I swore he stood up a little straighter each time.

Making my way to the ladies room, I went about my business. As much as I didn't want to lose the feeling of Brett being inside of me, I needed to clean myself up. I always enjoyed the feeling of his semen running down my inner thighs, reminding me of where he's been. I smiled to myself knowing he would like that as well.

While I was washing my hands, the door closed, a lock clicking in place. I looked up and found Anna leaning against the wall.

Her brown hair was pulled back in a tight bun, showcasing her beautiful porcelain features.

I may have been pale as well, but Anna might as well have been called fucking Snow White. She was just as gorgeous, if not more so.

I remained calm, wondering why the hell she would lock the door in the first place. "Problem?" I asked, drying my hands.

Anna chewed her bottom lip, her eyes frantically searching around the small bathroom before finally landing on me. "I...I saw you."

The back of my neck heated but I shrugged it off. "I know. I saw *you*."

Her cheeks reddened. "Is he happy? With you?"

I frowned. "Listen, Anna, I don't know where you think you get off questioning—"

"No. I'm sorry." She shook her head and took a step towards me. "And I'm sorry for walking in on you." Her cheeks flushed.

My face went red hot but I ignored it and noted the mascara around her eyes and the redness in them. "I know you're in love with him."

She gasped, her hand flying up to her chest. "I...no..."

"You don't have to lie about it. I can see it in your eyes," I said, leaning against the counter.

"I..." She sighed. "We were close in high school but after his parents died, he shut everyone out." Her voice became thick with emotion, making her British accent more pronounced.

"Did you ever tell him how you feel?" I didn't know why I was asking these questions. I guess I wanted to know more about him. A part of me felt jealous over not knowing him at a time where he was happier. Could I give that happiness back to him?

Anna scoffed and leaned over the counter while grabbing a paper towel. "I tried." She looked at me in the mirror. "He loves you. I don't...I don't want you thinking I'm here to ruin things for you. I'm not like that."

My gaze searched her face. I wanted to believe her but after the shit with Claire Morgan, I didn't know if I could trust her or any woman again for that matter.

Anna looked away. "I know you don't believe me. Hell, I wouldn't believe me either. Some random woman coming home with my boyfriend..." She laughed. "You handled it way better than I would have."

"Well I was surprised to see you. Brett never mentioned you at all." My stomach twisted. And why was that?

Anna's eyes saddened. "I figured as much. After high school, I moved. I needed…"

"To get away from him?" I finished for her.

She nodded. "I'm sorry, Evvie. I really like you. At first I thought I had a chance when you weren't in New York with him but then when I met you and saw the way he looks at you, I knew you had his heart."

My skin heated. "When was the last time you saw him?"

Anna cleared her throat. "Evvie, maybe—"

"Tell me."

"Two weeks before he came to New York. But I had no idea he was going to show up at Mathis' club," she said quickly.

"You were here?" I asked, trying to ease the racing beating of my heart.

She nodded and chewed her bottom lip. "We met up for coffee."

I gaped at her. Why didn't he tell me? If they were so close, why would he keep his friendship with her a secret from me?

"I'm sorry, Evvie. I didn't know about you…" Her mouth clamped shut.

My eyes widened. "He didn't tell you about me? At all?"

She shook her head. "Not until he came to New York but please don't think—"

"Anna, thank you." I walked past her and stormed out of the bathroom.

"Evvie, please. I didn't mean to cause problems," she said, rushing up behind me.

I stopped and placed a hand on her arm. "I don't blame you for falling in love with him. I get it. He makes it very hard to control your feelings. But I do blame him for not mentioning me to you when we were together while you had your coffee date."

She chewed her bottom lip. "I…I'll pack my things and be out by the end of tomorrow."

I shook my head. "No. Stay for as long as you need." I was going to make Brett fucking stew over this shit he's pulling.

I turned and headed in the direction of the open space of the dance floor. The back of my neck tingled and I knew Brett was watching me but I wasn't ready to face him. Yet. I was going to make him beg for my forgiveness.

Walking up to DJ Nitro, I requested a song and headed back to the crowd that was moving to the deep bass of the music.

I caught Anna's eye and motioned for her to join me on the dance floor.

She hesitated a moment before dancing along beside me. "Brett's watching you," she yelled over the music.

I smiled. "Good. Let's give him a fucking show." I grabbed her hand and we spun around each other, while moving our hips to the beat. Even though I was pissed at Brett, I actually was having fun. Anna and I laughed, danced and gave the men around us a taste of what they were missing.

I knew Brett was watching us. I didn't even have to look in his direction to know that he couldn't take his eyes off of the display of dirty dancing before him. The regulars and the staff knew that I was his. I laughed. I bet they were wondering what in the hell his girlfriend was doing grinding on another person, and a woman for that matter.

After a couple of songs, sweat ran down my back, my heart beating hard against my ribs. Adrenaline pumped through my body and my cheeks heated as the men surrounded us, no doubt fucking us in their minds.

The next song ended when Anna's eyes widened. She let go of my hands and took a step back.

Heavy arms encircled my waist, pulling me against a hard body. The scent of leather and man invaded my nostrils making my heart flutter.

"You have no idea how fucking pissed I am right now, do you?"

I smiled at the deep growl in my ear. I could guess but I didn't care. "Tell me."

His teeth grazed up the side of my neck, before nipping my ear lobe. "Do you like having all of these men watching you?" he asked, his fingers digging into my hip.

Call it immature of me but I got enjoyment out of his jealousy. "Did you like watching me, Brett? Did it turn you on seeing me dance with Anna?"

"Just you standing there turns me on, lover." His voice lowered. "Watching you use your body to get a reaction from men, pissed me the fuck off."

I tilted my head back and looked up at him. "You know you enjoyed watching me move my hips back and forth against her." I did the same to him. God, I loved teasing him. I loved seeing how far I could push him before he would break and I knew he liked doing the same to me.

His hand moved up to cup my jaw before he leaned down to my ear. "The only one that I want you grinding your ass against is me. Man or woman, I get jealous. Your body is fucking mine. You, are mine. Did you forget that?"

I swallowed hard at the deep husk of his voice.

A wicked grin spread on his handsome face. "I think you did. Do I have to show you how much you belong to me? I could bend you over and fuck you right here and no one would even notice."

Anna would, because she was standing right in front of us but just the thought of him doing something like that to me in public, made my core quiver.

I licked my lips. "I didn't forget. I think *you* did."

"Never." His fingers grazed down the vee of my dress before gripping my other hip. "I could never forget that you belong to me. Your body, mind, soul...all mine, Evvie. Even when you're mad at me, which I know you are, you're still mine."

Desire unfurled deep in the pit of my belly. The heat from his body radiated into mine and I couldn't help but want him right then and there.

I watched as Anna started dancing with a guy a few feet away from us. Her tall slender body moving to the beat of the music. The man was practically drooling over her and when she looked back at me, I waved.

She laughed and shook her head, shrugging before continuing to dance with the guy that couldn't keep his hands off of her.

I wanted Brett to be mad like I was mad at him. I wanted him to know how much I was hurt that he never once mentioned me to her or her to me. I wasn't a child. I didn't play games. If he was that embarrassed over me that he couldn't tell his old friend about me, then I was at least going to give him something to be embarrassed over.

I took a breath and moved my hips against him. I could feel the bulge in his pants grow as I ground my ass into him.

His nose brushed up the length of my neck, his hand grazing down the side of my body to my hip. He squeezed and I knew right then that he was losing it and fast.

Satisfaction flew through me and I reached behind me before cupping the erection between his legs.

His breathing picked up, his hips thrusting to the movements of my hand.

Just when I knew he was getting worked up, I released him and walked away. Heading in the direction of his office, I brushed a shaky hand through my hair.

Once reaching the hallway, I was pulled by the arm into a dark corner and pushed up against the wall.

Brett spun me, his nostrils flaring. His big body shielded me from the onslaught of viewers as his fingers grazed down the side of my neck to the vee in my dress. He didn't say anything. He didn't have to because I already knew that he was pissed but turned on just the same.

His hand pulled the top of my dress down, exposing my breast.

The cool air washed over my skin, making my nipple harden.

He licked his lips and brushed his thumb over the erect peak.

I inhaled a gasp, a jolt of pleasure shooting straight to my groin. I lowered the zipper on the front of my dress.

His gaze followed my movements. "Completely exposed for *my* enjoyment."

The way he growled *my* let me know that this was all for him. He would take what he wanted from me and he wouldn't stop until he got it. I loved when he got like this. The possessive need to mate. To mark me. Remind me who I belonged to.

He smirked and brushed his knuckles down my stomach to my panties.

Screw it. I gripped the sides of my thong and ripped it clean off my body and stuffed the fabric in his suit jacket pocket.

He leaned his head from side to side, cracking the tendons in his thick neck before he lifted me and pushed me up against the wall. "You like me fucking you in public, lover? You crave my body just as much as I crave yours. So much, in fact, that you're willing to fuck anywhere."

Licking my lips, I gripped his suit jacket. "You crave me more."

He grinned. "You have no fucking idea. I'm addicted to you."

Reaching between us, I undid the zipper of his pants, digging my heels into his ass. My core throbbed, aching for him. Needing him inside of me at that very moment.

He pulled out his rigid length and in a smooth move, lowered me onto him.

I whimpered, my body opening to meet the size of him as he fucked me slow and deep in the dark corner. Although we were in public, at that moment I didn't care.

Brett licked up the side of my neck, mixing kisses with bites, the scruff of his jaw scratching my chin. I knew it would leave red marks but I reveled in it. I craved the way he needed to cover my body with evidence of his love making.

He leaned his forehead against mine, his hot breath caressing my face. He stared intently into my eyes and brushed a finger down the side of my cheek like he was memorizing me. "Don't ever forget."

"I can't. You're all I think about. All I dream about."
Although I was mad at him, the power of our love took over,
simmering the anger I felt towards him.

I moaned, his thick cock swelling inside of me after each
stroke. God, he felt good. All hard and long, reaching the bundle
of nerves that were made just for him.

Holding under my knees, he brought them up to my chest
and pushed into me as deep as he could go.

I gasped, crashing over an explosion of ecstasy that hit me
fast.

A smug smile formed on his face when his thrusts picked up
speed. I reveled in the feeling of him losing control. Of him
going over that edge.

I dug my fingers into his shoulders and cried out as he came
inside of me while my own release washed over me for the
second time.

His orgasm was so strong, I could feel his semen pulsing
into me, coating me with remnants of him.

Brett placed a hard kiss on my mouth before putting me
back on my feet. "You, my little vixen, are going to be the death
of me."

"Serves you right," I responded, nipping his bottom lip. A
hot shiver ran down my spine as I felt his release run down my
inner thigh. I could never get over the feeling of him being inside
of me.

He frowned, released me and righted his pants. "What the
hell are you talking about?"

"Does having a coffee date with Anna ring any bells?" I
asked, zipping up my dress and attempted to shove past him

He grabbed my arm and pushed me back up against the
wall. "It wasn't a date."

I raised an eyebrow. "But you didn't tell her about me until
you got to New York."

Brett rolled his eyes. "Evvie, it was no big deal."

I scoffed. "How would you like it if I had a coffee date with
a guy?"

His brows furrowed. "Over my fucking dead body."

"Oh, but Brett," I said, feigning shock. "It wouldn't be a date. We're just friends, of course."

"Watch it, lover," he said, his voice full of warning.

I shoved a finger in his chest. "So it's okay for you to meet up with a woman, but it's not okay for me to meet up with a guy?"

His jaw clenched. "Damn straight."

I leaned against the wall and crossed my arms under my chest, knowing that there was no way in hell he was going to let me pass. "So how was your date then? Did you picture fucking Anna and I together?"

His gaze darkened. "Evvie…"

My heart raced. I couldn't believe those words just came out of my mouth. What the hell? "What? Or did you just fuck her in your mind? Did you dream about both of us while you were in New York? While you jacked off, was it me you were thinking about or Anna?" *Stop. Just stop, Evvie.* Oh God. What the hell was I even saying? Jealousy reared its ugly head deep inside of me. So deep that I never even knew this kind of feeling existed.

Brett snarled and pushed me face first against the wall. Slapping a hand beside my head, he leaned down, his hot breath scorching my ear. "The only person I thought of while I jacked off, was you. *You* invaded my thoughts while I slept, while I showered. Whenever I touched myself, *you* were there. I could smell, breathe, hear only you. It was so intense, I had to ask myself whether it was real or not." His hand ran up underneath my dress before cupping my ass. "Don't you ever fucking question me again. I would never fuck someone else in my mind, in real life or even my dreams. *You* are all I think about. Do you fucking understand me?"

I swallowed as his voice lowered, the deep rumble travelling through me.

He cupped my jaw and tilted my head. "Do you, understand me?" he growled.

I nodded.

"The reason I never told Anna about you was because I wanted to make sure that what we have is permanent," he said, fisting a hand in my hair. "Real."

"But you told me you loved me before then. If you didn't know if it was real, why would you say that?" I moved to turn when his grip on my jaw tightened.

"Keep your hands on the wall," he demanded.

My pussy clenched at the firm command and I did as he said.

"I love you and only you, Evvie. You are my first for many things and I want you to be my last. I was making sure that you would be it for me. You are my forever." He breathed hard against my neck and dug his fingers into the flesh of my rear. "You know that and it fucking pisses me off when you question my feelings."

I shook my head, swallowing a moan in the process. "I didn't—"

"Quiet," he snapped. "I'm going to take you to my office and show you what I did to you in my mind while I was away."

My body heated. *Oh dear God.*

He bit my shoulder. "And Evvie?"

I looked up at him.

He smirked. "It will be something that you will *never* forget."

Five

ON SHAKY legs, I headed down the hall to Brett's office. After the very fast orgasm he gave me, my mind reeled with thoughts at what he could possibly do to me that he hasn't done yet.

I was nervous and excited and although I had started out mad at him, right now, curiosity got the better of me. I craved what he wanted to do. I needed it and I knew he needed that control.

"Take off your shoes and dress," Brett demanded as he shut the door behind me, clicking the lock in place.

I kicked off my black pumps and unzipped the dress before letting it fall at my feet.

"Beautiful," he whispered.

My body heated at the compliment. I looked at him over my shoulder. "Like what you see, lover boy?"

"More than you could ever imagine." He rubbed his jaw, his eyes grazing over my naked body. "Now kneel on the floor by the couch with your back to me."

I swallowed past the dry lump in my throat and knelt. Anticipation flowed through me like molten lava.

"Close your eyes."

I squeezed my eyes shut. I wanted to argue. To scream and shout and tell him to just have his way with me already but words were frozen on my tongue. I found my body listening to him before I could even respond. It was like a battle was going on inside of me. A war of—

Something icy cold ran down my spine making me gasp. Arching my back, my nipples hardened to sharp peaks, goose bumps rising on my skin.

"Open."

Lost in my thoughts just a moment ago, I didn't even realize that Brett had joined me on the floor.

His handsome face was tense, his eyes dark with a hunger so strong, I was surprised he was—

51

The icy sensation ran back down my spine again and I cried out. "Holy—"

"Ice."

My heart raced, my breathing making my ears ring as he ran the ice down to my tail bone, in between my ass cheeks and to my center.

"I enjoy seeing your pussy glistening with my come," he whispered in my ear.

A hot shiver ran down my spine and I arched into his touch.

"When you push your ass against me, it makes it hard for me to be in control, Evvie," he husked.

I smiled and licked my lips. A moan escaped my mouth as the cool cube brushed over my opening before he inserted it...wait...I looked down and back up at Brett.

A smug smile formed on his face.

I shook my head. "Did you just...the ice cube..."

"It wasn't a cube." His eyes flashed with amusement. "Now turn around."

I did as he said and leaned back against the couch cushion.

"Spread your legs," Brett said, grabbing another ice cube...no, it was in the shape of a small ball, from the metal ice bucket on the floor beside him.

I bit my bottom lip and waited, spreading my legs like he asked.

His hand reached up and ran the small ice cube from between my breasts down the length of my torso before reaching my clit.

A cold shiver ran over my body and I whimpered as my pussy swelled. "Brett," I breathed.

The ice disappeared once it reached my core. "Your cunt's nice and hot. The ice won't stay inside of you for long."

I moaned, the walls of my center clenching around the small balls of ice. I could already feel them melting as they dripped down my inner thighs.

"One more and I think that will be enough." He cupped my jaw and placed a hard kiss on my lips, before licking his way into my mouth.

I gasped as a third ice ball was inserted into me. My body shivered, my pussy feeling numb. I couldn't even describe all of the sensations rushing through me. The ice burned but felt amazing all at once.

"I have another surprise for you," Brett whispered against my mouth.

"Hmm…" Something hard brushed against my clit before delving deeper. I frowned and opened my mouth to ask what it was when a strawberry was brought into my view.

Brett smirked and brushed the tiny fruit over my lips. "Taste yourself, lover."

I opened my mouth and brushed my tongue over the tip before biting down. The sweet taste of the fruit mixed with the essence of my body, made a flood of liquid seep between my thighs.

"I think you like the taste, Evvie," he said, eating the rest of the strawberry.

"Brett."

"What's wrong?" he teased.

"I need…" I shivered.

He grabbed another round piece of ice and brushed it over my mound. "Do you want to come?"

I threw my head back and panted. "Please."

His fingers separated my folds. "Your clit's nice and hard."

"I—" I whimpered when the ice pressed against it. "Holy shit. Oh God, that's cold." I grabbed his hand.

"Hands behind your back or I won't let you come," he said, his voice firm.

"Brett," I pleaded.

He arched an eyebrow.

I bit my bottom lip and did as he said.

Brett moved in front of me and knelt between my legs. He pushed the ice against my aching clit, rubbing it slowly back and forth.

It was pure and utter torture but it felt good. Oh God, did it ever feel good. The burning sensation of the ice mixed with the tingles from my erect clit made a warmth start from my toes and travel up my body. "Brett."

He spread my pussy lips wider and rubbed the ice harder against me. "Come for me."

I whimpered as I came fast against his hand.

He smiled. "Now turn around again. Keep your arms on the couch and lover?"

"Yes?"

"Hold on." He pulled his belt out of the loops with a snap.

My body shook as a shiver ran down my spine. My thoughts travelled to what that leather belt would feel like—

I yelped when his hand landed on my ass.

"Tell me what you were thinking," he demanded, rubbing his hand over the sting.

My cheeks heated. What if—

Another swat landed on my flesh making me jump but the delicious erotic pain flowed through me like melted chocolate. *More.*

"Tell me."

"Your belt," I panted.

"What about it?" he asked, a teasing lilt in his voice. He knew what I wanted but damn him for making me say it.

I chewed my bottom lip. I knew he liked mixing pain with pleasure but he had only ever used his body. I didn't know why and I didn't understand it but I knew that I needed more. "Use it."

He folded the belt in half and held it firm in his hand. "Brace yourself."

I did and gasped when the leather landed on my ass. It was gentle at first but still stung like a bitch.

The swats were tender, gradually getting harder and harder. My ass burned but my pussy swelled to the point of painful. I spread my legs.

"Now I'm going to show you what you really want. Breathe out as the leather lands against your ass. It will hurt less that way." His hand grazed down my back "And Evvie, you will come against my belt."

I opened my mouth to question how when the hard leather landed against me in a firm snap. I inhaled a gasp, tears burning my eyes at the rough impact. *Breathe, Evvie. You asked for this.*

Swat. Swat. Swat.

A shiver of ecstasy travelled down my back, desire unfurling deep in my belly. Oh God, it hurt but felt so good. Was that normal? Was I a freak because I liked the pain?

I yelped when the leather moved down to the backs of my thighs to my mound.

"Stop thinking. Feel, Evvie. Shut off your mind."

Swat. Swat. Swat.

The bite of the belt hit my clit and an unexpected cry escaped my lips.

"That's it. Let me hear how much you like the pain I give you," Brett growled and repeated his movements harder.

Tears rolled down my cheeks and I shook, sweat coating my body. The belt hit my clit repeatedly sending me over the edge. I gasped as an explosion so strong erupted deep inside of me and spread over my skin.

A zipper lowered and Brett moved behind me before thrusting into me so hard, I screamed. His name left my lips on a breathless gasp as the most intense pleasure rushed into my very being. My vision faded in and out, his name leaving my mouth until my throat turned raw.

As he continued to pump into me, I felt like I was floating on a cloud of bliss. His hands ran down my body, the soft touches tickling my skin.

His teeth grazed over my shoulder as he continued to power into me. As he bit down, I came hard again for the third time in a row.

My pussy squeezed his cock, milking him dry as I felt him release deep inside of me. My mind was fuzzy, light headed even as I leaned against the couch.

Soft kisses were placed on my shoulder blades before heavy arms lifted me. Wrapping me in a blanket and curling me against a hard body, he sat us on the couch.

"Brett?" I whispered, my throat burning at the use.

"Shhh…"

The scent of something sweet invaded my nostrils and I opened my eyes. They were heavy but not like a moment ago.

Brett smiled, his blue eyes warming. "Welcome back."

I frowned and sat up in his lap. "Where did I go?" My voice was hoarse and I cleared my throat a couple of times but it still stung.

"You fell asleep," he said, his voice soft. "Open."

I noticed the small piece of chocolate in his hand and opened my mouth, savoring the sweetness as he placed it on my tongue. "Mmm…" I moaned and snuggled against him. My skin vibrated, hypersensitive to any touch at all and I reveled in it.

"How are you doing?" he asked, brushing his hand over my ass.

I squirmed, my flesh burning at the touch.

Brett's eyes darkened. "Drink this."

He gave me a bottle of water and I downed half of it in one gulp, the cool liquid soothing my aching throat.

"Lay on your stomach," he said, lifting me off of his lap.

I moved to lay down when my muscles twitched. "How long was I sleeping for?" I asked as I stretched out on the couch.

"About a half an hour."

I looked back at him over my shoulder, watching him rummage through something in his desk. "What did you do during that time?"

His gaze met mine, his blue eyes twinkling. "I held you."

"Oh…isn't that boring?"

Brett chuckled. "Holding you is never boring, my sweet Evvie." He knelt at my side before opening a metal tin. "This will make your beautiful ass feel better." He dipped his fingers into the white salve and placed a kiss on the flesh of my rear before rubbing the ointment onto my skin.

I moaned. The cooling sensation easing the sting from his belt. His belt. His leather belt that I had practically begged him to use on me. And he did. Oh God. What did he think of me?

"Evvie," he said, placing a soft peck on my mouth. "Stop thinking so much."

My cheeks heated. "I'm just worri—"

"Are you ashamed of what we did?"

I thought a moment. "No. It's just…"

Brett lifted me and wrapped the blanket around me, holding me tight. "Then what's the problem?"

I brushed my thumb over the back of his hand. "I was worried that you would think something was wrong with me."

Brett pinched my chin and turned my head. "Just because you like pain, doesn't mean there is anything wrong with you."

"Yeah, but I had no idea I liked it *that* much."

He smirked. "Oh, I knew you did."

I frowned. "How?"

"From the first moment I spanked you, I knew. The way you moaned, the way your pussy dripped for me. I bet if I would have looked into your eyes, they would have been dilated."

He had a point. "Does it make you happy…"

"Of course I'm happy."

"I mean—"

"I know what you mean, lover. I like giving pain. You clearly like receiving it. Yes, that makes me happy but even if you didn't like it, I would never force it on you," he said, kissing my shoulder.

A breath left me on a whoosh and I rubbed a hand down my face. "I'm sorry for the things I said earlier. I didn't mean them."

"I know and I'm sorry for not telling Anna about you," he said brushing a hand down my arm.

I thought a moment. "As much as I try, I can't hate her."

He smiled. "I want you to be friends. She…it's not my place to say but she needs someone like you in her life."

I nodded and sat up, wincing as the flesh of my ass throbbed.

Brett's gaze heated, a smug grin spreading on his handsome face. "Seeing my marks on your pale skin, Evvie, makes me feel very satisfied."

My skin tingled. "I can feel you every time I move," I said softly.

"I know." He handed me my dress.

I put it on and shivered when his knuckles brushed down the cheek of my ass.

"Pure perfection."

My pulse raced.

"As much as I don't want you to, you should go clean yourself up," Brett suggested.

I nodded and headed into the bathroom, doing as he said. A couple of minutes later, I headed back to the couch and giggled when he pulled me onto his lap.

Brett brushed his hand up my inner thigh. "I'll just fill you with my come later."

If we had it our way, he would be inside of me forever. I loved knowing where he had been, the way my body swelled, ready and aching for him. I could never get enough and I didn't want to.

Brett cleared his throat and turned me in his arms. "Before I lose control and do what I really want..." His gaze raked over my face. "I have a present for you."

My heart skipped a beat. "Oh, what is it?"

He laughed and reached behind him before bringing out a small black velvet box. "Now this is not an engagement ring."

"Oh...okay." I couldn't hide the disappointment in my voice. Why was I shocked? It was way too soon. Wasn't it?

"Evvie," he said, pinching my chin. His eyes softened. "When I propose, I want to make sure that we're both ready because I don't want a long engagement."

I smiled. "Neither do I."

Brett winked. "If I had it my way, I would pop the question and then marry you that same day."

I liked that idea. Just him, me, a minister, two witnesses. It would be small. Intimate. Brett and I didn't do well around other people...clearly, so a small ceremony would be perfect.

"I can see the wheels turning in your beautiful head, Evvie. Do *you* like that idea?"

"Yes," I said, cupping his cheek.

"Good but first..." He opened the small box.

I gasped as a gold band lined with diamonds shone up at me. It was simple but breathtaking, much like the person who was giving it to me.

He took it out of the box and grabbed my left hand. "My Evvie, my lover and my best friend. This ring is my promise to you that I want to spend the rest of my life with you. I want to give you children, even if it's just one. To see something that we both created would be the happiest day of my life…besides marrying you, of course."

I laughed and wiped the unexpected tears that were flowing down my cheeks. We had never talked about children. We never even talked about marriage really. I knew we were going to spend the rest of our lives together. He didn't have to tell me that. It was etched deep inside of me. His love, his heart, his soul, it was all mine.

"This is my promise to you as well that I *will* marry you. In time. When we are both ready." He kissed my forehead. "Look inside the band."

I took the ring from him and gasped. *I love you deep* was engraved on the inside.

He slipped the ring onto my finger and kissed it before placing a soft kiss on my mouth. "I do. I love you deep. Deeper than ever before."

A sob of happiness escaped my lips and I threw my arms around his neck. "I love you," I whispered.

I couldn't help but stare at the ring on my finger. It fit perfectly, the small diamonds sparkling in the light.

I covered his face in kisses. "Thank you."

He chuckled and grabbed my hands, brushing a thumb over the ring. "This ring also lets you know that no matter what shit is thrown at us, we'll find our way back to each other. As long as we have each other, we can make it through anything, my sweet Evvie."

I swallowed past the hard lump in my throat.

Brett smiled but not before I noticed something flash in his eyes.

"Are you okay?" I asked and kissed the back of his hand.

He cleared his throat. "The ring was my stepmom's."

My heart thudded and I stared at the ring. "It's beautiful."

He nodded once. "And so are you."

My cheeks heated. "Thank you. For everything." I rose to my feet. The fabric of my dress brushing against my ass made me wince as a slight burn spread over my skin.

Brett kissed my neck. "It will be very hard for me to get any work done, knowing what I just did to you." He put his belt back on and did up the buckle.

My eyes followed the movement, memories of it touching me, making me have the hardest orgasm ever, reined full force in my mind.

Brett cleared his throat. "Something you like, lover?"

I smiled and licked my lips. "We can always do it again," I offered.

He chuckled and nipped just under my ear. "It's too soon. Don't want to do any damage to that hot little body of yours."

My stomach flipped. I loved when he called me *little*. I was short and curvy but compared to him, anyone would be small.

"I do enjoy knowing that the sweet juices from your body are on my belt," he purred. "I can smell you on me and it makes me *hard*."

A hot shiver ran down my back. God, I would never get over the way he spoke. Desire unfurled deep inside of me. Usually it was *his* scent on me but knowing that mine was on him, did something new to me. It was like I had claimed my territory without even knowing it. I pictured him walking into his club, his head held high knowing that both of us had been scented by each other.

His fingers brushed down my arms, the tiny hairs tingling under his touch. So much was said without him even needing to say any words. His communication through touch left me panting, wanting.

His large hand curled around my throat, tilting my head back against his chest. His dark blue eyes stared into me and I fell. Deep.

60

He leaned down and licked up the side of my neck to my jaw before delving into my mouth. The kiss was hard, slow and demanding. A reminder of who I belonged to. I didn't need reminding. I knew. I knew from the very first kiss, the first touch. I was his from the very start.

I opened to him, taking him all the way in as he held me restrained. My body relaxed, turning to mush at the gentle but commanding hold he had on me.

Every time he touched my throat, my body submitted to him before I could even process what he was doing. To trust that he wouldn't hurt me and give in completely made my heart flutter but I craved it. Needed it on a whole other level. As each day passed, I learned more and more about myself and him.

Brett nipped my bottom lip, sucking it into his mouth before licking down the other side of my neck. He inhaled, his hot breath scorching my skin. "I can feel your heart beat," he husked, grazing his finger back and forth against my pulse point.

My stomach tumbled and all I could do was stare into his depths.

He kissed my forehead. "Don't ever forget who you belong to," he whispered.

I shook my head. "Never."

Brett grabbed hold of my hand and kissed my ring finger before placing a soft peck on my lips. "I love you," he breathed against my mouth.

A light knock on the door sounded. "Boss?"

Brett opened the door to a pissed off looking Kane. "What's up?"

He huffed and ran a hand over his bald head. "A woman is here to see you. I told her you were in a meeting." His gaze flicked to mine before looking back at Brett. "but she refuses to leave."

"Thanks, my man," Brett grumbled.

My stomach twisted. A woman? Oh please God, don't let be another one like Claire.

Kane nodded once and left us alone.

Brett kissed my forehead. "Go grab a drink but only one. I need you sober for what I plan on doing to you later," he said, before landing a light swat on my ass.

I yelped, the tender flesh of my rear heating against the sting of his hand.

He winked. "Sensitive, lover?"

I shook my head and headed to the bar, the sound of his deep chuckle following me down the hallway.

Pulling my dress down as far as possible, my cheeks heated when I came into view of the customers and staff milling about. Jake Chan nodded at me from the bar and Tatiana Sweet winked as she walked by me. She usually smacked my ass in fun but her hands were filled with a drink tray and thank God for that.

Each step I took, the material of my clothing brushed against the sensitive skin. Did I have marks? Bruises? Welts even? The salve Brett had put on me earlier made the stinging go away some but it didn't help completely.

My stomach fluttered. What was I even thinking in asking him to spank me with his belt? Was it in the heat of the moment? Is that why I wanted it?

Once reaching the bar, I slid onto the stool and bit back a gasp. Images of not too long ago and what Brett and I did, invaded my mind. My heart thudded. Brett was right. Every time I moved, I thought of him.

"Hey Evvie."

I turned to Anna coming up beside me. "Hi."

She smiled. "Everything good between you and Brett?"

I nodded and looked down at my hands. The gold band flashed in the dim lighting. My heart flipped. A promise ring. After everything that had happened in the last hour or so, everything was very good. I couldn't believe how much things had changed in the past couple of weeks.

"Evvie?"

"Hmm?" I looked up at Anna smiling.

Her grin widened. "Distracted?"

My cheeks heated. "You could say that."

She laughed and then her smile faltered, her gaze landing on my left hand. "I like the ring."

"Thank you." I didn't know why but I felt kind of guilty, like I was waving it in her face that Brett was definitely no longer available.

My gaze caught sight of my oldest brother, Evan, approaching the bar. I gave a little wave and motioned for him to join us.

He smiled and then his face paled when his blue eyes landed on Anna.

I frowned and looked back at her. "Anna?"

She stopped twirling the olive in her vodka martini and met my gaze. "Wha…" Her eyes went cold as Evan closed the distance between us.

"Hello Anna," he grumbled, his eyes darkening. He shoved a hand through his short blonde hair, his stance hard and tense.

"Hi." She looked away, her back stiffening.

"Do you know each other?" I asked, frowning.

Anna scoffed. "No."

Confusion coursed through me. "Then what—"

"That's not my fault, baby," Evan sneered.

Okay, this was weird. "Evan…"

"I'll see you later, sis." He stormed off and headed towards Brett that I now noticed was standing against the wall.

My skin hummed, the flesh of my ass tingling as memories poured in over what we did just a moment ago.

Brett winked at me.

I blew him a kiss.

He captured it and cupped himself over his pants.

I coughed, choking back a gasp and laughed. Shaking my head, I turned back to Anna.

Her eyes flashed before she looked away.

Clearing my throat, my stomach clenched as guilt settled deep inside of me. I wasn't trying to rub what Brett and I had in her face. God, what was wrong with me? "I'm sorry."

She let out a deep breath. "It's fine." A small smile splayed on her face.

"What's going on with Evan?" I asked softly, remembering what Brett had said about her needing a friend.

Her cheeks reddened. "Um…"

"You slept with him, didn't you?" I mentally smacked myself. *Way to be gentle, Evvie.*

Anna sighed. "Yeah and now his ego is bruised because I left in the morning."

As much as I tried not to like Anna, it wasn't happening. She wasn't Claire. She was genuine and I could tell that she honestly felt bad for being in love with my boyfriend. You couldn't control your feelings though. I knew that first hand. Maybe her being with my brother wouldn't be a bad thing after all. If Evan could get his head out of his ass and stop being a douche.

"Well…" I caught a movement out of the corner of my eye and found Brett coming towards me. My body tingled, the small hairs on my skin standing on edge as he closed the distance between us. It was like I was set on a Brett MacLean radar. I was like a light bulb. Every time he was near, my body turned on.

"I'm going to head out." Anna placed her hand on my arm. "And Evvie?"

I looked up at her.

Her eyes warmed. "I know you don't trust me but I promise you, I would never do anything to hurt you or Brett. Especially not now. No matter what anyone says, you both deserve to be happy."

I frowned and opened my mouth to respond when she walked away. Confusion coursed through me. Well that was odd.

"Hey, lover."

I smiled as a soft peck was placed on my neck. Inhaling deep, the scent of leather and man mixed with a hint of sex, invaded my nostrils. Although my body was sore, it tingled, ready for his attention. "Hi—"

"What the fuck—" Brett shot to his feet.

"Brett?" I placed a hand on his arm.

He cleared his throat, his jaw tensing.

64

I followed his gaze as a tall brunette glanced our way. Her blue eyes raked down Brett and if I didn't know any better, I'd think she was checking him out.

"Who is she?" I asked, my stomach clenching.

He looked down at me and grabbed my hand. "Come with me."

I frowned but followed him back to his office. "What's wrong?" I asked after he closed the door behind me.

He scrubbed a hand down his face, his big body as tense as an elastic band ready to snap. He started pacing back and forth in front of me.

I walked up to him and placed my hands on his chest, stopping him. "Talk to—"

A soft knock sounded on the door before it slowly opened, revealing the woman from the bar. She was an older lady with wrinkles lining her face in a hard way. She looked like she had been to hell and back but her eyes…they were so blue, they were captivating.

My heart sunk. I had seen those eyes before. I looked up at Brett. "What's going on?"

His jaw clenched. "What the *fuck* are you doing here?"

The woman sneered. "Now is that any way to speak to your mother?"

I gasped. My stomach tumbled as shock tore through me.

"My mother is dead," he bit out.

The tension rolled off of him in waves, leaving me breathless. What the hell was going on?

The woman took a step towards me and held out her hand. "I'm Diane MacLean. Brett's *real* mother."

Six

HOLY. SHIT.

Brett grabbed my arm and pulled me behind him. "Don't you dare fucking touch her. Get out. *Now.*"

Diane bristled but held her stance. "I want to talk."

"*No!*" he yelled. "Leave me the fuck alone. You're dead to me."

The woman crossed her arms under her chest and tilted her chin. "You *will* talk to me. You'll have no choice, little boy. There are some things you should know. About Claire."

"I don't care." His voice was calm, even and that made me more nervous than if he were to continue yelling and screaming at her. "I don't care what either of you have to say. Get. The. Fuck. Out."

The woman smirked. "You are definitely my kid." At the moment, she turned and left, slamming the door shut behind her.

A breath left me on a whoosh and I quickly locked the door before turning back to Brett.

He shook his head. "Fuck me. Shit...I...Evvie."

Our whole relationship flashed before my eyes as I saw Brett crumple to the floor. I closed the distance between us and wrapped my body around his, holding him. Comforting him as best I could.

"God, I...I can't deal. I can't." He shook against me, gripping, pulling at my clothes like he was trying to get under my skin. "Let me touch you. Please. I can't...fuck."

The tremors that wracked through his big body made my throat tighten. That woman. She did this. She made him and then destroyed him. Took a gift that God had given her and crushed it in her hands.

"Shhh...I'm here." I didn't know what else to do, I didn't know what to say. So I just mumbled over and over again that I wouldn't leave him. That I was there for him.

He had told me his real mother had died. I didn't know why he had lied to me about it but at that moment I didn't care. He obviously had his reasons.

The look in his eyes when he saw her came into my mind as the realization hit me. He was terrified. Of her.

His hold on me tightened to the point of painful. "I thought I was over it. I didn't think seeing her again would affect me this way," His voice was thick. No matter how big or strong a person is, seeing someone that hurt you so deeply could bring anyone to their knees. I realized that when Brett broke against me. My heart pounded in my ears. I wanted a piece of her. The woman that made my strong boyfriend, the dominating Brett MacLean surrender all control. It made me want to rip her face off. That evil sneer. She knew she had gotten to him and it made me sick to my stomach.

Leaning back, I cupped his face in my hands and bit back a sob when our gazes met.

His jaw clenched but the bright look of fear in his eyes was proof that he had built up a wall around himself, around his emotions. Protecting monsters like his mother from barging in.

That's why he would never let me go. He let me in and I was stuck. Permanently and I wouldn't have it any other way.

He took deep breaths and looked away, his cheeks flushed. "I hate that woman. It's so strong. I have nightmares about killing her."

I bit back a gasp, my heart racing against my rib cage.

"After my father divorced her, he had her charged." Brett took another breath. "She plead insanity, saying God wanted her to punish me for my sins."

My throat burned, nausea settling in my stomach at what he was telling me. He was just a boy. A *child*. Her baby and she did this to him.

"Have you talked to anyone?" I croaked.

"No, not until you," he mumbled. His hands grazed under my dress, caressing my lower back as he leaned his head against my shoulder. "I can't deal, Evvie."

Tears threatened to escape my eyes. My big strong boyfriend was breaking before me and I had no idea how to fix it.

"I'm so sorry," I whispered. I was sorry. For not knowing how to fix things and for not helping him as a child. I knew that was silly but the need to protect him was so strong, I couldn't control it. I couldn't save him as a boy, but I would save him as a man.

"I'm sorry for lying to you," he said, his voice muffled by my shoulder.

My fingers grazed over his nape brushing through the short brown hair. "I'm sorry you felt you had to."

He lifted his head, his gaze warming. "I don't deserve you, at all but I love you and I thank God every day for giving me you. My angel."

My heart stuttered, my vision blurring. I swallowed past the hard lump that burned my throat. "I...I wish I could take away your pain."

He kissed my ring finger, placing soft pecks on the gold band before leaning his forehead against mine. "I miss..." his breath hitched. "I miss my dad. He would...he would know what to do. How to fix this."

At that point I lost it. All of the emotions I had felt over the past couple of months crashed into me, overwhelming my sense of control. Losing my mom years before. My dad having a heart attack only a couple of weeks ago. Tears flowed down my cheeks. I held him, with everything in me. I tried giving him the strength that I knew he needed. "I'm so sorry."

"Please. I...I can't." He swallowed several times before clearing his throat. "Just let me touch you. I need to feel your skin against mine." His hands roamed higher under my dress. His tense shoulders relaxed, like he was physically pulling the strength from my body.

I placed a soft peck on his mouth. "I love you. I'm here for you. No matter what. You can always trust in that," I said in between kisses.

"Don't leave me. Ever." His hands roamed over my lower body, pulling me tight against him. "My mother may have hurt me, fucked me up, but you..." his eyes darkened. "you could *destroy* me."

I shook my head, ignoring the thud of my heart. "Won't happen. You're stuck with me." I lifted my hand indicating my ring. "This is proof."

"Good. You're mine. I'm stuck in you, lover. Forever," he said, his voice firm.

My heart raced. "You...you want that? This?" I motioned between us. "Forever?" He had said it only a while ago but I needed to hear it again. I needed to know that this wasn't short term. That this was meant to be. *Real.*

He nodded. "I need it. I need you. I need this."

A flutter soared through my belly. "What are we going to do about your mom?" I hated to ask but we needed to prepare him for the onslaught of what was to come.

He breathed a heavy sigh. "I'll deal with it."

"Brett..."

His gaze hardened. "I said, I'll deal with it."

My stomach clenched. I had a feeling that there was more to her impromptu visit. She wanted something. And if it had to do with Claire... Whatever it was, would probably change our lives forever.

***

AFTER GETTING home from the club, Brett acted different, which, in fact, was understandable given who he had run into. His mother. His flesh and blood evil mother. I couldn't believe it. I understood why he had lied to me. Yes, it hurt that he felt he needed to, but I realized that it was during a time when our relationship was so new. Fresh. Now, I prayed that he would tell me anything.

I wrapped the blanket around me, trying to sleep but all I could think about was him. The look of terror as his mother forced her way back into his life. What did she want? It was

69

something to do with Claire but neither of us knew. Brett wouldn't talk about it. He had only told me so much about his childhood but he needed to talk to someone. A professional. I sighed. Only being with him for a couple of months, did that really give me a right to tell him what to do?

A part of me felt helpless, like no matter what I did, it wouldn't be enough. I wanted to help him but I couldn't figure out how.

I looked at Brett lying beside me.

His brow was furrowed, his handsome face strained like he was in pain. Small groans escaped his lips.

Oh God. He was having a nightmare. "Brett," I said, lightly touching his shoulder.

He moaned, moving his head back and forth.

"Brett," I repeated, my voice firm as I cupped his cheek.

He jumped and suddenly, I was pinned under him. I gasped and looked up into his deep blue eyes that were cloudy from sleep that soon turned dark with lust. "Brett?" I cupped his face, my heart racing.

His mouth crashed to mine, his hands roaming up my body, squeezing and massaging as they went. They were rough, needy, like they were trying to get under my skin. His thumbs brushed over my nipples, cupping my breasts in his hands as he took a hard peak in his mouth.

I moaned, throwing my head back at the rough impact.

The stubble of his cheeks scratched my skin as he licked his way back up to my mouth. Shoving his tongue between my lips, he sucked and pulled, devouring me.

His rock hard erection brushed against my inner thigh.

What was he dreaming about that got him so worked up? I tried to rationalize why he needed me so bad but my mind soared. As he continued to run his hands over my body, my emotions fizzled out and I just *felt*. The pull in my belly and the desire for this man curled deep inside of me. He needed me. I didn't know how I knew it but something tugged at my soul.

70

I moaned, wrapping my legs and ar sank into my body in a hard thrust. I cri opening to him as he took me rough.

He grunted, pushing into me as fe body was tense, his hips speeding up in ı.

If I didn't know any better, I would think he wa get as deep inside of me as he possibly could.

My hands scratched down his sweat slicked back when he sat back, pulling me into his lap.

I straddled his waist, circling my hips against him.

He groaned as my fingers dug into his skin. Running them through his hair, I tugged and pulled, deepening the kiss.

His tongue pushed against mine, devouring my mouth as his hands gripped my ass. Slamming my hips against him, I rode him hard, giving him what he needed.

He growled, fisted my hair and threw me face first down on the bed.

My body hummed, my core throbbing in anticipation. The animalistic desire that spread around us as he covered my body with his, sent my heart racing. God, he was hot as all get out. I had never seen this side of him. Yes, he always liked it rough but now, he was a savage animal. Feral with the need to mate. And the new masochistic side of me that I soon just discovered, loved every second of it.

He knelt between my knees, forcing my legs apart and pulled me to all fours before slamming back into my pussy.

I whimpered, gripping the blankets in my fists as he fucked me from behind.

After each hard thrust, my knees lifted from the bed. It was dark, possessive as he controlled my body. Taking what he wanted and giving me that much more in return.

The heady scent of sex washed around us and I moaned, inhaling deep the scent of him.

"Fuck," he growled. He pumped into me one last time before we came at once, crashing over waves of bliss together.

His name left my lips as a ripple of ecstasy exploded in my center.

ett's heavy body landed on mine as we both flopped onto
ed.

I sighed and wrapped his arm around me. Kissing his wrist,
reveled in the feel of him still semi-hard inside of me.

"I'm so sorry," he whispered into the crook of my neck.

"What for?" I asked, frowning.

"For attacking you," he bit out, his voice gruff.

I turned onto my back and cupped his cheek. "You did not attack me."

He looked away, shoving his head out of my grip. "I fucked you like an animal."

"So? I didn't complain, did I? You've been rough before. What's different about this time?"

His gaze met mine and he sighed.

"What's wrong?" My heart thumped hard.

He shook his head, closing up on me.

I huffed. How was I going to get him to talk to me? An idea came to me almost instantly and I rose off the bed before heading to the bathroom to turn on the tub. It was early in the morning but we needed this. *He* needed *me*.

I walked back to the bed and grabbed Brett's hand. "Come with me."

He raised an eyebrow. "Where?"

"We're taking a bath," I said, tugging on his hand.

He frowned. "Why?"

"Will you just come with me, please?"

He let me pull him from the bed and took a step towards me. "If you want me to fuck you in the tub, just say so."

I rolled my eyes and smiled, patting him lightly on the stomach. His rock hard abs twitched lightly under my touch and I inadvertently tried not to drool. "This isn't to have sex."

His gaze narrowed in questioning. "What are we going to be doing then?"

"Talking or relaxing. Whatever. Doesn't matter," I said and walked to the bathroom before stepping into the tub. The hot water sent a shiver up my spine as I sank into the large claw bathtub.

I watched as Brett tentatively walked into the room before joining me. He sat behind me and wrapped his big body around mine, pulling me tight against him. Always touching me. Always gripping me tight. Any harder and I wouldn't be able to breathe. That was one of the many things I loved about him. His need to touch me. His need to speak to me through his body.

"You expect me to just talk when you're sitting naked against me?" he asked, grabbing a cloth off the side of the tub.

"Yes," I said, leaning forward. "We don't always need to have sex."

He grunted. "You complaining?"

"No, but I would like to have an actual conversation with you."

His brows furrowed. "We talk."

"Yeah, after having sex." I didn't know why I was arguing with him but I didn't want to be one of those girls in a relationship based solely on sex. Yes, I loved every second of it but I needed more.

"Why are we here?"

I didn't know if he meant in the tub or in general so I just answered with honesty. "Because we need each other."

"You think so?" He dipped the cloth in the water and ran it over my shoulder and down my arm sending goose bumps over my skin.

"I know so." I looked at the gold band on my ring finger. The diamonds glistening in the light. Brett just got back a week ago and already so much had happened. "This is our time. Our moment to be one. It may sound corny or stupid." I waited for him to say something and when he didn't, I continued. "Since you got home from New York, things have felt different. I don't know. I just—"

"I think we should go to Mexico sooner than later."

My heart gave a start. "I agree." I wrapped my arm around his bent knee and kissed it before resting my head on my hand.

"I had a nightmare about my mom," Brett said a moment later. His body tensed behind me and I waited patiently for him to continue. "It was more like a memory playing over and over

73

in my fucking head. Evvie, when I saw her…" He took a deep breath. "I was serious when I said that I wanted to kill her."

I bit back a gasp at his admission.

"I know that makes me sound like a monster but it's the fucking truth. I will never forgive her for the shit she did to me. The shit she got her boyfriends to do." He sighed. "I…I was almost raped by one of them."

My head whipped around, shock tearing through my body. I didn't know why I was surprised. The way his mom looked at him like she wanted to eat him alive made me sick to my stomach.

His eyes were dark, stormy, pure raw hatred filling them as memories must have invaded his mind. "He whipped me with an extension cord. If you look at my back and ass really closely, you can see the marks. That's why I tan and…that's why I fucked you like I did tonight."

I frowned confused as to what he meant.

He ran a hand through his hair, drops of water sliding down his beautiful face. "I wanted to erase the horrible memories of my nightmare and when I woke, being inside you was the only way I knew how. It calmed me."

A hard lump filled my throat. I didn't know what to say.

A soft smile splayed at his lips. "You are the only reason I'm able to get through this."

I shook my head. "I had no idea it was that bad," I whispered.

"I don't remember most of it. I blocked it out I think but the things I do remember, threaten to destroy me every fucking day. Every time I close my eyes, I'm terrified that I'll have a nightmare. It's only since being with you, that I've been able to get a good night's sleep…until tonight that is." He leaned his head back against the tub and let out a frustrated sigh.

"I'm so—"

"Don't. Don't feel sorry for me," he snapped. "I just…I…fuck."

I wrapped my arms around his waist and leaned my head against his chest. "I'm sorry that you went through what you did. I'm not feeling sorry for you like you automatically assume."

A chuckle rumbled from his chest. "I love your brazenness."

I rolled my eyes and grabbed his hands, hugging his arms around me. "I'm here for you. Whatever you need. Whatever you want, just ask and I'm yours."

"Sometimes I don't know how to ask," he mumbled.

I looked up at him. I didn't know how to ask him either. "Then show me. Like you did tonight."

His jaw clenched. "That was a dick move on my—"

"Stop," I demanded. "I did not complain. It's not like you forced yourself on me, so stop it. This is what I'm here for. I'm your girlfriend, Brett. I'm here to help you through everything. I'm your forever, remember that."

"But I shouldn't have done that," he said averting my gaze. "I shouldn't have been so rough."

I turned in his arms and huffed. I was sick of him berating himself. I always took what he threw at me and I never complained. Not once. "You've always been rough. Why are you now upset for making love to me like you did?"

"That wasn't making love, Evvie. I was fucking rough."

I took a breath. "Listen to me and listen to me good."

Brett raised his eye brow, a hint of amusement flashing in his blue gaze. "Go on."

"I love you. I love everything about you. I enjoy when you make love to me like you can't get enough. Like you can't control the deep seeded need for me."

"Tonight I couldn't," he mumbled.

I cupped his cheek and placed a soft kiss on his lips. "Exactly. I'm not fragile. I won't break."

His eyes searched my face before he looked away. "I wanted to break you into submission."

My body tingled. I took a breath and cupped his cheek. "I've begged for you to break me. Maybe it was the heat of the moment. I don't know but I do know that I love you and that I want to help you in any way I can."

"I don't want to hurt you, Evvie," he added, his voice thick.

"There's a difference between hurting me and harming me, Brett," I said, turning back around. "You should know that. Look at the things we have done already."

His hand ran up and down my arm before he replied. "I'm scared that one of these days I'll be too rough, Evvie."

"Don't be. Yes, your passion overwhelms me sometimes but not because I'm scared of you."

"Then what?"

I thought a moment. "It scares me that I enjoy it so much and that I crave more." I realized as soon as the words left my lips, the revelation dawned on me. Brett liked administering pain for pleasure and I loved receiving it. Did that really make me a masochist? Was I a freak?

"No man ever spanked you during sex before?" he asked. It was like he read my mind.

I shook my head. "I thought it was weird but with you..." My cheeks heated. "God, the feel of your hands landing hard against my ass..." A hot shiver ran down my spine and I cleared my throat.

"I enjoy knowing that I'm your first...and last for many things," Brett said, his voice lowering.

I smiled. "You better be my last."

He smirked and kissed my forehead. "I am yours."

I watched as he entwined our fingers. It was a slow, sensual movement but it meant so much that in just that small touch, I could feel his love pouring between our fingertips.

"Does it bother you?" he asked softly.

"Hmm?"

He grinned. "Does it bother you that you enjoy the pain I give you?"

I chewed my bottom lip. "I'm...I don't know. During the moment, no, but when I go back and think about it, I wonder if something is wrong with me."

"Did it bother you that you asked for me to use my belt on you?" he asked, wrapping his hand around my throat.

My body instantly melted into his touch, relaxing at the restraint of him holding me. "No. Actually, it didn't." And that was the truth. "But this is all new to me. I just don't know how to deal."

He kissed my head. "We learn in time." His hand moved to the back of my neck. "I'm here to teach you."

"Does it bother you that I like the pain you give me?" As soon as the question left my lips, I felt dumb. Why would it bother him? *God, Evvie. You're such a—*

"No. Not at all. In fact, it makes me realize that I finally met my match. My one." He leaned down to my ear. "My only."

I smiled. We sat in silence for what felt like hours. Just enjoying each other. We had been dating for around four months but it felt like I had known him my whole life.

"I've always had this urge. This need to control. That's why I wanted to have my own business. Working for someone else? Not my fucking thing. And I've always been dominating."

I nodded. That was no surprise there.

"Even when my mother or her boyfriends smacked me around, I fought back. I tried to get as many punches in before they knocked me out."

As much as I didn't like hearing about his childhood, I knew it was good for him to talk. The fact that he was finally opening up after all of this time made me thankful for my bathtub idea.

Our eyes locked, my heart skipping a beat at the heat in his gaze.

"Lover, you are the only one that could break *me* into submission. That could bring me to my knees…willingly."

I shook my head. "I…no. I don't want that."

He pinched my chin. "If it meant being with you for the rest of my life and making you happy? I would gladly give up my control for good. For you."

"You did it once. That's enough."

"Evvie…"

"No," I snapped. I let out a deep sigh. "I enjoy giving up my control in the bedroom with you. I want that. I want you. I…" I chewed my bottom lip. "I need it."

A smug smile formed on his face. "I know but I'm just saying that if it came to that—"

"And I'm just saying that it won't happen again. That was enough for me. For us." Even though it was only the once, it really bothered me but also thrilled me to the core that he had done that for me. That he had let me control and dominate him as we made up but I didn't want that again. "I love you too much to put you through that. I could feel you holding back your need to control me."

"I always need to control you. The way your body submits under my touch, satisfies me."

"That's how I want it." It wouldn't be right of me to ask for anything else. It was one thing to play and attempt to dominate him but I knew deep down, it would never really happen. That's how I wanted it. I needed his control of me.

"Are you sure?"

"Yes."

"Because Evvie, I enjoy making your beautiful pale skin redden under my touch. And the way you moan when you're trying to fight back the pleasure you get from the sting of my palm. I also know you like it when I fuck you while your pussy is not quite wet enough but you like that pain, don't you? The tingle of my thick cock splitting you open," he breathed in my ear. "as I take you rough."

My eyes fluttered closed as I let his words wash over me. Everything he said was right. *He* was right.

"But when that happens, your pussy becomes instantly wet. I can feel it clench around me. Gripping me tight. Sucking me dry," he purred.

"Hmmm…" My body hummed. I could listen to him speak for hours, his deep voice caressing my skin like silk.

"I know everything about your body." He nipped my ear. "When you came against my belt?" He groaned. "God, it was the fucking hottest thing I've ever seen. I also know that it freaks you out when you like pain."

"It more shocked me than freaked me out," I whispered. "Am I a masochist?"

Brett smiled and kissed my nose. "Would it bother you if you were?"

"No, I don't think so."

"There is nothing wrong with it. As long as we are safe and both of us consent, that's all that matters. I do believe they need pain to get off but you…"

I looked up at him. "So did I."

His eyes darkened. "No. You only need my touch and you're putty in my hands."

I laughed, snuggling against him and thought a moment. "But pain enhances the orgasm."

"Exactly. The belt helped. My hands help," his voice lowered. "Giving you pleasure pleases me and there is nothing wrong with that whether you are a masochist or not. You crave the delicious sting."

I did. The hot intense tingle of heat spreading over my body as he spanked me with his hand or belt, left me panting and aching for more.

"Thank you for distracting me." Brett kissed my shoulder, letting his lips linger.

"Thank you for not making fun of me," I said, looking at our joined hands.

"Why would I make fun of you? It was an honest question."

I shrugged and sat forward.

His hand brushed down my spine and back up to my neck before wrapping around my throat.

A tingle ran through my body at the light but commanding touch.

"Look at me."

I swallowed hard at the firm tone and turned to him.

His thumb brushed over my mouth. "You wanted to know more about me. You feel that we don't know enough about each other."

I nodded.

His grip on my throat tightened.

A moan escaped my lips. I gasped, a flutter running through my belly.

A smug smile formed on Brett's face as he leaned closer to me. "I enjoy wrapping my hand around your throat. I can feel your body melt under my touch, submitting to me. That turns me on but makes me satisfied more. Knowing I can give you what you need as your lover makes me *very* happy."

Brett's blue eyes drew me in and all I could do was focus on his words as they held me captivated.

"This shit with my mother...I will deal with her on my own. Understand me?"

I frowned. "Brett."

"Do you understand me?" his voiced lowered, his jaw ticking as he demanded a response from me.

I nodded. "Yes. I understand." But it didn't mean that I had to agree with it.

His gaze softened. "Every chance I can, I want to please you. You won't stop me either, will you, my little vixen?"

I licked my lips and shook my head.

He grinned and placed a soft kiss on my mouth. Although it was gentle, it meant so much more.

All thoughts of his nightmare forgotten, I couldn't help but wonder at the back of my mind what his mother truly wanted.

Seven

"LOVER."

I moaned, stretching my arms out under my pillow. My muscles jumped and twitched, protesting at the movements.

"Lover." A deep purr caressed the back of my neck as a hard body covered mine. "Wake up."

"No, I'm dreaming," I said, my voice hoarse. And it was a very good dream. A hot man, a bottle of wine, a leather belt or two...

A hard swat landed on my ass making me yelp.

My eyes shot open. "What the hell?" I snapped. I hated mornings. Always have and always will.

Brett chuckled and bit my shoulder. "I love that you're not a morning person."

I huffed and stretched out my arm, reaching for the clock. "It's 5am. What is so—"

He covered my mouth with his hand while his other spread my knees apart. "You're going to shut up, let me fuck you and then I'm going to give you a surprise."

A shiver ran down my spine but I was still pissed at being woken up early on a Sunday morning. Since the guy didn't let me go to bed on time the night before, I deserved a full night's sleep. I normally didn't complain but it was 5am!

I opened my mouth and bit his palm.

He jumped and gripped my jaw tighter, snarling into my ear. "Do that again and I'll fuck you so hard, the neighbors will hear you scream my name."

Whatever. They probably already have anyways. He woke me up, so I was going to at least get something out of it. Morning sex with him was always raw, real and it had been so long that I wanted him every chance I could get.

I licked his hand before nipping as hard as I could before he pulled away.

He fisted my hair, pulling my head back at the same time he thrust into me.

I gasped at the added force and the feeling of him deep inside my core.

A sharp pain spread through my center that was quickly replaced with pleasure. The two senses mixed as one while he pumped into me hard and deep.

Brett gripped the edge of the bed, giving him that extra push he needed. "Spread your legs wide."

I did as he said, bringing my knees up to my chest. Since being with him, I had become limber but my muscles still burned at the forced stretch.

"I can feel my come still inside of you," he breathed against my neck.

No wonder. The many times he had taken me during the night caused me to pass out from pure exhaustion but I wouldn't have it any other way. Knowing he couldn't get enough of me, sent a thrill straight to the core of my very being.

He pushed into me hard and stilled. His cock twitched and pulsed, swelling to a length that filled me completely.

I moaned, my core clenching around him.

"I could stay like this forever," he whispered. His thrusts sped up.

I gasped when an electric surge shot through my body as I came hard around him.

The tight grip he had on the flesh of my ass heightened my orgasm. Bringing me over that edge of ecstasy.

He grunted, pulsing inside of me before he covered my body with his. "Never enough," he said softly, reining kisses on my shoulder blades.

I sighed in peaceful bliss.

"Now how about that surprise?"

"I think you surprised me enough already," I said, my eyes getting heavy.

"Well if you don't want it—"

I shot up and pushed him on his back. "No. I want the surprise. I was only kidding."

He laughed. "Shower and then surprise."

I pouted.

He chuckled and kissed my mouth. "Shower."

My body hummed at the demand. Before I could even process what was going on, he had me in the shower, pressed up against the cool glass, making use of my tired body.

***

"TODAY? WE'RE going today?" I squealed and jumped in Brett's arms, crashing us both onto his bed.

He laughed, wrapping his arms around me. "Yes. I need you to myself. Now get ready."

I reined kisses all over his face. "Oh, thank you."

He gently pushed me off of him and swatted my ass. "Pack light. I plan on having you naked every chance I get."

A smile spread on my face as I ran to his closet and pulled out a black gym bag, patting the bulky item. "Already done, lover boy."

He raised an eye brow. "Seriously?"

I nodded, my cheeks heating. "I packed as soon as you surprised me with the tickets."

He chuckled and shook his head. "Excited are we?"

"You have no idea. I've been counting down the days," I said, heading into his bathroom. To have him to myself, getting to know the man I love better on a level we both needed would do us some good. Being away from life, from others, people who threatened to destroy us.

"Good."

I smiled lightly and threw some toiletries into my bag and turned to him. My breath caught at the casual way he leaned against the door jam.

His brows furrowed, his stare boring into mine but he wasn't actually looking *at* me.

"Brett?" I walked up to him and placed a hand on his chest.

"Hmm?" His eyes focused and the corners of his lips turned up.

"What's wrong?" I asked, my heart thumping hard.

He shook his head. "Nothing." He captured my mouth in a soft kiss. "Nothing, Evvie," he whispered.

"If today isn't good, we can go some other time," I offered.

"No. I need this. I need you," he said, his voice firm.

"You have me." I gripped his shirt. "Always."

***

WHILE WE waited for the plane to finish boarding, I quickly sent a text to my brothers and Kane, letting them all know that today was the day we were leaving for Mexico.

"Call your dad," Brett said, brushing his thumb along the side of my neck.

I nodded and did as he suggested.

"Hey, sweet pea," my dad answered a moment later.

I smiled at the deep gravelly voice coming through the other end of the phone. "Hi, daddy. I just wanted to let you know that we're going to Mexico today."

"Be safe and let me know when you're there."

My heart swelled. "I will." I asked him about his health when I remembered the conversation that I had with Evan a week before. "Daddy, is everything okay?"

A pause. "Of course. Why wouldn't it be?"

"Just something that Evan said. Making sure you're alright."

"Going through some changes. I'm an old man, Evvie. 'Bout time I got my shit...er...crap together."

I frowned. Since when did my father censor his words? "Are you sure you're okay?"

"Yup. Now let me talk to that man of yours."

My stomach clenched at the quick demand and I passed the phone to Brett. Something was definitely different but I didn't know what. I wouldn't say that something was wrong but my father did seem...changed.

Brett placed the phone to his ear and winked at me. "Yes sir."

I didn't know what my dad wanted to say to him. I could only imagine it would be filled with some threats and promises if anything happened to me. Being the youngest child of four and the only girl sucked sometimes.

"I'll take good care of her," Brett said, his voice lowering.

My cheeks heated at the sexual innuendo.

He passed me back the phone and kissed my forehead.

"Evvie, that man reminds me so much of me, it's uncanny." My dad laughed.

I wasn't sure if that was a good thing or not. I said goodbye to my father, making sure to promise that I would call as soon as we got to the resort.

It was finally here. My heart jumped, my skin vibrating from excitement. I was like a kid on Christmas morning.

I leaned across Brett's lap and looked out the window. The large wing of the plane shone in the sunlight while the airport crew were doing security checks on the ground. Never being in a plane before, this was all new to me but it was simply fascinating.

"First time flying?" Brett asked, placing his arm across my lap.

I smiled, my cheeks heating. "Is it that obvious?"

He grinned and kissed my nose. "Yes, but it is adorable."

"Our parents never really had any money to take us anywhere so this is very exciting for me," I explained, stretching to see out the window again.

He chuckled. "I can see that."

The waiting while everyone got their bags in the overhead compartments and in their seats was tedious.

I sighed and snuggled against Brett.

"The novelty wears off, trust me," he teased.

I laughed and inhaled the scent of him. Nervous butterflies flew around my belly. The whole being in a big machine thousands of feet in the air was exhilarating but scary as hell. Man and soap invaded my nostrils, easing my racing heart.

"I love you," Brett whispered against my hair.

My eyes grew heavy. "I love you."

"Did I wear you out this morning?"

"Never," I breathed.

"You're lying." His hand wrapped around my throat, tilting my chin to meet his mouth.

My body relaxed, melting as he held my head restrained. My breathing picked up, needing more than just a kiss.

"Don't plan on getting lots of sleep these next two weeks, lover."

"Hmm...why not?" I asked, licking his bottom lip.

He smirked and brushed his mouth down to my ear. "I'm going to be buried deep inside you, fucking you, over and over again. Every chance I get. I will show you things about your body you never knew. I will satisfy those dark cravings of yours."

My stomach tumbled at his erotic words. They washed over me, heating me from within.

"I'm going to mark that pale skin so every time you look in the mirror, you're reminded of me. Every time you move, you *will* think of me."

The smug air surrounded him as he continued whispering to me, telling me the things he wanted to do to me. The things he *was* going to do to me. My body heated. Never being overly sexually active since before meeting him, this was all new to me but I wouldn't change it for the world. Whenever he woke me during the night, I allowed him to have his way with me. It happened where it was the other way around, too. He always gave in to me, giving me an inch of control each time but never enough where he submitted completely. Except for the one time.

"I'm giving you my control."

God, that was intense. Although it happened weeks ago, every time I thought of that moment, it made me sick to my stomach. As much as I liked being in control, if it meant destroying him, I didn't want it.

Eight

"FIRST TIME flying?" A deep smooth voice with a twang of a Southern accent invaded my thoughts.

I turned to the man sitting beside me and bit back a gasp. His piercing green eyes bored into mine like they were looking into my soul. His short blonde hair styled perfectly in a crew cut. He was good looking but he wasn't Brett.

"Yes," I croaked, my voice hoarse from lack of sleep. I decided right then and there that I hated travel days. The seats were uncomfortable, the plane food was gross and at that moment, I really wished I had a private jet.

The man grinned, his gaze filling with lust as they roamed down my body. He may have been hot but he was way too pretty for me. "Honeymoon?" he asked, his heated gaze stopping at my left hand.

I looked at Brett sleeping against the window and held back my frown, pasting on a friendly smile. "Yes, actually," I lied, gripping Brett's hand tight in my own.

The man nodded, his jaw clenching.

I almost laughed. Looked like he didn't expect me to lie. "Too bad."

Brett stiffened beside me but didn't say anything. Hmm...interesting.

Feeling the man's stare on me, I gripped my sweater closed and inched closer to Brett. He let go of me and wrapped his hand around my inner thigh, squeezing me tight.

My heart gave a start. Even while sleeping, he knew where I was and took full possession of me. I loved it. As every day passed, I craved his touch more and more.

Why couldn't people see that we were happy? Why did they have to try and ruin it? Were we being tested?

"Well," the man whispered in my ear. "If you change your mind and wanna test the waters—"

"Finish that sentence and I'll break your fucking face," Brett growled.

I gasped and looked between the two men.

The man chuckled and sat back. "I'd like to see that."

"Keep hitting on my girl and you will," Brett snapped, sitting forward.

I placed a hand on his chest. "Hey, it's fine. I'm fine. It was innocent."

"Nothing about me is innocent, beautiful," the man crooned.

Brett's jaw clenched, the tendons in his neck protruding. "Stop."

My heart raced. I cupped his cheek. "Brett."

His gaze met mine, his nostrils flaring. "Switch me seats."

The man laughed and rose from his seat before heading down the aisle to the bathroom.

I gripped Brett's shirt tight in my hands. "That's what he wants, Brett."

"I don't care. I'm not having him eye fucking you when we still have an hour left of the flight," he said, his tone harsh.

My head spun but I nodded.

His tense body relaxed as he let out a breath and we switched spots. "Why did you lie and say we were on our honeymoon?"

I looked up at Brett and leaned my head against the seat. "I thought maybe it would back him off."

His eyes heated. He pinched my chin and placed a hard kiss on my lips. "Mrs. MacLean," he whispered.

Mrs. MacLean. The way the name rolled off of his tongue made my insides melt. To be his wife one day, to get to that point let me know that he was definitely in this for the long run. It wasn't a fluff, hearts and flowers filled romance but raw, intense, painful. *Real.*

I imagined us sitting on the porch of our future home, being old and gray and laughing about all of this. The only question was, would we ever get there?

"Rest. It's going to be a couple of hours at least before you'll get to sleep," he whispered in my ear.

I smiled, knowing he wasn't just saying that because it would take a while to get to our room.

The next time I opened my eyes, I was greeted with beautiful blue depths.

Brett smiled and placed a soft kiss on my mouth. "We're getting ready to land. We're in Mexico, Evvie."

My heart jumped and I looked outside. The sun was shining bright as we landed. My stomach flipped. This was it. Two weeks. Alone. With Brett MacLean. My boyfriend, my lover, a piece of me I never knew existed until a couple of months ago.

No worries, no one else to ruin our moment. It was just him and I.

***

WE ARRIVED to our room mid-afternoon. I was tired but so excited, my body vibrated. The room was large. A king sized bed sat against the far wall with a small sitting area beside it.

I walked around the bright room, taking in the scenery before me.

When we landed and headed through security, we didn't see the guy from the plane again. He didn't even come back to his seat after going to the bathroom which I had thought was odd.

The sun shone into the white room, heating my skin as I stared out the patio doors.

The hairs on my body tingled and I smiled, taking a deep breath as I felt Brett approach me.

"Do you know what I'm thinking right now?" he asked, kissing the side of my neck.

I leaned into his touch. "I could take a guess."

"Go for it," he said, placing his hands against the patio door on either side of my head and leaned into me.

"You're wondering how many places you can christen in this room."

He chuckled. "Oh, I am thinking more than that but yes, that's the general idea."

I turned around and leaned against the cool glass. Memories of our first time reined in my mind as I brushed a finger down the cotton of his t-shirt. "Sex first and then tour the resort? Or tour the resort and then sex?"

He smirked and stepped back. "Strip and bend over the edge of the bed."

"Sex first then." I sighed dramatically. "I guess if we have to," I said, feigning a yawn.

A wicked grin spread on his face. "Lover, you will regret saying that."

I sashayed away and pulled off my clothes, leaving me standing naked before him. "Prove it. Show me what you want, Brett," I demanded.

He pulled his belt off with a snap. "I will break you."

"Tell me."

He took a step towards me and folded his belt in half. "I will *fuck* you into submission."

Oh dear God. Liquid seeped between my thighs. I couldn't wait. I needed him inside of me but this new game we were playing was hot as hell. I licked my lips not being able to keep my eyes off of the belt in his hand. Memories of the leather slapping against me made the flesh of my ass tingle. "You think so do you?"

His eyes heated as he circled me. He was like a feral animal, caging me in, waiting to make his next move before he struck. "Bend over the bed."

I did as he said. The bed was high off the floor and with me being short, it left my feet dangling in the air.

"Close your eyes," he demanded, running a hand down my naked back.

"You—"

A heavy hand covered my mouth, tilting my head back. "If you don't be quiet and do as I say, I will gag you."

I gasped. Now that would make for an interesting situation. Bound and gagged for his pleasure only as he took me how he wanted. My body heated. Yup, that's it. I was done.

He kissed my forehead. "Now, close your eyes."

My heart raced but I closed them.

"My Evvie. So beautiful. So perfect." His hand brushed down my spine before he grabbed my wrists, pulling them behind my back. "We'll start out slow but I promise you, by the end of these two weeks, you will hate the word 'anticipation'."

***

AS BRETT and I walked hand in hand around the resort, I couldn't help thinking back to only an hour before. My skin tingled. My core building with pent up frustration of epic proportions. Anticipation. Yup. Already hated the word. Not letting me have a release of any kind as he got me so worked up, I could have punched him.

"How are you feeling?" Brett whispered in my ear.

I growled and shoved him playfully.

He chuckled. "I told you, you will hate the word."

"I already do," I mumbled.

"Good. When I let you come, it will be the biggest orgasm you've ever had. Just think about that, Evvie," he said, grabbing my hand.

I sighed. To think that he had that much control over my body left me breathless.

He pulled me beside him and wrapped an arm around my shoulders. We toured the resort. It was small but perfect. Intimate. The warm afternoon air washed over my skin and although I tried to focus on the grounds before us, I couldn't help but wonder what Brett had in store for me later.

"I will fuck you into submission."

My body heated. Out of all the erotic words he said to me, that was the hottest. I craved it. His touch, his body, his love. I couldn't get enough. I was addicted now more than I was an hour ago.

"You have got to be fucking shitting me."

I frowned at the harsh tone of Brett's voice and followed his gaze. My eyes widened when they landed on the douche from the plane.

The guy glanced our way and waved, a wide grin spreading on his face as he continued chatting with some people at the bar.

I gripped Brett's hand. "Let's go."

Brett didn't move, his jaw tensing as he glared hard at the other man.

"Brett, I'm hungry."

He looked down at me and placed a hard kiss on my lips before wrapping an arm around my shoulders.

I sighed knowing the kiss was a claiming of sorts. Brett and his intense alpha cave man side were going to get him into trouble one of these days. It was only a matter of when.

***

"BRETT, WILL you stop looking at him like you want to gouge his eye balls out with a spoon," I said, taking a sip of my beer.

Brett scrubbed a hand down his face and turned to me. "I don't like the way he looks at you."

I scoffed. "You don't like the way anyone looks at me."

He grunted in response.

I moved from my spot on the couch across from him and sat beside him, placing my feet in his lap. "Foot massage?" I asked, kicking off my flip flops and wiggled my toes.

He smiled and wrapped his hands around my feet. "You always know how to calm me."

I leaned my head against the back of the patio couch and sighed. I knew that touching my skin helped him. I didn't know how deep down that went or what caused that but I didn't ask. I would always help him in any way I could.

My fingers lazily grazed through the hair at his nape. Only being in Mexico for two days, Brett had already gotten some color in his cheeks. I, on the other hand, would burn and I needed to apply the sun screen like it was a second layer of skin.

His thumbs pushed into the arches of my foot and I jumped. A hot tingle shot up my body. "We need to keep your skin protected this week."

"Hmm..."

He looked down at me and chuckled. "The only thing that is going to be making your body pink is me."

The back of my neck heated. "Jealous of the sun, lover boy?" I asked, stifling a yawn and moved my feet from his lap.

"Yes. I'm jealous of anything that touches you," he said, cupping my calf.

I would have laughed if I knew he wasn't joking. While his fingers continued to massage me, I took in my surroundings before noticing a young couple about our age standing by the bar.

The woman, average height and slender had a nice dark tan. The man she was with was pale like me but still had a glow from the sun. The woman threw her head back and laughed, a loud boisterous sound escaping her lips.

I smiled.

"What's so funny?" Brett asked, brushing the back of his knuckles down my cheek.

My heart lifted. "Just watching the couple by the bar."

He followed my gaze. "They're deep in love."

I nodded. The woman tilted her chin when the man placed a soft kiss on her lips. She grinned and looked our way. Her blue eyes twinkled and she gave a little wave.

Brett kissed my forehead and headed to the bar. The man started talking to him when the woman he was with headed my way. Her shoulder length dark brown curly hair bounced with each step as she neared me.

"Hi," she said cheerfully.

I smiled. "Hi."

"My husband is telling your man about the ways of the resort."

"I'm surprised my boyfriend isn't saying that he can figure it out on his own." I laughed.

She chuckled. "I know, right? Big strong Alpha men need to find out that crap on their own." She rolled her eyes. "Please." She giggled. "I'm Sydney."

"Evvie and he's Brett," I said, pointing at him.

He met my gaze and winked. My body flushed. God, one look and I was done.

"My husband is Alex. How long you guys been together?" she asked as the guys headed our way.

"Almost six months." I reached for Brett's hand as he sat down beside me.

"You talking about me?" he purred in my ear.

"Always, lover boy."

He chuckled and pulled my feet onto his lap. "Alex here was just telling me about the buffet times and a special little something just for you."

My eyebrow rose. "Oh?"

"Did you tell him about where you took me?" Sydney asked brushing her fingers through the hair at her husband's nape.

Alex winked. "Yes."

Sydney turned to me. "Girl, have fun."

"Okay." My heart thumped, nervous butterflies flew through my belly.

"And piece of advice." Sydney leaned towards me. "Hold on."

I frowned, confusion coursing through me. "Hold on?"

Sydney giggled.

Brett grabbed my hand. "It was nice meeting the both of you." He looked down at me. "Come with me."

My cheeks heated at his innuendo and I let him pull me to my feet. "I'm sure you'll see us around."

We said our goodbyes and headed down the walkway. "Brett—"

"Well how's my favorite couple doing tonight?"

We both bristled as the guy from the plane stepped in front of us.

"The name is Stefan Price," he said, holding out his hand.

Brett snarled. "You touch her—"

"Brett." I smiled at Stefan. We had to put up with the guy being in the same resort as us for the next two weeks. Might as well play nice. "It's nice to meet you."

"Evvie," Brett said, his voice full of warning.

I ignored him and returned Stefan's handshake. "Evvie Neal and this is Brett MacLean."

Stefan nodded once and crossed his arms under his chest.

Brett ran a hand in small circles over my back before grabbing my hand. He fingered the gold band on my ring finger.

Stefan's gaze followed his movement, his eyes turning cold before meeting mine.

I swallowed. Luckily we were in public so the guys had to behave. Somewhat. "So Stefan. Here alone?"

"Yes. It was supposed to be me and another woman but she fell ill," Stefan said, taking a swig of his beer.

"Evvie."

I looked at Brett.

His jaw clenched. "We should go back to the room. You're tired."

No I wasn't. "But I—"

"I said, you're tired." His eyes searched my face, daring me to challenge him.

My stomach tumbled and I yawned for added affect. "It was nice meeting you, Stefan. I'm sure we'll see you around."

Stefan's brown gaze travelled down my body. "Yes. I'm sure I will."

Brett's hold on my hand tightened and pulled me along. "You are way too fucking nice, lover."

"Well what do you expect," I asked as we walked away. "We have to put up with the guy for two weeks."

"No. We don't."

"Brett." I grabbed his arm, stopping him. "I'm just trying to make this easier on us."

His eyes softened before he placed a hard kiss on my lips. "I don't like the idea of any man touching you or talking to you."

"You are the only one that I want touching me but you can't stop a man from talking to me," I said, trying to keep up with his quick strides.

"No, I can't but he so much as lays a finger on you, they'll have to fly him home in a box," he snarled.

95

My stomach hurt. "You didn't act that way when Alex spoke to me."

Brett's jaw clenched. "That's because he only had eyes for his wife."

I sighed. "Where are you taking me that he suggested?"

"You'll find out tomorrow," he mumbled.

Anxiety crept in as we headed back to our room. The time away was supposed to help us. Do us some good but instead, it looked like the problems from our lives followed us to paradise. "Brett?"

He swiped the key into the door of our room and pushed it open. "Yeah?"

I kicked the door closed and leaned against it.

He walked to the bed and faced me. "What?"

I licked my lips, letting my gaze travel down his body. His loose beige pants hung low on his hips, the light blue t-shirt showing off tanned thick arms. My mouth watered. Veins protruded from his forearms. Every time he moved, his muscles rippled fluidly.

A grin spread on his face as he closed the distance between us. By the time he reached me, we were both naked. All thoughts of people trying to ruin our relationship forgotten.

Nine

"CLOSE YOUR eyes and open your mouth," Brett whispered in my ear. Although his voice was quiet, low, it was firm and strong. I listened. Willingly.

I did as he said when something round pressed between my lips. My tongue licked over the ball that was in my mouth. The metal soon became hot as my breathing deepened. After being woken the next morning by a light swat on the ass, my brain was still fuzzy.

Soft fabric covered my eyes before Brett tied it behind my head. "*Feel*, lover. That's it. No touch, no sight, no speaking. Just feel. Feel my hands on you." He made a point of running his hands down the length of my body, massaging and kneading a path in their wake. "*Feel* me."

I nodded. I did. I felt him everywhere. Before he touched me, I knew what it would feel like. My body, familiar and accustomed to his ways but he always surprised me. Left me panting and wanting with need. A desire so strong, it was mind controlling.

"Your skin is vibrating," he crooned, placing sharp bites and soft kisses on my shoulder blades.

I moaned and whimpered. Mewing sounds left the back of my throat as the two senses mixed as one. He would bite and then kiss and then bite again, not giving me enough time to get over the first nip. His mouth grazed down my spine, his teeth biting into me every so often. My mind reeled. My eyes rolled back into my head. Who knew that being bit could feel so good?

"I could eat you up. Devour your body completely," he husked. "Leaving you aching and panting for more. You always want more, don't you, my little vixen?" he breathed against my tail bone.

I nodded.

"I'll give you more. I'll give you everything you ever dreamed of. Those erotic fantasies that you were too ashamed to share with your other boyfriends." He gripped my ass, digging his fingers into my flesh. "Well my sweet Evvie. With me? You won't have to be ashamed. I will please every dark, passionate, delicious," he husked between kisses. "fantasy."

My breath caught in my throat. I did have fantasies. Always about a dark lover who could please my every waking desire and more. What woman didn't? She was lucky enough to find that one person who could appease her appetite. Her hunger. I found mine in Brett.

"You would like that, wouldn't you? You want me to fill that hunger deep inside of you? Curb your craving for dark erotic love making?" He fisted my hair and pushed my face into the mattress, breathing hard against my neck. "Is that what you want?"

I frowned. Or tried to with a ball shoved in my mouth.

"I don't make love?" he asked, taking the question right out of my thoughts.

I nodded.

"Every time, I'm inside of you, it's making love. No matter how rough, how gentle, how delicious," he purred. "It's always making love to you."

I panted. But I wanted more. I wanted proper normal love making. At least once. I wanted to know what it would feel like with him. He knew that. I just had to be patient.

"But right now..." He leaned into me, his erection pressing against my ass. "It won't be making love. It will be pure raw animalistic fucking."

My pussy throbbed, the liquid from my center running down my inner thigh. God, he hadn't even touched me yet and I was turned on more than ever.

"I *crave* you," he growled and grabbed my hands before pinning them behind my back. He tied something around them and grunted in approval.

My heart raced. I was completely and utterly restrained under him.

"I always preferred to have your hands on me but right now, seeing you bound and gagged, spread open for me…" His hand caressed my ass. "I think I prefer this. I can do whatever I want and you can't stop me, Evvie. Now this is *control*."

My breathing picked up and I moaned when his fingers dug into the flesh of my rear.

"Your cunt is soaked and hungry for me. Your greedy body wants my cock." He leaned down to my ear. "You like being restrained, Evvie?"

I nodded, spreading my legs more.

"Do you want me to fuck you?" he asked, moving down the length of my body.

I whimpered and nodded again.

His rough hands spread me open, kneading into my ass cheeks. "God, I love your ass."

I cried out when teeth bit into the flesh. The white hot pain spread over me and when Brett did it again, I bucked, arching under his touch. *More.*

He lifted me onto all fours, holding onto my bound hands while he brushed the tip of his cock over my core. "Prepare to be fucked, lover."

I inhaled a gasp as he thrust into me hard. A shudder tore through me, my body opening to him as he drove in and out of me with a speed we both craved. My cries of pleasure were muffled by the metal ball in my mouth but that didn't stop me from letting him hear how good he was making me feel.

Tingles spread over my skin as his thrusts deepened. His long thick cock hit the bundle of nerves setting me off. I screamed, my body clenching around him. I shook and trembled but that only encouraged him to power into me harder.

"Come again," he demanded.

I moaned, my muscles contracting and twitching from the hard use.

"Your pussy's nice and hot." His thrusts slowed and he pulled out of me. "Nice and swollen."

My body shook as his fingers pushed through my folds, rubbing gently over my engorged clit.

The tip of his cock ran from my center to the puckered opening between my ass cheeks, coating me with the juices from my center. "You're going to take me everywhere, Evvie."

Although I couldn't see anything with the blindfold on my face, my eyes widened.

Brett grabbed the ball from between my lips. "I want to hear you scream my name as I take complete possession of your body."

My heart raced. "I…"

"What, Evvie?" he asked, rubbing his cock over the tight opening at my rear.

"No man has ever…" I swallowed, my throat dry.

"I know." He placed a light kiss on my tail bone. "I'll be gentle…at first."

***

MY BODY stirred, the sound of clicking keys invading my thoughts. I rolled over onto my side, opening my eyes to find Brett sitting across from his laptop, working away.

I looked at the clock. 9:00am.

We were on vacation and he was still working. Had he even gone to bed yet? He woke me originally at 6:00am and let me go back to sleep after he bound and gagged me.

The skin around my wrists were tender, tingling to the touch. Red lines marked them and I smiled, knowing what he had done. Where he had been. Oh God, he had taken me everywhere. To new heights. New beginnings. Many firsts for me and I loved every moment of it.

I rose from the bed, the cool air caressing my naked skin, sending a shiver down my back.

I stepped up behind him and wrapped my arms around his shoulders, placing a soft kiss on his neck.

"What are you doing up, lover?" he asked, while he continued to type away on the keyboard.

"I could ask you the same thing," I said, my voice hoarse from lack of sleep and the many times I screamed his name through the night. I curled my hand around his throat and nipped his jaw.

He grabbed my wrist, kissed the red marks and in a quick move, pulled me onto his lap. "I should bend you over my lap and spank that delicious ass of yours for interrupting my work."

I grinned and straddled his hips, pushing my naked chest against his. "You work too much, lover boy."

His hands roamed down my naked back before cupping my ass. "It's not really work when I enjoy it."

Running my hands through his hair, I placed a soft kiss on his mouth. "Do you enjoy it?"

He searched my face, his lips turning up at the corners. "I do. It gives me a sense of security for me and mine."

I smiled. "But you need to take a break every now and again."

"Do I? And what kind of break would that be?"

I licked between his lips, the scruff of his jaw scratching my cheeks.

"Hmm…you want something, my little vixen?" he asked, smacking me hard on the ass.

I jumped, the slight pain turning into burning pleasure as my skin heated under his touch. "Yes. Please," I breathed.

"Then be a good girl and show me," he demanded and let go of me.

Not wasting any time, I reached into the waist band of his sweat pants and pulled out his cock.

He groaned, his eyes closing as I stroked him hard.

My core pulsed and although I was sore, tender from the many times we had made love already, I couldn't get enough of this man.

His length grew under my touch, his hips bucking when I brushed a thumb over the tip.

I brought my hand up to my mouth and licked the pre-cum off of me.

His nostrils flared. "It makes me so fucking hard knowing you love the taste of me."

I covered his mouth with mine and lowered myself onto him, my body stretching to meet his size.

He swallowed my moan and grabbed my hips, pulling me hard against him as I rode his rigid length. "You're wet already and I haven't even touched you," he husked.

I circled my hips, slamming against him as I gave us what our bodies needed. "I woke up wet for you." I breathed.

He growled and deepened the kiss, running his hands up and down my back. His calloused fingers ignited my skin on fire.

"That's it. Harder, Evvie. Use your body to please me." He gripped my ass, pulling me flush against him. His fingers dug into my flesh as he thrust into me as deep as he could go.

I whimpered.

"You like my dick deep inside that sweet pussy of yours?"

"Oh God, yes," I cried out, my thigh muscles burning from the over use.

"Good. Now come with me." He cupped the back of my neck and brought my mouth down to his, shoving his tongue between my lips. He kissed the hell out of me as I rode him hard.

We came together, crashing over waves of pure bliss. He grunted, filling me and I screamed, the sounds of our pleasure mixing as one.

He continued to thrust in me slow and deep as he devoured my mouth.

The heady scent of sex mixed with the sounds of our bodies meeting, heated my skin.

"Can you hear how much your body enjoys being fucked by me?" he breathed against my mouth.

I panted and sucked on his bottom lip.

He growled and gripped the back of my neck, squeezing before plunging his tongue back into my mouth. "My body owns you. Don't forget that."

I smiled and pushed against him, challenging him. "Right now, I think it's my body that owns you."

He released me and pushed his laptop to the side. "Say that again."

I swallowed hard at the wicked glint in his eyes. "I. Own. You," I said, pointing at his chest.

In a quick move he lifted me onto the table. "Again."

"I own you." I laughed.

He smirked. "Are you sure?"

I licked my lips and nodded. "Yes, lover boy."

His thumbs brushed over the folds of my pussy. "Last chance to take that back."

"Never." I shook my head. "You're mine. Always have been. *My* body owns *you*."

"We'll see about that." He placed his hands on my inner thighs, pushing my legs apart. He spread me open to him as far as my body would allow. He winked and covered my clit at the same time he thrust two fingers into me.

I bucked under him, my eyes rolling into the back of my head as he sucked the hardened nub. "Oh God. Brett."

His fingers plunged into me, a growl escaping his lips. His lips closed over the nub sending a jolt of electricity straight through my body.

Just when I was about to come, he stopped.

My eyes widened as he lifted his head, his lips glossy from my juices. "I wish my come would stay inside of you, marking you as mine from the inside out."

A hot shiver ran down my spine and I moaned as he pushed his fingers into me as deep as possible.

"You want to come?"

"Yes," I begged.

"Then say it."

I frowned. "Say what?"

He grinned and dove at my center again but ignored the spot where I wanted him most. His finger brushed over my pussy before sinking back into me. "Say it."

I had no idea what he was talking about. "I…" I panted. "Please."

His finger was replaced by two, thrusting into me hard as he brushed his teeth over my clit. "Tell me and I'll let you come."

"I don't know—"

His mouth closed on my inner thigh, his teeth biting down hard.

I cried out, tears burning my eyes at the sharp pain but oh God, did it ever feel good. The deep thrusts of his fingers mixed with the bite sent tingles spreading over my body. A sheen of sweat coated my skin as he continued to ignore my begging for a release.

"Tell me," he demanded, reining small but sharp bites over my inner thighs. His lips reached the crease beside my pussy. "I enjoy seeing my marks on you, lover."

I enjoyed it too. It let me know where he's been, always reminding me of his touch. "Brett, please. I can't take it anymore."

"Who owns who?" he asked, pushing his fingers into me as far as he could.

I gasped, gripping the edge of the table. "You. You own me. Please, I can't...I need—"

His thumb rubbed over my clit. His teeth bit down on the crease between my thigh and pussy and his fingers thrust into me at a frantic rate.

My body shook as I gasped for air, the multiple sensations mixing as one. Just when I thought I was about to break, shattering from the ecstasy, his finger pushed into the tight hole at my rear, setting me off. An explosion erupted inside of me. It was hard, making me scream loud enough that my voice went raw.

The orgasm was so intense, I felt like I was floating, having an outer body experience as I came down from the high of the release.

Strong arms lifted me before placing me on the bed as a warm body covered mine.

My eyes grew heavy when a deep chuckle sounded in my ear.

"How was that?" Brett asked, pushing his hips between my legs.

I ran my hands down his back, scratching my nails into his skin. "Best. Orgasm. Ever."

"Good." His tongue licked up the side of my neck before delving into my mouth.

I swallowed the sweet taste of my juices mixed with the saltiness of his previous release and lifted my hips as he lowered into me.

His movements were slow but deep.

I moaned, my muscles jumping, my core pulsing. A tingle spread through my center and I whimpered.

"That's it. I want you with me," he breathed against my mouth.

My nails dug into the hard muscles of his back as we came together. We swallowed each other's sounds of ecstasy as our bodies moved as one.

I sighed in bliss, running my hands down his sweat slicked back.

He chuckled and placed a hard kiss on my lips before releasing me completely.

I watched as he rose from the bed and righted his pants.

He pulled me into his arms, wrapping the blanket around me and placed his laptop on my lap. "I want to show you what I've been working on."

A couple of clicks later, an advertisement popped up on the screen.

Benefit Against Drunk Driving
Making people aware
Saturday, November 10th, 2013
All proceeds go to families affected
6pm – 10pm
Location: The Red Love

My breath caught in my throat and I looked up at him before glancing back at the screen.

He smiled lightly.

"Anything I can do to help?" I asked, pulling the blanket tighter around us.

"Just you being there beside me is all the help I need," he said, shutting his lap top closed. His eyes took on a faraway look.

My heart hurt, wishing I could take away his pain. My mom had died from cancer. Natural causes. I couldn't even begin to imagine what he and his sister had gone through. Having both of your parents die due to a drunk driver hitting them was something you could never get over.

"Are you okay?" I asked, cupping his cheek.

"Yeah," he answered, his voice thick as he placed the computer back on the nightstand.

Tears burned my eyes.

"Hey, Evvie, don't." He kissed me on the nose. "You've cried enough over me."

I shook my head. "This is different."

"Stop. I can't deal. Even though it was years ago, it still..." he swallowed. "It fucking hurts."

With a shaky breath, I wrapped my arms around his neck, holding him. Pouring the love I felt for this man into my touch.

"Thank you," he whispered.

I leaned back. "For what?"

"For being you. For not leaving even though I can be a dick."

"I love you," I said, cupping his face in my hands. "I'm sure I'm not the easiest person to get along with either."

He scoffed. "Evvie, you are perfect."

I laughed. "I'm many things but perfect is not one of them."

Brett's eyebrows narrowed as he grabbed my wrists. "You are perfect for me. You're still here even after all the shit I've put you through."

My stomach clenched. "I love you. We both make mistakes. You thought you were looking out for me but realized that you needed me more."

"I couldn't deal with any of this without you. I'm...I'm not strong enough," he mumbled and looked away.

I sighed and brushed a thumb over his bottom lip. I didn't know how to make him see reason. How to make him not be so hard on himself. Maybe there was something wrong with me that I still stuck around but I loved him. It was all consuming, all powerful, like he told me when we first started seeing each other. "I'm not leaving you, Brett."

He nodded slightly. "I know." He took a breath. "I know that."

Did he? "No matter what. This?" I motioned between us. "Is strong. Permanent."

He looked away, his jaw clenching.

"Brett," I demanded.

His eyes twinkled as he met my gaze.

"Don't look at me like that."

He raised an eyebrow. "Like what?"

I kissed him hard. "With doubt in your eyes."

He laid us down, pulled off his pants and wrapped his arms around me. Bringing the blanket up and around us, he held me tight, pressing his body against mine. "It would destroy me if you left me," he whispered into my hair.

"Stop. I'm here. I'm always here. I'm not leaving." I grabbed his hand, pulling him tighter around me. I would crawl under his skin if I could. Curling up into a little ball in the corner of his warmth. He was my safe place. My forever. My one. My only.

"I couldn't deal with the shit about my mom either if it wasn't for you," he mumbled, his voice getting heavy from sleep.

"I'm here, Brett. You're safe."

His body relaxed as he kissed my shoulder. His breathing eventually turning deep and even.

I lay awake, staring at the ceiling as I listened to the sounds of Brett's hot breath against my neck.

I loved the man that had his body wrapped around me. His hold on me was tight, like he thought he would wake up and I would be gone. Never. I was his. I knew that now.

Ten

I BROUGHT our nightly bath time ritual to Mexico with us. Except there, the tub was huge and I could sit across from Brett. My body leaned against the white cool basin. The scent of lavender and vanilla invaded my nostrils, a sigh of bliss leaving my lips.

"Do you know how hard it is to control myself when you're sitting there naked and soapy?" he said, holding my foot in his hands. He brought it up to his mouth and nibbled my heel.

I giggled. "This is our time, remember? No sex." I enjoyed just spending moments like this with him. We had our issues but it was like as soon as we were together in our bath, all thoughts of the outside world left us.

Brett grinned, his blue eyes twinkling. "But if it turned into a shower, then we can?"

"Yes." Those were the rules. Even if we didn't talk and just sat there, there was no sex allowed in our baths together. Call it lame or corny, but we needed this. A relationship couldn't be based on physical needs. I knew that and so did he, even though he wanted to deny it.

"Are you having a good vacation?" he asked, pushing his thumb into the arch of my foot.

A moan escaped my lips. "Yes. You?"

He winked. "Oh yes."

My cheeks heated and I shook my head. It was a week into our vacation and although he hadn't wanted me to get touched by the sun, my pale skin was a little tender. But it was darkening nicely into a light tan so I didn't feel so much like a ghost.

There had been no sign of Stefan since our first encounter with him. We had stuck to the beach and our room, getting room service whenever we were hungry. Brett got enjoyment from feeding me or eating the food off of me and I was saddened with the fact that one more week and this would be over.

***

J.M. Walker

THE NEXT morning after breakfast, we decided to head down to the beach. Lathering on the sunscreen, I had a moment of jealousy that Brett's skin could golden and mine would burn. Damn my blonde hair and blue eyes. My brother's? Nope, they had no issues tanning at all. I was the unfortunate one.

"Swim?" Brett asked, rubbing the cream on my shoulders. I shook my head. "I think I want to read first."

"I think we should swim first," Brett said, grabbing my hand. His gaze travelled down my bathing suit clad body, heating my skin on fire.

I swallowed. I brought three bikinis with me to Mexico and after much debate over which one I would wear, I chose the sexy red one-piece. It still hardly covered anything but I told Brett that we would never have to see any of these people again after our trip. "I want to read. It's a really good—"

"Lover, I will throw you over my shoulder if I have to. Either way, you're going swimming," he said, his voice firm.

I frowned, attempting to pull my hand from his grip. "I want to read and besides, you wouldn't dare."

A wicked smirk splayed on his face. He pinched my chin and brushed his mouth along mine before biting my bottom lip. "Try me."

My heart fluttered. I playfully punched him in the stomach forcing him to let go of me.

An evil glint flashed in his eyes before he hooked an arm around my middle and threw me over his shoulder.

I squealed, gripping the waistband of his bathing suit shorts. "Brett, put me down!"

He chuckled and started jogging to the water. "I will."

My cheeks heated as the chuckles sounded around us. Women giggled and I looked up as we neared the water.

Their gazes heated, jealousy soaring through the air. *Eat your hearts out girls. He's mine.*

"Brett, put me down please," I said, smacking him on the ass.

"You *will* pay for that," Brett growled, gripping my hips. He swatted my rear making me yelp. So he was allowed to smack my butt and not the other way around? I grinned. We'll see about that. I repeatedly slapped his hard delicious ass when I was suddenly, thrown over his shoulders.

I landed in the cool body of water, coughing and sputtering as I choked down the salty water. Rising to the surface, I splashed Brett. "You are a douche monkey."

He laughed and wrapped his arms around me. "Douche monkey? You can't come up with something better, lover?"

I struggled in his grip. "Sorry. All the salt has clouded my judgment."

"Well you'll be calling me something else in a moment," he said, swimming with me in his arms.

I wrapped my arms around his thick neck, holding on tight as he swam with me against him. "Oh? Like what?"

He winked. "Something like, Oh-Brett-yes-harder-harder-faster-you-are-amazing-you're-a-fucking-God. Would that work?"

I tapped my chin. "Hmm…I don't know."

"Or how about, Yes-Brett-Oh-yes-harder-fuck-me-harder-make-me-scream," he said, raising his voice to imitate me.

I rolled my eyes and giggled. "I do not sound like that."

"No? Then tell me, Evvie, what do you sound like?"

"Oh-yes-yes-wait-you're-done-already? How's that?" I laughed.

His eyes darkened making my breath catch. "Are you challenging me, my sweet Evvie?"

"Now why would I ever do such a thing?" I teased.

"You won't be asking me why I'm done already in a moment. With my cock buried deep between your creamy thighs, you'll be begging me to stop." He placed a hard kiss on my lips, not giving me a chance to process his words. "You'll be screaming my name so hard, your voice will go raw."

"Hmm…sounds like a good idea," I breathed against his mouth. "I like this playful side of you," I whispered.

110

He grinned and cupped my ass before wrapping my legs around his waist. "You bring out the best in me," he whispered.

I placed a soft peck on his mouth when I was pressed up against a rocky wall. Looking around us, I realized that we had swum around the bend. The waves moved against us, hitting hard against the side of the small mountain.

"Is this safe, Brett?" I asked, squeezing my thighs tight around him.

"Don't worry, lover. I got you."

My heart gave a start. His words meaning more than just at that moment. I cupped his cheeks, staring intently into his deep blue eyes. "And I got you."

His mouth crashed to mine.

I reached between us, pulling his rigid length from his swimming trunks. Pushing my bathing suit bottoms to the side, I lowered my body onto him.

He groaned, pushing into me with the added force of the waves.

"Brett," I breathed against his mouth.

His hold on my waist tightened.

I gasped, an eruption of pleasure exploding inside of me. Cries of ecstasy escaped my lips, the sounds of the ocean swallowing my screams.

***

"WHERE ARE we going?" I asked Brett as the black town car drove us through Cancun.

His hold on my hand tightened. "I have a surprise for you."

"Really?" We were leaving the next day. What kind of surprise could he have for me so close to the end of our trip?

He winked and placed a soft kiss on my forehead. "We're here." he said.

I turned and looked out the window. My eyes widened. A large white building stood before us, sporting *Rouge L'amour,* on a sign in red neon letters.

"Is this...yours?" I asked Brett in awe.

He grinned. "It's actually ours."

"Really?" I gaped at him. *Ours?*

"I was serious about wanting to spend the rest of my life with you, Evvie." He brushed his knuckles down my cheek before pinching my chin.

My heart stuttered at his words. "I can't believe you opened another club and in Mexico of all places."

"This place is booming. The tourists rolling in constantly will make us a killing."

The way he said *us* made my heart skip a beat. There was no way that I could accept this though. How could I pay him back? "Why do you do it?" He clearly didn't need the money. It's not like he was poor or anything.

He rubbed his strong fingers along his jaw and thought a moment.

"I'm sorry. That was rude—"

"No. It wasn't. I honestly don't care about the money. I get a thrill out of making people happy." His eyes twinkled. "To have people spend time in my clubs is almost as satisfying as you having an orgasm. That's how much I like being in control."

My body hummed. I would never get used to his constant references to sex. I watched him as he looked out the window, glancing around us. His body was relaxed as he let out a deep breath.

He looked back at me. "What?"

My cheeks heated at being caught staring. "I'm proud of you."

His eyebrow rose. "You're proud of me?"

I nodded and grabbed his hand. "You're so young and look at what you have accomplished."

He grinned and cupped the back of my neck. "You haven't seen anything yet, my sweet Evvie." He brushed his mouth along mine. "When you marry me, *that* will be my biggest accomplishment ever and all of this, every single one of my clubs, will be yours."

A breath escaped me on a whoosh. Just the thought of marrying him, left me speechless. "Brett, I can't pay you back for all of this."

His eyes narrowed. "You don't have to. Work with me and we'll help it grow. This is ours."

My heart thumped. Chewing my bottom lip, I looked around us. The sun had set so the lights of the city were glowing in full force. Almost looked like a mini Las Vegas. This was mine. This club. *Mine.* I looked back at Brett.

His face was passive like he was waiting for me to freak out. To run and scream into the high heavens saying that my boyfriend was crazy. Maybe he was. Maybe I was the crazy one for falling for it. But I would be there for him. No matter how crazy we got, we would be together.

His eyes twinkled. This man. *Mine.*

Brett cleared his throat. "Let's go before I can't control myself any longer."

I laughed and watched as he left the car and walked around to my side, opening the door for me.

Placing my hand in his, I let him pull me out of the vehicle.

His arm slid around my shoulders. "One request. I want you by my side. At all times. We're both in this together. Not 50/50 but 100/100."

I nodded.

"By my side, Evvie," he said, kissing my forehead.

People milled about, mostly tourists from all over the world. News media stood outside the club, waiting to speak to someone when I heard his name being called.

"Brett MacLean, how does it feel being one of the youngest club owners in Mexico?"

"Are you planning on opening clubs in other countries?"

"Anymore clubs being opened in Mexico?"

"Brett, who's the beautiful lady with you?"

Brett grabbed my hand and pulled me beside him as he answered the rapid fire questions that were thrown his way. I knew his club in the U.S. was pretty popular but never like this. Of course, I wasn't there on opening night so I didn't know how that went but I couldn't imagine it was anything like this. Hundreds of people stood outside the club, waiting to be let in. Mathis had taught him well.

"How are you doing, lover?"

I smiled up at Brett and gripped his arm. "This is amazing. Mexico loves you."

He grunted. "As long as you love me, I don't care about anyone else."

My heart swelled. "I do. More than anything."

He kissed my forehead, inhaling deep before stepping back. "Remember, I want you by my side. This is all yours, too."

My heart raced as I took in the vast expanse before us. My stomach clenched when a thought crossed my mind. I couldn't ask him now as he mingled, answered questions, showed people around but I would have to ask him later.

"Miss."

I turned to a small woman standing beside a cameraman.

She smiled. "Would you mind if I asked you a couple of questions?"

"Um...I..." I looked around and caught Brett's gaze. He smiled, noticing the news woman standing before me and nodded. My anxious nerves eased and I turned back to the woman. "Okay."

"Thank you. Ignore the camera and focus on me." She patted my arm. "You'll do fine."

I took a breath. Easy for her to say.

"Mary Foster reporting from Cancun, Mexico at the new highly anticipated club, *Rouge L'amour*. I'm standing here with..." She looked at me.

"Evvie Neal," I said into the microphone.

She smiled. "Evvie Neal. Is this your first time here, Evvie?"

I nodded.

"And you are the girlfriend, wife....of the owner?"

"Girlfriend."

She winked. "I can tell by that huge smile on your face that you are deeply in love with him too."

114

I laughed, the back of my neck heating. "Is it that obvious?"

"It's all good, but I do have to say, God, you sure are beautiful."

"Yes, she is." Heavy arms wrapped around me and a light kiss was placed on my neck.

I smiled up at Brett.

"Speaking of the owner. Brett MacLean, it's so nice to finally meet you."

"Evvie is the owner, as well. The club is ours," Brett explained, holding me tight beside him.

I had completely forgotten about that. In my whole life, I never owned anything bigger than a car.

Mary's smiled widened. "Well that changes things. A partnership that's going to explode into 2014."

"In more ways than one, Mary," Brett said, caressing the small of my back.

Mary winked and looked between us both. "Your girlfriend is so sweet." She asked us several other questions, including me in the interview as much as Brett.

She ended the interview and shook both our hands. "You are the new couple of the year. If I have it my way, I will make it possible."

Brett and I laughed but by the serious look on her face, I had a feeling that she wasn't joking.

"Stay and have a drink. Anything you want, it's on the house," Brett said, wrapping an arm around my shoulders.

Mary smiled. "Rick, baby, it's party time."

The cameraman, Rick, shook his head and took the microphone from her. "Lead the way."

"How was your first official interview, lover?" Brett asked, cupping my chin.

"It was good. Mary is funny and nice. I wasn't too nervous," I said, looking up at him.

"Get used to it, Evvie." He placed a soft peck on my mouth.

Camera flashes went off but all I could focus on was Brett's soft lips against mine. He released me a moment later. "Let's get a drink."

"Will this interview be on TV back home?" I asked as we walked hand in hand to the bar.

"It should be but if not, I'll find it online for us to watch."

We sat at the bar and while Brett spoke with his or our staff, I guess it was, I ordered a beer.

"What's wrong?"

I ran a finger around the rim of the brown bottle and shrugged.

"Talk to me, Evvie," Brett said, grabbing my hand.

I sighed. "How am I going to pay you back for all of this?" I asked, motioning to the large expanse before us.

Brett frowned. "I told you that I don't want you to pay me back, Evvie. We're in this together."

"But…what about a…"

"What?"

I took a breath and braced myself. "What about a prenuptial agreement?"

Several emotions flashed on his face before he cupped the back of my neck. "If I was worried about you taking my money, we wouldn't be sitting here." His eyes softened. "I love you. I want to spend the rest of my life with you. What's mine is yours."

"Then how come you don't believe me when I tell you the exact same thing?" I blurted and regretted it a moment later when he pulled back.

He didn't respond.

I bit my cheek to keep from lashing out when a hand curled in mine. I looked down at our entwined fingers. The gold band that I had become so used to wearing, flashed in the dim lighting of the room. Brushing my thumb over it, I sighed.

"Say the word and you don't have to be any part of this. I'll remove your name from everything that has to do with owning the club." He pinched my chin, forcing me to look up at him. "I want you happy. What do *you* want?"

I chewed my bottom lip and searched his face. We had come so far in a short amount of time. I had only known him for six months but felt like it was a lifetime. He was my one. My only. My soul mate. What he wanted, I wanted. "I want this."

"Are you sure?"

I nodded. "I want to do this with you. I want to be by your side every step of the way."

His warm mouth captured mine in a soft but demanding kiss. "Thank you."

"No, thank you. This is all a little overwhelming but I couldn't ask for a better business partner."

He kissed my forehead. "I'll teach you the ropes, my sweet Evvie."

I smiled as he released me and took a sip of my beer.

"Two drinks and no more, lover," Brett whispered in my ear. "I want your body sober for when I take my pleasure from it later."

"Hmm...what about my pleasure?" I teased.

He kissed my bare shoulder. "I can guarantee that you will be screaming from more than just pleasure in a couple of hours."

My throat went dry at what he was suggesting. "What do you mean?"

"I mean, pure, raw, hot, ecstasy as I dive deep inside of your body."

Oh dear God.

He laughed and kissed my cheek.

I shook my head and smiled. This new playful side of him was something that I could get used to. Knowing it was just revealed for me and only me, made a surge of desire spread through my body. As each day passed, little bits were revealed from us both. We became more comfortable with each other and as much as I missed home, I didn't want this time with Brett to end.

***

"LOVER, WHAT'S wrong?" Brett asked me, brushing a hand down my arm.

I stared out the window of the plane the next day and sighed. "I don't want to leave."

He kissed my head. "I know."

I still couldn't believe that I was part owner of a club. "You'll go back to being busy with the club and I'll go back to working behind the bar." I couldn't help it but a deep depression was threatening to settle in and I was having difficulty fighting it.

"Mathis will be having me travel more in the next couple of months. I want you to come with me and we can come back to Mexico anytime you want...partner."

I smiled. Partner. I liked the sound of that but then my stomach clenched. "I can't pay my bills if I'm not working though."

"I'll take care of it."

I shook my head. "I appreciate that but there's no way I'm living off of you."

"You wouldn't be." Brett thought a moment. "You can be my secretary. I'll pay you. I'm sure Mathis would be fine with it. I'll get him to pay you if you think it's too weird but sleeping with the boss would be getting you some extra benefits."

I laughed and snuggled into his side, the heaviness in my heart lifting. I watched as the plane taxied down the runway before we lifted into the air. "I just know what we're going home to."

"You have nothing to worry about. Anna and Claire—"

"It's not just them, Brett." I turned to him and cupped his face. "There's also your mom."

His gaze hardened. "If I never have to see her again, it'll be too fucking soon."

"That's what I'm worried about."

"Don't worry about me," he said, kissing my knuckles. He paid special attention to the gold band on my ring finger.

"Why wouldn't I worry about you?"

"Evvie."

"No." I pulled my hand from his grip and crossed my arms under my chest. "So much is trying to keep us apart. I can't

118

explain it. Maybe it's all me." A hard lump formed in my throat. "But it's like we're not meant to be."

He looked away, his jaw clenching. "You are mine. No one is going to change that."

I breathed a heavy sigh.

"Move in with me."

My head shot around. "Excuse me?"

Brett pinched my chin. "Move in with me. We now have the club together, we will be getting married eventually, so move into my apartment."

My heart raced. "Isn't it too soon?"

"Why? I love you. You love me." He shrugged. "I want you all to myself. I want to go to bed with you beside me and wake up with you next to me. These two weeks were a tease and I want more."

Well I did practically live at his apartment anyways. I did while he was in New York. "What about Anna?"

"She'll be back in her own place soon enough. I'll kick her out if I have to. I want you. With me."

My stomach flipped. "Okay."

A cheesy grin spread on his face before he crashed his lips to mine. "Are you sure?" he asked, cupping my cheeks.

I nodded, chewing my bottom lip. "I'm nervous, but yes."

He frowned, pinching my chin and pulled my lip from the onslaught of my teeth. "Why are you nervous?"

I scoffed. "You do remember my family right?"

A wicked smile spread on his face. "If they only knew how corrupted their little Evvie has become."

I laughed. "You would be buried alive."

Brett chuckled and wrapped an arm around my shoulders before placing a peck on my forehead. "I will make it so you don't regret it."

I didn't and I knew I wouldn't. I loved him. I knew that I wanted to spend the rest of my life with him. It was everyone else that had a problem with it.

Eleven

THE TWO weeks in Mexico flew by. Before I knew it, it was over. But we did go out with a bang. Our club. Our celebration of it later that night. My body bloomed as memories of Brett demanding his pleasure from my body invaded my mind.

I sighed. My heart was heavy as I sat at the bar while Brett worked away in his office getting ready for the benefit later that week. I brushed my finger around the opening of the beer bottle. We had been home for three days and I hardly saw him. Yes, I was moving in with him, but we had decided to wait until the weekend so he could help me. I didn't want to disturb him so I would wait. I had to.

He was so wrapped up in work, he hadn't been sleeping. I didn't want to distract him so as much as it pained me, I spent the nights at my own apartment by myself since Kane was still doing his thing with Tatiana. I didn't know what was going on there exactly, but if he was happy, then so was I.

We broke the news to Kane that I was moving out and he was ecstatic. I could tell that he was a little sad but he would never mention it.

My brothers were not so understanding and freaked out when I told them via text messages. I didn't want to deal with their shit. I called my dad and let him deal with them. He didn't like that I was moving in with my boyfriend so soon. But after explaining to him that I did live with Kane for five years, he got over it.

"Evvie Neal?"

My thoughts were interrupted as I turned and saw a tall man approach me. I frowned and then my eyes widened as recognition kicked in. "Nick Rowan?"

He grinned and closed the distance between us. "Look at you. You're absolutely stunning."

My cheeks heated as I rose to my feet. Nick was taller than I remembered. His short brown hair cut into a crew cut, his deep

brown eyes that I had remembered being captivated by years
before, took me in.

"It's nice to see you again, Nick."

He pulled me into a hug before holding me at arm's length,
his gaze glancing down my body. "Wow. How long has it
been?"

My stomach clenched at the heated look in his dark stare. I
looked around the vast room. Brett was nowhere to be found. He
would not be happy at all if he saw Nick's hands on me. For the
guy's safety, I pulled away and sat down on the stool. "It's been
around ten years. Drink?"

He nodded and stared at me.

Okay...odd. I cleared my throat and walked around the bar.
"What will you have?"

He frowned. "You work here?"

"I do." It was my night off but the club was slow and Jake
was busy so I didn't see any harm in making the drinks myself.
Not like Brett would notice anyways or care for that matter.

"I'll have a beer," Nick said, rubbing his fingers over his
mouth.

Back in high school, I had the biggest crush on the guy but
now, I wasn't so sure what I saw in him. He came off as a smug
asshole. I bit back a laugh. Brett was no different but he didn't
look at me like I was a piece of meat. A toy for his little game.
God, what did I ever see in Nick?

"So, are you single, Evvie?"

Well, he moved fast. I placed the bottle of beer in front of
Nick and moved around the bar but not before I saw Brett
heading our way. My stomach clenched. *Oh shit.*

"Evvie?" Nick said from behind me.

"No, I'm not single," I responded, not taking my eyes away
from Brett.

He closed the distance between us and cupped the back of
my neck before capturing my mouth in a hard demanding kiss.
"Lover," he snarled in warning.

My heart thudded and I gripped the front of his black suit
jacket. "He's an old friend, Brett."

His blue eyes searched my face. "Friend or ex?"

I swallowed. "Both."

Brett growled and pulled me beside him before wrapping an arm around my shoulders.

Nick rose to his feet and met Brett's glare head on. "This the boyfriend, Evvie?"

I nodded. "Brett, this is Nick Rowan. Nick, Brett MacLean. He owns the club."

Nick raised an eyebrow. "You're dating the owner?"

"Yes." I frowned. "Why?"

Nick's brown eyes turned cold and accusatory.

What the hell did he think was going on between me and Brett? Did he think I was sleeping my way up the ladder? Little did he know, Brett approached me first. *Asshole.*

"I'll catch you later, Ev." Nick placed a card on the bar top in front of me. "We'll chat over coffee."

Brett tensed. "Like fu—"

"Brett," I said, turning to him as Nick walked away. "You need to calm down."

He leaned down to my ear. "I will calm down when I'm deep inside of you."

I pushed him onto the stool and sat beside him. "You can't get jealous over every guy that talks to me."

"He's your fucking ex, Evvie." His strong jaw clenched and unclenched. "Did you sleep with him?"

"Yes," I said, crossing my arms under my chest.

Brett frowned. "Did you lose your virginity to him?"

"Brett, I don't—"

"Answer the fucking question," he snapped.

My cheeks heated as customers near us looked our way. Okay, Brett needed to really calm down or else he was going to cause a scene. "Yes. Happy now?"

"No. Knowing that it wasn't me that you lost your virginity to makes me furious," he said through gritted teeth.

I rolled my eyes. "That was years ago. You didn't lose your virginity to me and you don't see me losing my shit over it."

"That's different."

122

"How so?"

He grabbed my hand and kissed my ring finger, the gold band twinkling under the light. "How many men have you fucked?"

"Does it really matter?"

His nostrils flared. "Tell me."

"Four." But none of them had compared to Brett. At all. "And that includes you." What the hell was his problem? "How about you, Brett? How many women have you slept with?"

His eyes narrowed.

I huffed. "Your whores kept coming back for more."

"I have fucked many women in my time but none compared to you, Evvie," he growled.

"You're being an asshole, you know that, right?"

"How old were you?" he asked, tightening his hold on my hand.

I huffed. "I was seventeen when I lost my virginity. It had been years since I had sex before meeting you." What can I say, I went through a very long dry spell. But I never craved sex like I do now since meeting Brett.

A twinkle of amusement flashed through his eyes as he pulled me closer to him. "How long did you sleep with him?"

"Brett, honestly. Forget about him. Nothing will happen."

"I saw the way he looked at you, Evvie. He wants you."

I rolled my eyes and went to pull my hand from his grip when he tugged me into his arms.

"Roll your eyes at me again, lover and I'll bend you over my lap and slap that delicious ass."

My body heated but I glared at him instead. "Yeah? Well you're the one that's being difficult. I can't control when another man hits on me. You need to calm down and trust me."

Brett's gaze turned cold. "I don't need to do shit. *You* need to know your place."

My muscles quivered and I pushed him. "Yeah? And where's that, Brett? With my legs wrapped around you as you bound and gag me? Or at your feet, bowing to your every dark sadistic desire?"

"Watch the tone," he growled.

I pulled out of his grasp and sat back on the stool. "Whatever."

"Office. Now," he demanded.

I took a swig of my beer, ignoring him.

A heavy hand cupped the back of my neck. "If you know what's good for you, you will listen to me."

I smiled. I couldn't help it. The whole thing was ridiculous but he pissed me off. His jealous rage although hot at times, at this very moment I was ready to kick him in the balls. "I'm drinking my beer and enjoying the music."

"Lover."

"What?" I turned to him. "You want me to go to your office so you can fuck me and pretend everything is fine? Cause it's not, Brett. You can't always get out of our fights by using sex."

His grip on my neck tightened. "You never complained before."

I shrugged. "So? Right now, I'm enjoying my drink." I lifted the bottle when it was snatched from my hands and thrown across the bar. Glass and beer flew everywhere as it shattered against the wall.

"Oh real mature, asshole," I snapped, pushing out of his hold.

His eyes darkened to the point of being black. "Get in my fucking office. *Now.*"

"Really, Brett?" I tried not to notice the people staring at us. "You're causing a scene."

He pinched my chin, forcing me to look up at him. "I don't care. Everyone can hear what I have to fucking say to you. I don't give a shit."

"Then say it, Brett. Tell me how jealous you are. How much you wanted to punch Nick in the face for even talking to me. You going to do that with every guy? What about Kane? Jake? My fucking father! You going to punish me for letting them talk to me? Or do I have to go around with a sign on my chest saying, *I'm sorry, I'm taken. Don't talk to me.*"

Our chests rose and fell as we sat and glared at each other. My body flushed with heat.

"Office," he snarled.

I jumped to my feet and headed in the direction of his office. With a shaky hand, I opened the door when I was tackled from behind and pushed to the floor.

"I want you so fucking bad right now," Brett snarled, fisting my hair in his hands.

"Show me." I rolled over onto my back and gripped his shirt. My blood pumped in my ears as I ripped the dress shirt in half. Button's flew around us, pinging off the wall and floor.

He growled and pulled at my clothes.

I struggled out of my panties and arched my back as he split my black cotton dress down the middle. My body throbbed, aching for him in a way that was dark and delicious. "Brett," I begged.

He undid his belt and towered over me before crashing his mouth to mine.

My fingers trailed inside his shirt, scratching into his skin.

He lifted me in his arms and sat back at the same time as he impaled me.

I gasped, wrapping my arms around his neck. My body opened to him, taking him deep as I circled my hips against him.

"Hard, lover. Fuck. I need you rough."

I moaned and rode him like he asked. Our bodies slapped together, my fingers digging into his muscles. "You feel so good." I licked up the side of his neck to his jaw, the scruff of his five o'clock shadow scratching at my tongue. My body buzzed.

Anger and frustration circled around us as we used each other's bodies for pleasure. Taking what we wanted and needed.

His teeth grazed over my collar bone before biting down. His hands pulled and kneaded at my skin. "Harder, Evvie. Use. Me. *Possess* me."

Sweat ran down my back as I gave him what he demanded. What both of us craved. My muscles burned. It was rough, intense and I wouldn't change anything about it. We scratched and pulled at each other, needing the connection more than anything.

A tingle spread from my tailbone to my neck before crashing into me hard. I screamed, his name leaving my lips as his hips sped up.

Brett lowered me to the floor and licked between my lips.

I smirked and pushed him onto his back. Brushing my nose up the side of his neck, I inhaled. The scent of leather, man and sex invaded my nostrils making my core clench around him. I was drunk with desire for this man. "I want to eat you."

He growled and pushed me off of him before kneeling between my legs. His hands spread my knees apart. "Beautiful."

I licked my lips as Brett pulled off his ripped shirt, his muscles straining and rippling under the movements. Red scratches marred his skin, sending a shiver down my body. *Mine.*

His eyes darkened. "The way you're looking at me right now is fucking hot."

I spread my legs as he towered over me. "How am I looking at you?" I asked, scratching my nails down the hard contours of his torso.

He nipped my ear, trailing bites along my jaw. "Like you want to eat me alive."

I shook my head. "I want to *devour* you."

He growled. "Take my thick cock," he demanded, lowering back into me.

I moaned, my muscles stretching as he pushed between my legs. My thighs burned as he powered into me, my legs restrained under him. "Harder, Brett." I swallowed a gasp and ran my fingers through his hair.

He grabbed a fistful of my blonde curls and pulled my head back. "Who do you belong to?"

"You," I panted.

"Again."

"You. Oh God, I belong to you."

His hips sped up. "*Mine.*"

I scratched my nails down his back, marking him in my own way.

126

"That's it. Scratch me. Mark me as yours, lover. Hurt *me*," he demanded, breathing hard against my neck.

I pulled at his hair, scratched at his skin and met him thrust for thrust. My teeth grazed over his collar bone before I bit down.

His big body covered mine as he continued to demand his pleasure from me and I gave in. Willingly.

My pussy throbbed, aching from the rough force of his thick length. Sweat coated our bodies, our clothes were torn, hanging off of us in pieces. It was rough, passionate. *Delicious*. But I had the insatiable urge to do it over and over again.

The sounds of sex filled the air and I moaned, spreading myself wide for him.

Brett's large hands cupped my inner thighs, squeezing tight as he powered into me with a ferocity we both craved.

His cock swelled as he pushed into me, filling me to the hilt as his body shook. He came hard, spurting his warmth into me.

My body relaxed, like I was melting into the floor.

He sat back on his hunches. He wiped the tip of his cock over my aching core, his release coating me. "Spread yourself for me."

I reached between us and spread the folds of my sex, revealing my engorged clit.

He groaned and pushed the head of his length over the aching nub.

I whimpered, thrusting my hips to match his movements. "Oh Brett."

He smirked and sped up his thrusts. "I'm going to come all over you, Evvie."

I moaned. "Please. Mark me. I need you everywhere."

He chuckled. "Oh I have been, don't you forget it."

I smiled and licked my lips. He had touched every part of me. He owned me and he made damn sure that he reminded me constantly.

***

"ARE YOU sure you wanna do this?"

I rolled my eyes at the fifth time Kane asked me if I wanted to move in with Brett. It was finally the weekend and I was getting my stuff ready to head over to his apartment. "Yes, Kane."

"What about your furniture?" he asked, grabbing a box from my arms.

"Donate it." I didn't need to bring much with me. Just my clothes really.

We moved the last box into Brett's apartment and I sighed, taking in the vast space around me. Anna had moved back home but not before she gave me a hug. It threw me, but I returned the embrace.

"You need anything, you call me. You'll always have a home at our apartment."

I turned to Kane.

His hands were shoved in his pockets, his black t-shirt stretched over a massive chest. He rubbed his bald head and looked away.

"What's going on, Kane?"

He sighed. "Rumors are going around." His jaw clenched. "Just be careful. Brett's become...moody."

Become moody? The guy was always moody. "That's nothing new."

"Not usually." He pulled me in for a hug. "Just be careful."

I nodded and watched him leave. Shutting the door behind him, I leaned against it and took a breath. Trying to ease my racing heart, I closed my eyes and inhaled. Was I making the wrong decision? Kane was right. Brett *had* become moody. Since our big fight a week ago that had turned into amazing hot messy sex, I hardly saw him. But every time I did, he would make sure to kiss me. To touch me. To love me.

My phone dinged, startling me from my thoughts.

All moved in, lover?

I smiled. *Yes,* I typed and hit send.

Good. Now go to our bedroom.

My stomach flipped. Our bedroom. Why did those two little words get me all excited?

I want you naked. Kneeling on the bed. With your back to the door.

My body heated. *And if I don't?*

I could almost hear him chuckle. I loved playing games with him. He liked that I gave him a challenge. I knew that. He knew that. He also knew that I would be ready and waiting for him. Always.

The keys jiggling in the door made me gasp. *Shit.* I ran to the bedroom but not before Brett saw me dart away.

"I see you didn't listen to me," he yelled from the doorway.

I backed up, holding my hands to shield him off. My heart raced, my body blooming as I tripped against the bed and fell on my ass.

A bubble of laughter left me and I pushed to all fours when my feet were pulled out from under me.

"Why are you not on the bed naked like I asked?"

I rolled my eyes. "You didn't ask. You demanded it."

He bit the side of my neck. "And?"

I struggled out from under him. "I'm making you work for it."

He chuckled. "Oh, lover." He reached under my dress and ripped my panties. "I sure love a fucking challenge."

***

"I CANNOT believe you just told me that," I laughed and shook my head at Tatiana. Not having many girlfriends, she was one that I could always count on to tell me straight up how it was.

It was a couple of nights later and she and I had decided to meet up for coffee to give our boss a much needed break while he stressed the hell out.

She blinked innocently. "What? You asked, I told."

I sat back and took a sip of my coffee. "Kane is my best friend. Please don't give me any more details about your sex life."

She giggled and ran a hand through her shoulder length dark purple hair. The piercing in her eye brow twinkled in the dim café shop lighting. "You happy, babe?"

I smiled and sighed. "Yes." And I was. Living with Brett for just over a week felt normal. It was like Mexico all over again. We didn't fight. Unless you counted arguments about who got a shower first which then in turn ended up with both of us taking a shower at the same time.

"Are *you* happy?" I asked, placing my cup on the table between us. I waved at Anna as she came into the coffee shop.

Tatiana shrugged. Her caramel skin glowing as she blushed. "For now. It is what it is." She smiled at Anna as she joined us.

Tatiana tried to play it off that her relationship with Kane was casual but I knew they both had feelings for each other. They just needed to get their heads out of their asses and realize that before it was too late.

Speaking of that... "Anna, have you talked to Evan?"

Her smile faltered. "No. He won't...uh...return my calls." She cleared her throat. "How was Mexico?"

I bit back a frown and sighed at her change in subject. "It was wonderful."

"We heard you guys opened a club," Tatiana said, crossing her legs as she sat back in the couch.

It didn't surprise me that the news had travelled fast. When we got home, a newspaper was at his door with a picture of the two of us smiling for the cameras in Mexico.

I nodded and explained what had happened. It was fun, exciting, exhilarating but also scary and overwhelming. I knew nothing about running a business and Brett promised he would help but the benefit that he was holding was the next day. He was stressed to the max. His controlling side wanted to make sure that everything was perfect. My nurturing side wanted to please the tension in his body but I hadn't seen him enough to take care of that. You'd think living with the guy meant seeing him more but not so much. I saw him if I woke during the night but that was it.

"You talk to Claire?" Anna asked, ringing her hands in her lap.

My stomach twisted at the mere mention of that woman's name. "Not since she showed up at Brett's birthday party." Everyone had found out about Claire and that she originally said she was pregnant with Brett's baby. After having a miscarriage, it was like she fell off the face of the earth. No one knew who the father of the baby actually was except for her and it wasn't like she was going to admit that anytime soon. It could have been Brett's or Ethan's. My brother. God, what I wouldn't do to end that situation. I made a mental note of visiting him.

"Evvie?"

I looked up at Tatiana. "Hmm?"

She smiled. "You lost in thought?"

"Sorry. I was…" My gaze landed on someone as they came into the coffee shop. Someone I never thought I'd see again.

Stefan Price.

What the hell was he was doing here?

Twelve

"WHY, HELLO again, Evvie."

Tatiana and Anna both looked at me. Their eyes filled with curiosity.

"Tatiana, Anna, this is Stefan. We met him in Mexico," I mumbled.

They both watched as he sat down beside us, casually crossing his ankle over the opposite knee. It was like he thought we were lifelong friends but really, he bothered me. I couldn't quite put my finger on it but something was off about him. Different. I didn't trust him. At all.

"What are you doing here, Stefan?" I asked, my gaze darting from him to the door every so often. Brett was working so I didn't expect him to show up but it wouldn't surprise me if he did. It's how he was. I wouldn't even be surprised if he was there now, watching this whole messed up interaction. Waiting to strike when the moment was right.

"I wanted coffee. So here I am," he said, shrugging.

Anna rolled her eyes as Tatiana scoffed and fiddled around with her phone. Her gaze met mine before quickly glancing away.

I frowned. "Who did you text, T?"

"No one." She looked at Anna. Anna's eyes drifted down to her phone, her cheeks flushing when they popped up to meet mine.

"Tatiana," I said, my voice firm.

She looked back at me. "I didn't text," she glanced away again. "anyone."

My heart raced and I reached for her phone, quickly grabbing it before she had a chance to react. I swiped my fingers across the small screen while ignoring her protests. My stomach sunk. "You texted Kane?"

Stefan chuckled. "And here I thought my night was going to be boring."

I threw the phone on the table.

"I'm sorry, Ev," she said, her voice small.

Kane would tell Brett that Stefan was here and then Brett would definitely show up. I loved him, with all of my heart and more but his jealousy was going to get him into trouble. Why the hell did no one see that but me?

"Evvie, why don't we go back to your apartment?" Anna offered.

"Yes, Evvie, why don't we do that?" Stefan suggested, licking his lips.

My stomach cringed at the innuendo that rolled off of his tongue.

I ignored the girls and watched for the door. Under normal circumstances, it wouldn't be a big deal if Brett showed up. But Stefan was here. He had caused enough problems in Mexico. Brett had just finally gotten over the whole issue with Nick. Everything was starting to feel…normal. For us anyways. Anna moved out, Claire disappeared, and his mother hadn't tried contacting him again. It was the calm before the storm, we both knew that, but took advantage of the peace and quiet anyways.

"You shouldn't be with a guy that's so jealous, Evvie."

My gaze slowly glanced at Stefan. "What would you know about the guy that I'm with?"

Stefan smirked. "I know more about Brett MacLean than you think, darling."

My stomach clenched. "What the hell are you talking about?"

He grinned. "Let's just say that we have a mutual friend and I've heard all the juicy details about that man of yours."

"Please. The only one that knows the true Brett MacLean is my girl," Tatiana scoffed.

"I'm not going to sit here defending my relationship with Brett to you or anyone else for that matter," I snapped. My blood boiled. At that point, I came to the conclusion that I couldn't stand Stefan. So much for me being nice. He was going to get the full wrath of the Neal family way if he didn't watch out.

"Oh? Is that so? How were those pictures that I sent you, Evvie? Did you get a good look at your boyfriend fucking Claire?"

A mutual gasp erupted between Anna and Tatiana.

I stared him, my mouth set in a firm line. I wouldn't let him know that he got to me but I wasn't Brett, I didn't have a poker face. My emotions showed in my eyes and I couldn't change that. "What happened before me is none of my business."

Stefan looked at me hard. "Hmm…guess I thought you would have reacted differently."

I did. When I got the pictures. Now that I knew who they came from… "How the hell did you get those pictures?"

He grinned. "A little slow are we?"

"Answer me," I demanded.

"Like I said, Brett and I have a mutual friend."

I swallowed hard. *Claire.*

"I see the light bulb turned on this time." He laughed.

Tatiana slammed her cup on the table. "That's it. Listen asshole, whatever you want with Evvie—"

"No, you listen, bitch. This has nothing to do with you."

"What the hell do you want?" I demanded.

Stefan grinned. "You'll see. In time."

Chewing my cheek, I waited. Anxiety swirled deep in the pit of my belly. Screw it. "Tatiana, Anna, I'll see you later." I couldn't sit there anymore. I rose to my feet and headed out of the small coffee shop. Just as I rounded the corner, I bumped into a hard body.

An arm reached out, stopping my fall.

I looked up into deep blue eyes that had captivated me from the very start. "Brett."

He smirked and cupped my cheek. Rubbing his thumb along my bottom lip, he placed a hard kiss on my mouth. "Where do you think you're going, lover?"

I took a breath. "I…I was going to see you."

Brett leaned down and brushed his nose along the side of my neck, inhaling deep. "I want coffee."

"Brett…" He was lying. He wanted to see Stefan and pound his face in. I could tell by the cold look in his eyes. "Take me home."

"Hmm…home," he purred.

My heart soared. "Please. I don't want anything to happen."

He nibbled my palm and kissed the band on my ring finger. "What do you think would happen?"

"I think you'll end up punching Stefan in the face…" I frowned as Brett's gaze turned icy cold.

"Stefan? That fucker from Mexico is here?"

My heart dropped. "Yes. I thought that's why you're here."

"No. I came to see *you*. Tatiana texted Kane and he told me to meet you here but no one mentioned Stefan," he said, his voice rising.

Shit. "Okay, well…" I swallowed. "Take me home."

A wicked grin spread on Brett's face before he grabbed my hand and pulled me back into the coffee shop. "We don't want to be rude, Evvie. Let's say hi to our dear old friend."

My heart raced, thumping hard against my rib cage. "Brett, please, just take me home."

His hand wrapped around my neck and he leaned down to my ear. "I will, but right now, I'm going to remind Stefan, who you belong to."

"Brett," I cried and grabbed his arm, stopping him. "He knows Claire."

Brett paused in his steps and turned back to me. "He does?"

I nodded. "He's the one that sent those pictures of the both of you to me."

His jaw clenched, his eyes turning black. "Now we definitely have to say hi."

I frowned and followed behind Brett as he led us back to the table where Tatiana, Anna and Stefan were still sitting. All three of them looked up as we neared it. Tatiana's eyes widened and Stefan sneered. Anna chewed her bottom lip, brushing a dark strand of hair behind her ear.

"Well well well. Now isn't this interesting?" Stefan said, rubbing his chin.

Brett grunted and held me tight beside him, practically placing me on his lap.

"Um…we should go." Tatiana grabbed her stuff.

Anna nodded. They both gave me hugs.

"Whatever happens, Brett loves you," Anna whispered in my ear and headed out the door before I could protest. I stared after her. I knew Brett loved me. It was the one thing that I was certain of.

Now that he knew who was responsible for the pictures, I didn't blame him for being furious.

I didn't know what Brett had in mind when it came to showing Stefan who I belonged to. I knew how he showed me in the past but it was unlikely he was going to have sex with me in public. Even though he had threatened it several times before.

The jealousy that Brett had, took over sometimes. I wasn't even sure if he was aware of it. He needed to not worry and trust me. Trust in the fact that there was no one else for me. That he was it.

As I sat there watching the guys have a macho he-man stare down, my stomach clenched and twisted. Anxiety swirled deep in my belly. If Brett wasn't careful, his jealousy would get the best of him or worse. It would destroy what we had worked so hard at getting back.

Thirteen

AFTER SITTING for what felt like forever in uncomfortable silence, my nerves got the better of me and I couldn't take it anymore. "Stefan, what do you want?"

Stefan smirked and rubbed his chin. "Now what makes you think that I want something?"

I rolled my eyes. "I told Brett about the pictures."

"I know. That's why I told you about them in the first place." Stefan shrugged.

Brett stiffened beside me and grabbed my hand. "You hassled us on the plane, in Mexico, and now here. What the hell is your deal, fucker?"

"Paranoid? Worried I'll take your girl, Brett?" Stefan laughed.

My stomach twisted.

"That'll never happen, asshole," Brett growled.

"Brett, we should go. He's clearly not going to tell us what he wants." I rose to my feet when my hand was tugged.

"Sit," Brett demanded.

I sat back down and huffed.

"You going to let him boss you around like that, Evvie?" Stefan frowned. "If you were mine—"

"Well, she isn't. So shut the fuck up." Brett gripped my hand tight.

I looked between the both of them, my heart thumping hard against my ribs. "Okay, this needs to stop. I don't know what your problem is, Stefan, but—"

"The problem is Claire."

"Claire. What does she have to do with this?" She had left us alone. I didn't know if that was good or bad but neither of us had heard from her since Brett's birthday party. I made a mental note to call Ethan and asked him if he talked to her.

"She hired me to send you those pictures and I haven't been fucking paid. I want my money and then this will all go away."

My heart sped up and I looked at Brett.

"I'll pay you. How much?" he barked.

Stefan rubbed his chin. "1 million."

I gasped. "You can't be serious."

"I don't have that kind of money," Brett ground out. "Even if I did, that's a lot of cash to be handing over to someone who could be lying."

"Either way, I will get my money." Stefan rose to his feet. "You should also know that she hired me to go to Mexico. I wasn't there on vacation. I was paid to watch you and report back to her."

"Why the hell are you telling us this?" Brett snapped.

I couldn't believe my ears. Shock tore through me at what I was hearing.

Stefan shrugged. "She fucked me over."

Brett grunted. "She does that."

Bile rose to my throat.

"Get me my money," Stefan demanded.

"Get me proof and I'll see what I can do but I'm not giving you a million dollars." Brett sat back and casually spun my ring around and around on my finger.

"You better—"

"If you want the issue with Claire gone, you will take what I give you once you get me the proof that I need. Until then, leave me and my girlfriend alone." Brett's voice was firm as he stared at Stefan head on.

Stefan stood up and stretched. "One last thing, you need to treat her better."

I gasped.

Brett shot to his feet. "Listen, mother—"

"No, you listen to me, asshole."

"As if you're here telling me how to treat my girl. You just asked me for a million dollars," Brett said, his jaw twitching.

Stefan pushed him. "Paranoid, Brett?"

"Guys, stop. Please," I said, shoving between them.

"Not on your fucking life, asshole," Brett snarled.

"Stop. Now. Both of you," I cried.

"Yeah, Brett. Listen to your whore. Claire was right about one thing, she is a little slut."

I gasped and before I knew what was happening, Brett dove at Stefan, knocking him to the ground. His fist flew so fast against Stefan's face, bones crunched under the contact.

"Brett," I screamed and grabbed his shoulders. With all of my strength, I pulled him off of Stefan, landing hard on my ass.

"Fuck, you broke my nose," Stefan said, sniffing past the blood pouring out of his nose.

"Get out, now," a deep voice barked.

We all looked up as a large man came into view wearing a shirt uniform for the coffee shop.

Brett stiffened in my arms. "I'll pay for the damage—"

"Not you. Him," he pointed at Stefan.

Stefan glared. "What the hell?"

"I heard what you said about this young lady. You're lucky she's not mine or else I wouldn't have let her pull me off of you," the older man snarled.

Stefan rose to his feet and wavered. "You can't make me leave."

The man took a step towards him. "No? Try me."

Stefan looked between the three of us before his gaze landed on Brett. "I hope Claire makes your life a living a hell."

My eyes widened.

"The name's Sam," the larger man stated as Stefan left the small café shop.

"Thank you, Sam," I mumbled and rose to my feet before sitting on the couch.

Brett joined me and rubbed his red knuckles. "I am sorry about the damage."

Sam's chocolate brown eyes warmed. "No need. The damage already left. How about some ice for that hand?"

Brett nodded and wrapped an arm around my shoulders. "I'm sorry."

I sighed. "Are you okay?"

He smiled. "I am now. Shit. Mathis will hear about this."

"Here." Sam placed an ice pack in my hand and smiled before heading back behind the counter.

I held it against Brett's knuckles when his phone rang.

He huffed and cringed when he looked at the screen.

"Let me."

Brett's jaw tensed.

"Trust me," I said sweetly.

"I don't need you doing my dirty work, Evvie," he said, his voice hard.

I rolled my eyes and snatched the phone from his hand before snuggling into his side. Pressing the talk button, I held it to my ear and waited.

"Brett, you stupid mother…"

I almost laughed at the string of very colorful profanity that left Mathis' lips. His slight European accent became more pronounced when he was pissed. It was kind of adorable. I would never tell him that though.

"Mathis?"

His cursing stopped and he took a breath. "Why, hello, beautiful."

I smiled. "Bad night?"

"That man of yours is going to give me an ulcer. I'm too young for this level of stress."

"Baby, what's wrong?"

I frowned when I heard a woman's voice come through the phone.

"Nothing, love. Go back to bed."

Shock tore through me at the softness in his voice.

Brett noticed my reaction, his eyebrow raising.

Mathis Verlinden had a sweet side to him? He had been nice to me but that was only because he wanted something. "Mathis?"

"Yeah."

"Who was that?" I asked, with a teasing lilt to my voice.

He cleared his throat. "My wife."

I gasped. "Excuse me?"

Mathis huffed. "Why is everyone so damn surprised?"

140

"It's you. I just saw you a couple of weeks ago. You're married?"

Brett's head whipped around. Clearly, he was surprised as well.

"Yeah, well it was kind of sudden but I wouldn't change it for the fucking world. Now stop trying to change the subject," Mathis demanded.

"I need to meet this woman," I said, curling my feet under me.

"She would like you...wait, Evvie, put Brett on the fucking phone."

I laughed and handed Brett the phone all the while Mathis complained in the background about women and distractions.

Brett grinned and winked at me. "So who's the pussy now?" He laughed. "Yeah...I wasn't expecting you to find out so soon. I don't know...Claire...yeah..."

My stomach twisted at the mere mention of her name. Stefan knowing Claire made things a whole lot more interesting.

"I don't care what your sister in-law wants...I..." Brett breathed a heavy sigh. "I know. Stefan demanded a million dollars."

I leaned my head against his shoulder and held the ice against his knuckles. He punched Stefan for me. Because he called me a whore. My stomach twisted. What would have happened if I wouldn't have been able to get Brett off of him?

I listened as Brett explained what had happened and what Stefan was after. And the pictures. The pictures that almost destroyed our relationship. I forced the images to the back of my mind, swallowing past the lump in my throat.

"We can fly out whenever is good for you, my man. Company jet?"

I looked up at Brett.

"Two weeks? We'll be there." Brett hung up the phone and stood up. "Mathis wants us in Vegas to help promote his club, *Club Maroon*, at the end of the month."

"Us?" I asked, letting him pull me to my feet.

Brett pinched my chin and tilted my head before placing a soft kiss on my mouth and forehead. "He knows now that where I go, you go. It's either both of us or nothing at all." His gaze darkened. "We can join the Mile High club, lover."

My body vibrated.

"Imagine me fucking you, 35,000 feet in the air," he purred against the side of my neck.

"Okay," I breathed. I couldn't control it. The thought of him between my legs, up in the air, giving us what we both desired, sent a thrill down my spine.

I had never been to Vegas and I would get to meet the woman that captured Mathis' heart. It was funny. I hadn't known Mathis for long but he reminded me so much of Brett, it was unreal. I wondered if Mathis was just as possessive. I bit back a scoff. No one could be as possessive as Brett. He took that word to a whole other level and even though at first I fought it, now, I craved it. I needed the sense of being possessed by him. Without that? Without that all-consuming need? There was nothing.

Fourteen

THE NEXT morning, I woke, stretched and groaned. My body hurt in places I never knew existed before meeting Brett. You'd think after all of this time, I would be used to it.

Brett, of course, was not beside me. The guy worked way too much. Since we had the Vegas trip in two weeks, he needed to get the benefit under way, which was tonight.

I yawned and trudged to the bathroom. Turning on the bath, I glanced in the wall length mirror beside the shower and gasped.

My heart gave a start as I neared the image staring back at me. Dark spots marred my skin. Purple and brown bruises covered my ass. Scratches lined my pale back. My heart thudded. I knew we had been rough the night before but I had no idea…a breath left me and I took a step closer to the mirror. Turning, I grazed my fingers over the pink flesh of my rear. Memories of his palm swatting me sent a warmth spreading over my skin.

My muscles twitched and ached every time that I moved. My skin burned when I touched the marked spots. My stomach tumbled. I felt possessed, used. *Owned.* It was the most exhilarating moment of my life. I felt wanted.

"Do you like seeing my marks on your body, lover?"

I jumped, my gaze meeting Brett's in the mirror. He leaned against the doorjamb and rubbed his chin. He was a beautiful sight. His black satin pajama pants hung low on his hips, the muscles of his naked chest, stretching as he breathed.

My core swelled, attuned to him in a way I never thought was possible. I didn't think it could be done but every time I saw him, I became more and more attracted to him.

Words frozen on my tongue, all I could do was nod.

He closed the distance between us and stood behind me before wrapping a hand around my neck. "I have a surprise for you," he said, inhaling the scent of my skin as he grazed his nose up the side of my neck.

"What?" I breathed. Something hard landed against my chest and I looked down. My eyes widened. An 8x10 picture frame held a black and white photo of me with Brett's large hand wrapped around my neck. You wouldn't know it was me by the angle of the picture. All you saw was my mouth and down to my collar bone. But Brett's hand was what drew me in. His long fingers gripped my neck in a powerful, yet seductive way. It was utterly captivating. The skin around my throat tingled.

The picture showed the viewer strength, domination and control. My lips were parted and the camera caught the hint of my tongue. The photo oozed love but most of all, possession.

"Do you like it?" he asked softly.

I couldn't help but stare at it before I noticed the four letters written at the top of the dark wooden frame. *Mine.*

"Brett...I...wow...I love it," I said, stumbling over my words.

He grunted in approval. "There's more where that came from."

"Really?" I had no idea he could take such beautiful pictures. We had played around during the night, him snapping photos of us with his new digital camera. But I didn't realize they would turn out that good.

"None of the pictures show your face or mine. Just body parts."

Seeing images of us around our home sent a thrill to the center of my very being.

"I'll put them all in frames and have words describing each one," he explained and took the photo from my hands.

"I never knew that you were so talented."

He chuckled and brushed his knuckles down the center of my body before cupping my sex.

I gasped as he held me tight against him. His one hand wrapped around my throat and the other in a spot that couldn't get enough of his touch. I was restrained, utterly submitting to him.

"I have many hobbies. Just not enough time for them." His finger dipped inside of me before bringing it to my mouth. "Did the picture turn you on, Evvie?"

My body hummed, the scent of my arousal on his finger invading my nostrils. "I...I don't know." Did it?

"I think it did." His gaze met mine in the mirror as he brought his finger to his lips. He groaned. "Like honey," he breathed and licked the tip clean. "Watch how your body responds to my touch, lover." His fingers grazed over my nipples. The dark pink buds hardened to sharp peaks. His hand around my neck tightened sending goose bumps over my skin.

My chest rose and fell and the more he kept teasing me, the more I could see my clit peeking through the folds of my pussy.

"I want you to watch as I fuck you."

I frowned, confusion swirling deep inside of me.

A zipper lowered. "Place your hands on the sides of the mirror and hold on."

I did as he said, my knuckles turning white.

"Watch your eyes darken from lust, your mouth part with small bursts of air as I pound my cock into your sweet pussy." He brushed his hand down my spine, his deep sapphire gaze trailing down my naked body before colliding with mine. "Ready?"

I nodded.

He thrust into me hard and I whimpered.

"My favorite sound." He fisted my hair and pulled me upright before wrapping an arm around my waist. "Watch, lover."

I held onto the mirror as his thrusts picked up speed. The veins in his arms protruded, his powerful thighs helping the deep strokes of his cock. "*Watch*," he demanded.

My eyes darkened like he said they would, my full lips parting as my breathing picked up. My full breasts bounced with every movement but watching him, us, moving as one sent me over the edge of bliss. It was beautiful and highly erotic the way he made use of my body. Forced the pleasure from me.

Our gazes met and a wicked smirk spread on his face. His hand wrapped around my neck as he pushed into me as hard and fast as he could.

The mirror became wet from the condensation of my breath. My palms were sweaty as I tried to hold on while he gave me what I wanted and he took what he needed.

He grunted. "Your clit's hard. Stroke it for me. Pinch that little cherry until you scream my name."

His hold on me tightened and I did as he said.

Pushing my finger through my folds, I flicked it back and forth over the erect peak and squeezed, sending a jolt of electricity through my body.

"That's it. Make yourself come for me," he breathed against my neck.

The movements of my finger became attune with the deep thrusts of his cock. I screamed as a shatter of ecstasy erupted through me leaving me breathless.

His name left my lips three times before his length pulsed, spilling his semen inside of me, coating me with his essence from within.

I moaned, falling back against him.

Brett lifted me in his arms and carried me to the bath before placing me in it. He quickly undressed and sat behind me.

My eyelids grew heavy and my skin tingled, reveling in the feel of him washing me.

"I want pictures of you in my club," he whispered.

"Hmm…okay."

"I want to show people your beauty."

I looked up at him and cupped his cheek. "What if someone says something bad about it? Or a man makes a comment?"

His eyes narrowed and he took a breath. "If I can't deal, I'll take them down."

Through the foggy orgasm induced haze of my mind, a thought came to me. "No one will know it's me?"

He shook his head. "No. The hall leading into the main club will be lined with black and white pictures of you, my sweet Evvie."

146

My stomach flipped. "Did you just plan this or have you been thinking about it for a while?"

He winked, his eyes twinkling. "A while."

"I'm surprised you want to share me."

His jaw ticked. "I don't. People will think it's just some random black and white photo of a woman. No one will know different. I will never share you, Evvie. You're mine."

A breath caught in my throat at the finality of that statement.

"The pieces will be called, *My Heart*."

"My Heart." I liked the sound of that.

"You should see the one I took in Mexico while I had you bound and gagged."

My eyes widened, my cheeks heating. "You didn't."

A mischievous grin spread on his face. "I did and this photo…" His hand trailed up my thigh. "will no doubt turn you on more."

I licked my lips. "What's it called?"

"*Controlled*."

***

MY CELL rang as I reapplied my lip gloss. Reaching into my pocket, I pulled out my phone. "Hey Evan."

"Hey sis. Where are you?"

"At work," I said, looking in the mirror of the club bathroom.

"I heard you own a club."

My stomach twisted and I mentally smacked myself. How could I forget to tell my family, of all people, that I now owned a club? "I'm sorry. Things have been crazy since getting back. I was going to tell you."

"I know. So I guess you and Brett are serious?"

"Yes." My heart gave a start at the mention of his name. "We are. I wish you would warm up to him." Ethan got along with him after Brett punched him in the jaw for thinking he was hitting on me. But Evan was cold as ice when it came to him.

147

Evan sighed. "No matter who the guy is, I will never like him. No man is good enough for you, Evvie."

"I understand where you're coming from, Evan. I really do. But you're going to have to get used to him. He's not going anywhere." And that was final.

"You hear from Everett?"

I smiled at the change of subject and left the confines of the bathroom. "No, not for a while."

"If you do, please call me."

"Why? Is something wrong? Is dad okay?"

"Dad is fine. Stubborn as hell but stronger than ever." Evan laughed.

A breath of relief left me. "Oh good."

"You happy?"

"Yes, Evan. I am. I have to get back to—"

"Just don't do anything stupid, Evvie. Don't change for anyone. Be yourself and if he doesn't love who you are, dump his ass."

I frowned. "I think you should practice what you preach, dear brother. Have you called Anna?"

He scoffed. "Anna was a one-time thing."

I laughed. "Yeah. Okay." I knew the men in my family. Once a woman had them wrapped around her fingers, they were hers forever. The Neal men fell in love and they fell in love hard and fast. Realization dawned on me. I was the same way. Why didn't I think of that before?

Evan and I chatted a few more minutes and we made plans to get together with Ethan and go visit our father. Hopefully by that time, Everett would be around.

Heading back out in the dance area, I walked around the bar as Brett slid onto a stool.

He grinned and winked at me, crooking his finger for me to come closer.

My body heated and I closed the distance between us. Leaning over the counter, I placed a kiss on Brett's mouth.

He chuckled against my lips. "The boss shouldn't be fraternizing with his staff."

148

"I quit and then you rehired me after we got back together so that doesn't count." I smiled.

He shook his head, his bangs falling in his eyes. "Yes, it does."

I laughed and brushed a strand off his forehead.

His gaze searched my face. "Everything okay?"

"Yeah, just got off the phone with Evan."

"And?"

"Everything's good. Just checking in, in his usual big brother way," I said, brushing a strand of hair off his forehead.

"Good." Brett grabbed my hand and kissed the back of it before placing a kiss on my ring.

My heart gave a start every time he did that. It was almost like he was reminding himself that I was in fact his and he was mine.

Tatiana rolled her eyes and pretended to gag. "I think I just puked in my mouth a little."

"Whatever. You're just jealous," I teased and playfully nudged her shoulder.

She grinned. "Why, when I have that hunk of meat filling my...needs every night?" she asked, indicating Kane.

He licked his lips when his gaze landed on Tatiana.

"Ugh...gross. He's my best friend, T. I don't wanna think about what he's filling at all," I joked.

Tatiana laughed and grabbed the tray of drinks, shimmying her hips as she left.

I shook my head and wiped up the counter. The benefit was a huge success. People of power and business men alike donated thousands of dollars to the proceeds to help families affected by drunk driving. I was impressed with how many people it had reached. Now everyone mingled, ate and partied. Brett had also made sure taxi vouchers were available for everyone that had been drinking.

Finally taking a moment to himself, Brett joined me at the bar after receiving much arguing from me of course.

"Why don't you take a break, lover?" he purred.

A shiver ran down my spine. I would never get used to Brett's deep voice whenever he talked to me. "Can't. I don't want to get in trouble with the boss."

Brett's blue eyes darkened, raking his gaze over my body. "If you get in trouble, I'm the sure the boss would punish you in ways you never imagined."

My core clenched. *Oh dear God.* "I—"

"Brett. My darling baby boy."

I cringed as Brett's face changed from a look of hungry desire to downright rage in a matter of seconds.

We both turned to the sound of his mother's voice she walked up to us.

My stomach twisted, my heart racing a mile a minute. This would not be good. Not good at all. It had been weeks since we've seen her. Weeks since we've seen Claire, as well. The only person I had to deal with lately was Anna but we were becoming fast friends.

"What the hell do you want?" Brett bit out.

Diane sneered and sat on the bar stool beside him. "To talk." She looked at me, her gaze going cold. "Can we talk somewhere private?"

"No. Either you talk here or get the fuck out," Brett said through clenched teeth.

At that moment, a large man came into view. "Hello son."

I swore I heard Brett growl. His tense body, big and strong as he stared down the new visitor but the look in his eyes showcased terror. A little boy that had been abused by the one person who was supposed to love him. I needed to get him out of there but my limbs were frozen as I watched the scene play out before me.

"What..." Brett croaked. He cleared his throat. "What is he doing here?"

Diane smirked. "He's my husband now. Meet your stepdad."

"You married this asshole? After what he did to me?" Brett yelled.

150

Several people turned our way and I couldn't help but be embarrassed for him. He didn't need his personal life aired in public and he didn't need to face the wrath of Mathis either. To find out a person you worked with was a ticking time bomb waiting to explode would not look good in the new partnership.

"He didn't do anything that you didn't deserve, little boy," Diane said, grabbing her husband's hand.

Brett rose to his feet. Veins protruded from his thick neck and he cracked his knuckles, taking a step towards the large man.

Oh shit.

I motioned to Jake Chan.

He quickly walked up to me, his brown eyes frantically moving back and forth as the onslaught of the nightmare took place before us. Always the worrier. But this time, he had every right to be worried.

"Please take over."

He nodded. "Of course."

I squeezed his arm encouragingly and walked around the bar, staying a foot behind Brett.

Diane glared at me, her cold eyes boring into me like hot knives. Well I didn't care. She was messing with the wrong woman if she thought I was going to sit back and let her destroy my boyfriend's life.

"Tell your little whore to leave us be. This is a family matter. Doesn't concern her," Diane said casually, checking out her manicured nails.

Whore? Really? "At least I'm not the one who ruined my kid's life."

Diane looked around. "He seems to be doing fine all on his own."

I stepped between her and Brett. I knew I shouldn't have gotten in the middle of their issues but he was mine. There was no way I'd let him deal with this shit on his own.

"Leave. Now," Brett growled.

"No. Not until we get what we came here for," the older man stated.

"Yeah? And what's that?" I asked, ignoring the warm tense body behind me. I could feel the rage pouring off of Brett.

"Brett."

I stared at Diane. That one word confused the hell out of me. What did she want with him? "Don't you think you've done enough damage? Leave. Both of you," I demanded.

Diane rose to her full height. Unfortunately she towered over my five foot nothing frame but I was a Neal woman. I was not backing down.

I tilted my head and stared up at her, owning my place.

"Brett will come with us," she sneered. "We have some family matters to deal with that don't concern you."

"Everything you say to me concerns her. If you don't talk now, then get out," Brett demanded.

"We have some business to attend to, Brett, in private. You *will* talk to us," Diane stated matter-of-factly.

"Not on your fucking life. You're dead to me. From the first moment you hit me, you were no longer my mother," Brett snarled.

The words leaving his lips broke my heart.

Diane's gaze looked past me and if I didn't know any better, I'd say she was checking out her son.

Bile rose in my throat. What kind of sick person was she? Oh God. Please tell me she never…I shook my head. Brett said the abuse was never sexual. But with the way she was looking at him like she wanted to eat him alive, it made me wonder if he blocked out those memories.

I turned and placed a hand on Brett's chest, pushing him back. "Let's go." Something tugged at me, telling me to get him the hell out of there. I needed to save him. From his mother, her husband and the judgmental stares of the onlookers surrounding us.

His jaw clenched, his stare dark and cold.

"Brett, please," I begged.

"Did you tell your whore how much you liked it when I beat you?"

After those words left his mother's lips, everything happened so quickly, it was like I was watching a movie.

"Leave. Now. Get out of my club," Brett yelled.

"Next time you want a real man, give me a call." The man smiled at me, licking his lips.

Brett snarled. "Get the fuck out. Now. I hate you. I fucking hate you. Both of you," Brett screamed. He grabbed hold of the nearest table and flipped it over, the contents crashing to the floor. "Out. Now."

Kane hurried over to us and grabbed hold of Brett's shoulders but he fought him off. I stood there frozen in place and before things could get worse, I mentally smacked myself.

Taking control of the situation, I grabbed onto Brett's suit jacket. "Come with me. *Now*," I said with as much force as I could muster.

He looked down at me, his nostrils flaring. Something at that moment changed. I fell into the depths of his dark stare, captivated by what I saw. He was looking at me like he could see into my soul, see into my being at that very second.

I didn't know how I could tell but I knew he needed me in a way I never thought was possible.

"We'll be back for you and your little whore, Brett. I'll show her what a real dick feels like."

I cringed and looked behind me, watching Diane and her gross pervert of a husband being ushered out of the club by Kane.

I realized then that I shouldn't have done that. I shouldn't have broken eye contact with Brett because when I looked back at him, I saw something in him that I never thought I would see. *Fear*.

153

Fifteen

I SWALLOWED hard and grabbed Brett's hand, dragging him away from the onslaught of the viewers around us. My body vibrated like the tension from him was pouring into me.

Once reaching his office, I let go of him and the door slammed behind me.

I looked at him over my shoulder and gasped.

His eyes were black, cold as ice as he slowly sauntered towards me. His back hunched over slightly like he was waiting for me to bolt so he could catch me. I was the prey and he was my predator.

"I need you," he growled, taking a step towards me. His voice. Oh God, his voice. Deeper than ever before. The vibrato travelled over me, caressing my skin.

I swallowed hard and glanced down at the massive erection in his pants. "Brett…" I shook my head. As much as I always wanted him, this was way too inappropriate. "This isn't the time. You need to calm—"

In a quick move, he closed the distance between us and wrapped a hand around my throat. His nostrils flared, his chest rising and falling with ragged breath. "It's always the time, Evvie." The way he snarled my name let me know that this was going to be a fight. I didn't understand the need for sex that controlled him. I wanted to help him but I couldn't deal with the guilt he faced. Whenever he fucked me after his nightmares, he closed up. What if one of these days he closed up completely?

"Brett…

His jaw ticked, his grip on my throat tightening. "I can't fucking…I can't deal with this. I need inside you."

My stomach clenched at the desperation in his voice. Since the first time he saw his mother a couple of weeks ago, the sex was intense. But nothing compared to this.

"We…we should talk," I said, grabbing onto his wrist.

"No," he growled and gripped my shoulders.

I gasped as his fingers dug into my skin. My pulse raced. I didn't know this man standing in front of me but I had to stand my ground. He would thank me for it later. "Brett, stop."

He backed me up against the wall and brushed his nose along the side of my neck. "I know you're turned on. I can fucking smell how wet your pussy is."

My jaw tensed. "You need to—"

Brett crashed his mouth to mine, shoving his tongue into my mouth in a rough stroke.

I opened to him instinctively until a small voice sounded in my head. *Stop him, Evvie. He'll thank you later.*

I bit his bottom lip igniting a deep snarl from the back of his throat.

He released me, his tongue grazing over the small cut in his lip. His eyes narrowed, turning darker than night.

I darted around the couch and gasped when a heavy body tackled me to the ground. Struggling under his hold, I pushed to my knees when my legs were pulled out from beneath me. "Brett, stop. Please."

My panties were ripped off of me, my skirt hiked up to my waist and although the timing was so fucking inappropriate, I was turned on like never before. This couldn't happen. Not like this. He was somewhere else. Rage took control of his body.

Brett grabbed my hands, holding them above my head and breathed hard against my neck.

I pulled out of his grasp and turned onto my back.

His hands were rough, needy as he towered over me.

I fought against his hold, my heart racing at the adrenaline pumping through me. "Brett," I said in a firm voice.

He pulled me under him and licked up the side of my neck.

Using all of my strength, I pushed him but he was too strong for me. Bile rose to my throat. *Please God, help me stop him.* "Brett, stop now dammit," I cried.

He kissed his way up to my mouth, the sound of a zipper lowering.

My stomach cringed and I pushed him again. Shoving him with all my might, I geared up and slapped him.

He shook his head, momentarily dazed. His eyes that were dark before slowly lightened like my slap had shocked the rage out of him.

My chest rose and fell, my palm stinging.

He looked down between us, assessing his actions and what he had done.

My gaze followed his. My clothes were wrinkly from his touch, his belt and zipper were undone.

"Fuck me," he whispered.

Tears stung my eyes.

"I…you said stop. I wasn't going to stop," he mumbled. His shoulders tightened, his breathing picking up. "Shit…I…"

I frowned as small bursts of air left his lips. "Brett?"

He gripped the collar of his shirt, ripping it open. The top four buttons flew to the floor, pinging off the carpet. "I can't…I can't breathe."

I sat up and pushed him onto his hunches. Cupping his face, I stared into his eyes. "Breathe with me. Deep even breaths."

"I was…I almost…I didn't stop…" he said in between breaths.

"Brett, breathe with me," I said, my voice firm.

Tears welled in his eyes. "I needed you too bad. God, Evvie…I'm…"

"Stop." A lump formed in my throat, bile burning my tongue. I took deep breaths and he mimicked my movements.

He grabbed my wrists, rubbing his thumbs slowly over my pulse points. "I'm so sorry," he repeated over and over again.

I leaned my forehead against his. "It's done, Brett." Would he have stopped if I didn't slap him?

His breathing became calm. "Fuck, Evvie. I'm so sorry." His voice cracked. "Shit."

I shook my head. "What happened, Brett?" I croaked.

He released me and righted his pants. His body shook, tremors wracking through him. With a shaky hand, he scrubbed it down his face and squeezed his eyes shut like he was trying to ignore what was going on his head.

156

My heart shattered into a million pieces. I was losing him. Before my very eyes, he was pulling away and I didn't know how to fix it. The man that came at me wasn't the man that I fell in love with. This man was broken, damaged, a dark reflection of himself.

I took a breath, easing my racing heart and cupped his cheeks.

He jumped under my touch, his eyes focusing on my face. "I'm sorry. I'm so fucking sorry."

He had mentioned before that he was worried he would hurt me but nothing came of it since the last time he saw his mother. Our nightly baths had calmed us both and it helped but now that he saw her again, all that hard work blew up in our faces.

"Talk to me," he said, swallowing hard.

"I don't…I don't know what you want me to say." My emotions were all over the place. I didn't know how to react to what had just happened but I knew I couldn't leave him alone. Something told me that he needed me on a deeper level than I ever imagined. A level that was just revealed a moment ago when he attacked me.

"Tell me you forgive me. Tell me you still love me. Tell…" He closed his eyes and gripped my wrists in a tight hold. He pulled me onto his lap, hugging me against him. "I'm sorry." He repeated those words over and over until his voice turned raw.

"You scared me," I said softly.

His breath caught before he let it out in a heavy sigh. "I know. God, I know."

"Talk to me. Please," I begged, brushing a hand through the hair at his nape.

"*I'm* scared," he whispered. "I don't know what's going on with me. I've been fine but…since my mother came back…I'm a fucking mess and then tonight…it stirred up memories."

I leaned back and gripped his shirt.

"No, touch me. Please," he pleaded, grabbing my hand and putting it against his thick neck.

My heart stuttered.

"I need the feel of your skin on me." His eyes fluttered closed, his body relaxing.

I rubbed my thumb back and forth, his pulse beating under my touch. "It'll take time but we'll deal with it. With her." And her creepy husband that made me sick to my stomach.

Brett shook his head, landing his blue gaze on me. "I'm a mess." He pointed to his temple. "In here. I don't know what's going on, Evvie but being inside you is the only thing that calms me. You're my safe place. My center. I can't..." His jaw clenched. "You keep me grounded."

I took a breath. "That's what I'm here for. To help you."

He huffed. "No. You don't fucking get it."

He moved to get up but I latched onto him, cupping his face in my hands. "Then make it so I do. Talk to me. Tell me what's going on in here," I demanded and brushed a finger over his forehead.

"I...I wanted you so bad. It was like I was looking down at myself, not really understanding what I was doing." He looked away. "I could see the fear in your eyes, Evvie."

My breath caught. "I'm sorry."

"No. Don't be. You have every right to be fucking scared of me," he said, his jaw clenching.

"How are we going to fix this?" I asked softly.

"When I see her, I get so worked up, the only way I can calm myself is by fucking you." His breath caught. "I can't control it. I'm losing my mind."

"You should talk to someone," I suggested.

He didn't respond but leaned his forehead against mine. "Brett..."

He cupped my cheeks and reined kisses on my face. "I love you. I fucking love you so damn much. If I ever hurt you like that, I...I would never be able to forgive myself. I'm a...I'm a monster."

"No," I snapped and pushed out of his hold. "You are not a monster. Don't even think that. You won't hurt me. What happened just now was intense and yes, it s-scared me but..."

"But what?" he asked softly.

"I'm more scared *for* you. I feel like I'm losing you slowly. I'm not a doctor but I know that your mother is a trigger for this rage inside of you." A tear rolled down his cheek and I brushed it away with my thumb. "I love you. *You.* Yes, what your mother and that man did to you is disgusting and unforgivable but who fucking cares about them? This is about you. You, Brett," I said, shoving a finger against his chest.

He let out a shaky breath. "That's why I moved. To get away from her. This rage I feel has never been this bad. I thought I was over it."

"You can't get over something like that, Brett, but you can learn to deal with it. I'm here and I'm going to help you."

Brett wrapped his arms around my shoulders, squeezing me tight like I was his life line. "I don't deserve you. Any part of you."

"Stop. We deserve each other. You're stuck with me," I said, trying to ease the tears that were burning my eyes.

"I love you. I don't know where I'd be without you, Evvie. I…" He leaned his forehead against mine and sighed, the tears now rolling freely down his face.

Seeing him cry was one of the hardest things I had ever experienced. My big bad possessive boyfriend, emotional and distraught. It broke my heart and I don't think I would ever forget the image of him breaking before me out of my head.

His finger brushed down my arm. "You're my center, Evvie. Without you, I couldn't deal with this. With me. It's like a furious battle of control deep inside of me. That's why there was all the women."

Jealousy burned through my stomach but that was over. His past.

"I need to be controlling during sex. I swore to myself that I would never allow someone to force me to submit again…until I met you. I…I think I need help."

My breath caught. I never wanted to see him submit again. "We'll get you help."

"Thank you," he whispered. "Just…thank you."

I nodded and swallowed past the hard lump in my throat. How was I going to get him the help he needed? Every time he saw his mother and that man now, would he need sex to calm himself? What if it went further? What if he hurt himself? What if I wasn't enough?

"Stop."

I frowned. "What?"

"Stop over thinking. We're in this together," he said, using my words. "You're mine, lover. Only you. You *are* enough for me."

At that point I let the tears fall freely down my face. "How…how did you know what I was thinking?"

He pinched my chin and placed a soft, tender kiss on my mouth. There was nothing sexual in the least about it. It was pure raw love. A claiming. An ownership. He was letting me know that I was his. That I *was* enough.

I think I fell in love with him all over again.

Sixteen

A COUPLE of nights after we saw his mother and stepdad, Brett and I walked into *The Red Love*, before it opened. Things had been off since he saw them but cooled down a touch. He was timid around me, like he thought the wrath of his rage would take control again and he wouldn't be able to stop it. I tried reassuring him but that hadn't worked.

"Wait," Brett said, stopping me in my tracks. "Close your eyes."

I frowned. "Brett, I don't really—"

"Close them," he demanded.

I huffed and did as I was told.

Heavy hands gripped my shoulders and pushed me a couple of steps further into the hallway. "Okay, lover." He kissed the side of my neck. "Open."

I opened my eyes and gasped as my gaze fell on the photos lining the hall way. Spotlights centered above each large black and white canvas. The pictures...of me...of us...tears welled in my eyes.

"What do you think?" he asked, grabbing hold of my hand.

I shook my head. "They're beautiful." Each photo had me in a different position with Brett's large hand touching me in some way. Either with it wrapped around my throat, spread out on my lower belly or holding my bound wrists...it was simply breath taking. The pictures held a hint of sexuality but not enough to be deemed inappropriate. They let the viewer know that the models loved each other on a deeper level that couldn't be explained by words.

"They're not as beautiful as the model."

I smiled and cupped my hands over his.

"But I'm hoping that they capture the love I have for you, Evvie," he said softly, wrapping his arms around my middle. "I also hope that they inspire someone to find that person. That someone that makes them love...deep."

My heart thudded. "No one knows that you took them or that it's us in them?"

"Nope. Not even Kane."

To have this kind of secret with the man that I loved was thrilling. I couldn't wait to hear what people thought of them. Whether they liked them or not, the pictures were beautiful and I couldn't wait to take more.

***

A MONTH had passed since we had heard from Brett's mom or stepdad. I thought it was strange that people were leaving us alone.

The sound of a door shutting erupted through the small apartment. I stepped out into the hall and smiled when my gaze landed on Brett standing in the doorway. "Hey, lover boy. I..." My smile faltered when he took a step towards me.

"Run," he growled.

"Brett?" My voice cracked. My heart hammered, my palms going sweaty at the feral way he stalked towards me. Things had gotten back to normal. Or so I thought.

He leaned his head from side to side, the tendons in his neck cracking.

My mind travelled back to a couple of months ago when he told me to run the first time. The chase was thrilling and the sex was damn near mind blowing but this...this wasn't the Brett that caught me then. This was the Brett that needed sex to calm himself or else he would lose his mind. Something had happened. Something was wrong.

I didn't like who he was becoming. Yes the sex was amazing but I was losing him and fast.

"Evvie, if you don't want me to fuck you here out in the open, I suggest you head to our bedroom."

My skin hummed and although I hated the feeling of being used, I knew it wasn't his fault. It wasn't. Was it? It hadn't been like this in weeks. Every step forward we took, something always set us back. Was it my fault? I promised that I would help him but I hadn't yet.

I took a breath and headed in the direction of my bedroom but I didn't run. I needed some sort of control when he got like this.

Sashaying my hips, I pulled off my dress. A hot shiver ran down my spine when I felt him close in on me. I knew he was close. I could feel it. We were connected on a level that wasn't normal. A level I never even knew existed until meeting Brett MacLean.

"Bend over the edge of the bed."

I jumped at the deep smooth voice in my ear and did as he said.

A heavy hand fisted my hair, pushing me face first against the mattress. His fingers moved to my core before sinking into me deep.

I moaned, my body clenching around him.

"I'm not going to be gentle," Brett said, his body shaking like he was trying to hold himself back.

I nodded, words frozen on my tongue. I knew that. I could sense it.

He thrust into me hard, lifting my waist off the bed.

I whimpered. Every time he got like this, even though I knew what to expect, shock still tore through me after each session. I wanted to help him. Curb his cravings. I wanted to heal him from the onslaught of his mother and the things going on in his head.

"Stay with me, lover. I need...I need you with me." He grabbed my hand, holding it tight as his hips picked up speed.

God, he felt good but why did I feel dirty all of a sudden? Why did I feel like a whore even though I was his girlfriend? Was this normal?

A lump formed in my throat and I squeezed my eyes shut, fighting back the burning tears.

"Fuck, Evvie. Don't. Please...shit." His hands roamed down my body, massaging, kneading, and pulling at my skin. Marking me as his. Even though his words were soft and pleading, his actions proved he had no control. He took me rough. I was ashamed to say this or even think it and although my mind was fucking with me, I enjoyed every minute of it.

***

"ARE YOU okay?" Brett whispered in my ear as he held me tight against him.

"Yup," I lied. My throat closed up, threatening to choke me. I took deep cleansing breaths, easing my rattled nerves.

"Evvie." His voice hardened.

"What? What do you want me to say, Brett?" I pushed out of his hold and sat up, scrubbing a hand down my face.

"I'm sorry—"

"You keep saying that but you don't do a fucking thing about it, Brett," I snapped. I didn't mean to explode but after keeping all of these emotions locked away, I couldn't control it. But after, it felt like a heavy weight had been lifted off of my shoulders.

"I told you that I need help."

My head whipped around. "So because I haven't called a shrink to get you the help you need, it's *my* fault that you keep attacking me?" I gasped and slapped a hand over my mouth as soon as the words left my lips.

Brett's gaze darkened, his eyes going cold.

"I'm sorry," I said, my heart racing. "I didn't mean for it to come out that way."

He didn't say anything as he rose from the bed and pulled on gray sweatpants.

"Brett, please," I pleaded. "talk to me." *Oh God, what had I done?*

With his back to me, he stopped in his tracks. "Without you, I am nothing. I don't exist."

My jaw dropped at his deep words. "That's not true. You exist. To me."

He looked at me over his shoulder, his gaze distant. "Do I? I told you that I have a problem but yet you still threw it in my face."

I rose from the bed, quickly pulled on one of his white t-shirts and took tentative steps towards him. "I'm sorry," I whispered, my stomach clenched at the guilt that tore through my very being.

His jaw ticked. "I came to you, the one person I thought I could count on. I trusted you. I thought you wouldn't judge me."

"You can," my voice cracked. "You can count on me. Always. And I would never judge you."

His eyes narrowed. "Really, Evvie? I told you things about me that no one knows. I confided in you," he said, his voice rising.

I took a step back until I reached the door.

"You gave me a piece of you and I gave you something in return. Something that I've never given anyone before in my fucking life."

My stomach churned. "Brett…"

"I gave you my heart. I was hurt before. I told you that. I told you I wouldn't go through that pain again but you, you pulled me in, you consumed me. Possessed me with this urge to dive deep into your soul. Fuck, Evvie." He started pacing the room. "I'm fucked up. You know that. *I* know that. Not being able to control myself around you scares the shit out of me. I *told* you this."

I chewed my bottom lip. "I'm sorry."

His gaze hardened. "You keep saying that, Evvie, but you don't do a fucking thing about it."

My stomach twisted as my words were thrown back at me. "I don't know what you want from me."

He stopped pacing. "You. I want you. That's all I've ever wanted. Don't you see that? I'll go see a shrink, I'll talk to someone but if you're not with me by my side, there's no fucking point."

"Why do you keep saying that? Do you think I'm going to leave?"

He looked away, his jaw clenching.

I laughed. "And here I thought that I would be the one worried about you leaving. You left me first, remember?"

His gaze met mine. "I said I was sorry about that."

"I know." I sighed. "What I'm saying is that I should be the one that's worried, Brett. Not you. I'll never leave you."

"Evvie," his voice softened.

"But it's not just me that you have to do this for, Brett." I closed the distance between us and grabbed his arm. "You have to do this for you. You need to heal."

He gripped my wrist. "What if I don't want to heal? What if I want to hurt? What if I deserve all of this shit that's going on in my head?"

I frowned. "What are you talking about?"

"I've made mistakes, Evvie. Things have been covered up. Things that I've been a part of." He shook his head. "My mother was right. I am paying for my fucking sins."

"No," I snapped. "Listen to me when I tell you that you're a good man, Brett. We all have things in our past that we're not proud of. Some more than others. But what that woman and those men did to you, is not the way to deal with it. They had no right to put that judgement into their own hands."

"Evvie, I saw a man get fucking killed in front of me," he yelled.

I gasped, my hand slapping over my mouth. "Well there has to be a good explan—"

"He was a bastard. Deserved everything he got and I helped cover it up." His eyes searched my face like he thought I would run. Like I was scared of him. But I wasn't. Not in the least. I was scared of who that woman was making him turn into.

"Brett." I grabbed his hand and sat on the bed.

He knelt at my feet with his head in my lap. "You deserve better than me." His deep voice wavered.

"Stop. I'm a grown woman. I can make these decisions for myself."

"You deserve someone you can bring home to your family—"

166

I pushed him and gripped his jaw, staring intently into his eyes. "Brett, I love you. Do you hear me?"

His gaze saddened but a hint of lust flashed through the deep blue depths at my attempt at control. *Control.* That one word left us both undone. "Ev—"

"Every time I go visit my family, I'm proud to bring you with me. After all of the shit they've done and have put me through, they have no right at all to tell me who I can and can't be with. If my mom were still alive, she would love you." A lump formed in my throat at the mere thought of her treating him as one of her own.

"I want you happy. I want to give you the world and more."

"You have. You've given me more than I could ever ask for, Brett. Don't you see that? You've opened up something inside of me that no one else could. It was meant for you."

"I'm sorry. I…shit," his voice cracked.

As we sat in silence I couldn't help but think that all of this work was for nothing.

"You need to talk to someone," I suggested as I ran my fingers through the hair at his nape.

"A fucking shrink isn't going to do anything. I'm too far gone," he mumbled.

I pushed him back and cupped his face. "You are going to listen to me and you're going to listen to me good. Do you hear me?"

His brows furrowed. "There's no point—"

"Shut up. I'm sick of this inner turmoil that you have going on inside of you. You will talk to someone or else I will drag you kicking and screaming if I have to."

"What if it doesn't help?" he bit out.

"You can't expect it to be resolved in one day, Brett. It'll take time. But I'll be there with you. Every step of the way. We're in this together." I took a breath and braced myself for his reaction. "If you can't see that, then what's the point?"

His eyes searched my face. "Don't leave me."

"I won't stand by watching your mind destroy you. If you don't get the help you need…" I swallowed past the hard lump in my throat. I didn't want to threaten him but I refused to watch him wallow away in self-pity and slowly kill himself.

"I'm calling a psychiatrist tomorrow," he mumbled. "My sister recommended him."

I nodded. *Thank you, God.*

His gaze met mine. "Will you come with me?"

I leaned my forehead against his letting out a deep breath of relief. "Of course."

***

AS WE pulled up to the small brick building, I gripped Brett's hand tight in my own.

His body tensed as he white-knuckled the steering wheel. "I don't want to be here."

I looked up at him. "I know." I didn't want to be there any more than he did but he needed this. I needed this. After our fight last night, I was concerned that his reactions to his mother showing up would eventually destroy us. I didn't know how much longer we could deal with…what, I wasn't even sure. His nightmares, his belief that sex with me was the only way to calm him. God, I was so confused. An unbiased view from a person might be good for us. It had to be. I prayed it helped or I didn't know what else to do.

Nothing was resolved from the night before. I felt him pulling away before my very eyes and before he disappeared completely, he needed to talk.

He sighed and scrubbed a hand down his face. "My dad tried getting me to talk to someone."

"Did you?"

His gaze met mine. "No. I threatened to never speak again if he pulled that shit and," he looked back at the building standing before us. "here I am."

I brought our joined hands up to my lips and kissed his knuckles before releasing his grip. "The sooner we go in, the sooner we can leave."

He grunted in response and exited the car.

I slid out of the vehicle and joined him.

Brett wrapped his arm around my shoulders and kissed my head, inhaling deep before grabbing hold of my hand.

I looked up at him.

His jaw was tense, the stubble on his jaw darker than usual.

My heart thudded. I was worried for him. It had taken me so long to get him to open up to me but now, I felt like he was locking down his emotions. A part of himself that he never revealed to anyone except to me. Hiding. Protecting himself from others and...me?

We entered the small office building, the bright light of the foyer making me blink several times before I was able to focus.

Brett tugged me along and pulled me beside him.

"You must be Brett MacLean and Evvie Neal," a tall man said, approaching us. His dark eyes twinkled that showed domination and superiority.

"Dr. Santos?" Brett asked, returning the man's handshake.

"Yes. Please, follow me." Although it was said as a request, it was smart not to question his authority. I didn't know how I knew that but the slight smirk he gave me made my stomach tumble. It was almost like he knew what I was thinking.

"You okay?" Brett whispered in my ear.

I looked up at him, my heart swelling. "I should be asking you that."

He shrugged. "I'm fine," he mumbled and looked away.

Liar. I bit back a sigh as we followed the doctor into his pristine white office. It was brighter than what I expected. The hard-edged doctor of some sort of Latin decent took me as the dark wood kind of guy. The white furniture with gray and dark blue accents didn't seem like his style.

Dr. Santos closed the door as we sat on the couch across from a large chair.

"So, tell me why you're here."

Brett stiffened beside me and grabbed my hand, holding it tight in his lap.

My heart thudded.

Dr. Santos watched the movement and crossed his arms under his chest, waiting for either of us to speak. "I do have all day but the sooner either of you speak, the sooner you can get out of here," he said, the corners of his lips twitching.

Brett huffed. "I don't know where to begin."

"That's understandable." Dr. Santos nodded and ran a hand through his short crew cut black hair. "Some people feel the need to speak on their own terms. Others want questions thrown at them to get them to open up. Which do you prefer, Brett?"

I curled my hand around our joined ones, praying that I could give him the strength he needed to talk.

Brett spun the ring around and around on my finger. I realized it was something he did when he was nervous or feeling uncomfortable.

Since my mom had passed when I was a child, I gave up on church and the whole religion thing. But I still believed. My mother had instilled that part of herself in me as best she could even though I was so young. I didn't know what else to say but I hoped that one word would be enough. *Please.*

"My mom used to beat me."

$\mathcal{S}$*eventeen*

I WAITED for Dr. Santos to start hammering questions at Brett. What caused him to make his mother hit him? How did he feel about it? What did he do to deserve it? The usual questions that people automatically start wondering.

"How old were you the first time it happened?"

I breathed a sigh of relief when none of those questions left the doctor's lips.

Brett squeezed my hand, his body tensing and ran his fingers under the sleeve of my sweater. Touching me. Pulling strength. From me.

"I was…eight," he croaked.

A lump formed in my throat. Eight. Just a boy. My stomach burned. God, I could kill Diane.

Dr. Santos' jaw ticked but other than that, his face was passive. No emotion displayed on his tanned features but if he was a normal human being, I bet he wanted to destroy the people who hurt his patients.

His piercing brown eyes flicked my way every so often. At first, I thought maybe he was questioning why I was there. Why I was with Brett when he's so broken, destroyed but then I noticed his gaze soften. The corners of his lips twitched before he turned back to Brett. "How often," he asked, his mouth set in a grim line.

Brett tensed beside me. "It started out slow. Once every couple of weeks. Whenever I did something bad in her eyes. She always used the excuse that God wanted her to punish me for my sins. I was fucking eight years old!"

Tears welled in my eyes.

"Where was your dad in all of this?"

"My…he didn't know." Brett looked down at our joined hands. "I never told him. I was a child. A little boy. I thought my mom…" His voice cracked. "I thought she loved me."

As sob escaped my lips. I could no longer control the tears as they rolled down my cheeks. "I'm sorry. I…" I squeezed my eyes shut, taking deep breaths, attempting to ease the heaviness of my heart. My chest felt constricted, like someone was sitting on it.

"Did you need some air?" Dr. Santos asked me.

My eyes popped open and I shook my head. "No. I'm not leaving him."

The doctor smiled. "Good girl."

My belly gave a flip at the praise in his voice.

Brett's hold on my hand tightened to the point of painful. "It's funny," he said a moment later.

I frowned and looked between the two men.

"I blocked it out until she showed up a couple of weeks ago. I was fine. I was." He took a breath. "I was," he whispered.

I wasn't sure who he was trying to convince but I knew he wasn't fine. He was never fine. He was always on edge.

"When did your dad find out?"

Brett took a deep breath. "He walked in on…on…I was strapped to the bed and…"

Dr. Santos nodded. "Was there ever any sexual abuse?"

My stomach twisted in knots waiting for Brett's reply.

"No," he murmured.

A breath left me that I didn't realize I was holding. I thought back to the horrible things his mother and stepfather had said only a couple of weeks before. Brett was a grown man. Could they still try and do—

"When was the last time you saw your mom?"

Brett sighed and scrubbed a hand down his face. "A couple of weeks ago and shit has been downhill since."

Dr. Santos raised an eyebrow. "Between you and Evvie?"

Brett looked down at me, his eyes searching my face, no doubt thinking back to our fight last night. "I have urges…always have but I've been able to control them up to this point."

My heart thudded as I listened to Brett's admission.

"What kind of urges?"

Brett's eyes narrowed, his jaw clenching. I could just imagine what was going on in his head. He probably wanted to tell the doctor to go to hell for asking all the questions even though that was his job.

I placed a hand on his arm. "Brett."

He jumped and shook his head, smiling slightly at me. "In the beginning I held back. But then I could see in Evvie that she needed what I knew I could give her. That dark part of myself that I was so scared to show. To anyone. Fuck." He grimaced and shoved a hand through his hair. "I can't believe I'm saying this."

"What else has been going on?"

"I keep having nightmares." He turned back to Dr. Santos who nodded for him to keep going. "Evvie wakes me up and then I..." He paused.

I squeezed his hand in reassurance.

"Attack her," Brett finished.

"Attack her how?" Dr. Santos asked, crossing an ankle over the opposite knee.

"Brett," I whispered. "Tell him." As embarrassing as it was to have our sex life on display before a stranger, Brett needed help.

He took a deep breath. "When I wake up from these dreams, the need to be inside her, consumes me." He looked down at me, his eyes filling with apology. "I can't explain it but I feel...I can't control it."

"And that scares you," Dr. Santos added.

"Yes. God, yes." With a shaky hand, Brett brushed his fingers up higher under my sleeve. The touch, although small, calmed his shaking.

A lump formed in my throat.

"Evvie."

I met the doctors brown gaze.

The corners of his lips tugged which I could only assume was a hint of a smile. "I see the love you have for him."

My cheeks heated and I nodded.

"You want to protect him."

I nodded again. I could feel Brett looking at me but I ignored it as Dr. Santos' warm dark eyes held me captive.

"From what or who?"

I took a breath and thought a moment. What was I trying to protect him from? His mother? "Himself."

Dr. Santos looked between us before settling back on me. "Does it scare you when he attacks you as he says?"

"No," I said without hesitation but then I remembered back to the night a couple of weeks ago at his bar. "But..."

Dr. Santos raised an eyebrow. "But something does scare you," he prodded, his voice soft but demanding.

I looked up at Brett. He averted my gaze. He knew where I was going with this. "When we saw his mom and stepdad a couple of nights ago..." I took a deep breath and explained to the doctor what had happened and how I had to fight Brett off of me. "I don't consider it attacking me, except for that night, even though I threw that it in his face. I'm just...I'm scared of who he's becoming since seeing his mother." The word-vomit poured from my lips and I couldn't stop it. It was like the doctor had reached deep inside of me and pulled the truth from my mouth, spilling all for Brett to hear.

Dr. Santos didn't question anything I said. Didn't say that I was crazy for feeling this way or judge me and for that, I was grateful.

He placed his hands on his knees and leaned forward. "I can tell you that Evvie is very strong for fighting you off. I can see the guilt on your face. Have things been back to the way they were since then?"

Brett grunted. "Not really."

I sighed.

"Brett, your mother is a trigger. I can also tell you just from talking with you for a half an hour, that you have PTSD," the doctor said in a soothing tone.

Brett stiffened and then relaxed. "Yeah...what do I...how do I...*shit*."

Curling my feet under me, I wrapped an arm around his shoulders and brushed my fingers through the hair at his nape. "How do we help him?"

"Be there for him. Calm him in any way that you can." He looked at Brett. "You need to get control of that urge to strike before thinking."

Brett scoffed. "Yeah, like that's going to happen."

"Why won't it?"

"I'm possessive, obsessed with the need to control everything around me but most of all, I *need* to dominate Evvie. I can't stop myself. It's like at moments I have an outer body experience and I'm looking down, watching myself. Especially after my nightmares." He shook his head. "I'm a fucking monster."

My stomach clenched. "You are not a monster. How many times do I have to tell you that?"

Brett looked away.

I grabbed his jaw, forcing him to look at me. "I love you. I'm sorry for the things I said last night. I know you're still pissed but it infuriates me when you believe what that awful woman tells you."

He tried shoving his head out of my grip but my fingers tightened. At that point, I didn't care that we weren't alone. Our relationship was hanging on by a thread. My boyfriend was breaking as each day past and it was destroying me. *Us.*

"I don't want to hurt you," he whispered, his deep blue eyes filling with unshed tears.

A hard lump formed in my throat. "You're hurting me when you hurt yourself. I know we've only been together for a couple of months but what I feel for you is strong. You demanded my love. Remember? You knew how I felt before I did. You told me that you were in this for the long run. Please," I swallowed hard. "stop pushing me away."

His gaze searched my face. "Never. You're mine."

I squeezed his hand. "My one."

He kissed my forehead. "My only," he said softly, inhaling deep. He leaned down to my ear. "I crave your smell on me," he whispered.

My heart jumped.

"That right there proves what a good woman you have, Brett." Dr. Santos rose to his feet and walked to his desk before turning back to us.

He didn't say anything about our moment. Maybe he was used to people breaking down in his office.

"First thing, I want you to keep seeing me. We'll set up weekly appointments and if you feel that you need more, call me."

"What if..." Brett looked down at our joined hands in his lap.

Dr. Santos raised an eyebrow. "What if this never gets resolved?"

"Yeah," Brett mumbled.

"Then we'll keep talking. This won't be easy, Brett, but you need to open up and not just to me."

***

"HEY, SWEET pea. How are you doing?"

I smiled at my daddy's smooth calming voice coming from the other end of the phone. A couple of days after the session with Dr. Santos, Brett made regular appointments to start seeing him once a week. Brett knew he had a problem. He had a temper. He was dark, brooding and possessive. He knew it. I knew it. Was I scared of him? No. Did I love him and would do anything to fight for him and that love? Yes.

"I'm alright, daddy. How are you feeling?"

He grunted. "Can't eat fucking burgers. Doctor's orders."

I laughed. After his heart attack, he was put on a strict diet. Edward Neal loved meat and if he couldn't have his burgers, he was a testy man. "You need to get healthy. Try vegan burgers."

He scoffed. "Please. No meat? No treat."

I rolled my eyes. "Did you really call me to complain about your forced diet?"

"No. How's that man of yours?"

I sighed at my dad's weekly check in. If he could have it his way, I'd still be a virgin and living at home under his roof until I was old and gray. "My man." I walked by Brett's office and stopped, brushing my fingers down the closed door. Since his meeting with Dr. Santos, he hadn't been the same. It was like he was scared to touch me. Scared that he wouldn't be able to control himself or hold back the urge to go further.

"Evvie?"

"He's...getting there," I mumbled and slid down the opposite wall.

"He sick?"

"No. Just...he has some things going on right now."

"Tell him to take it easy. He treating you good?"

I smiled. "Yes." At least I thought he was, even though he thought different at times. I chatted with my father for a couple more minutes as he filled me in on my brothers. I also ended up finding out that my middle brother, Everett, had disappeared, which in my brother's case, meant he ran. He didn't even say goodbye. That hurt. A lot. But I knew he would call me.

"Why are you on the floor, lover?"

I looked up and met Brett's gaze not even realizing he had opened the door. "I was talking to my dad."

He nodded and headed back into his office before slumping down in the chair.

I followed him and wrapped my arms around his shoulders. "I love—" My eyes landed on the computer screen. "What's that?" A word doc entitled, *Mine*, shone back at me. I saw my name several times and before I could read anything more, Brett clicked a button that brought up a screen saver. Black and white images of us, danced along the large monitor.

"My Evvie."

"What was that?" I asked as he pulled me into his lap.

"Nothing," he whispered against my ear.

"It was something. I saw my name." I moved to grab the mouse when he wrapped a hand around my neck and pulled me against him. I gasped at the rough hold, desire unfurling deep in my belly.

"Curiosity killed the cat," he said, running his other hand up my jean clad inner thigh.

Yes. Touch me. Own me. *Want* me. "What are you writing?" I couldn't help it. The need to know was driving me mad.

"Don't worry about it," he purred against my neck.

I frowned. "Brett."

"I said," he nipped my ear. "Don't worry about it. You can read it when it's done."

"Is it about me?"

His hand cupped my sex, while the other unbuttoned the fly of my jeans. "Yes. Now do you want me to fuck you against my desk or are we going to continue talking?"

Brett's growing erection under my ass sent a thrill down my spine. I moved my hips, grinding against him. "Depends."

He brushed his nose up the side of my neck, inhaling deep. "On what?"

I licked my lips. "On if you talk dirty to me."

***

"TELL ME," Brett growled, gripping my jaw tighter.

"What?" My heart raced at the deep heat in his sapphire gaze. The look of lust and love filled them as they darkened with a hunger that left me breathless and wanting. Always wanting.

He smirked and licked along my bottom lip before diving into my mouth. Our tongues explored.

A shiver of desire soared through me and I reached between us, wrapping my hand around his thick cock. The veins protruded beneath my touch as he lengthened against my fingers. My thumb ran over the tip, his pre-cum coating me.

A groan rumbled from his chest as he pushed his tongue deeper into my mouth. The kiss turned hot, heavy, as I ran my hand down the length of him.

Instead of fucking me against his desk like he promised, he brought me to our bedroom. I would never get used to the big bed and even though it was huge, I always fell asleep wrapped in Brett's arms and woke up just the same.

"Tell me, lover," he demanded.

178

"What do you want me to say," I breathed and lowered my hand to the heavy sac beneath. Squeezing lightly, I wrapped my other hand around the base of him.

"Fuck," he moaned. "Who do you belong to?"

I smiled and nipped his bottom lip. "You."

His hand moved to my throat and he pushed my head back. "*Again.*"

I licked my lips, swallowing the gasp of my head being restrained. "You. I belong to you, Brett."

A smug grin formed on his face. "Let's see how flexible you've become."

I frowned wondering what he was talking about when he grabbed my ankles and pushed my legs up over my head.

I gasped, my ass sticking in the air as he held down my ankles on either side of my head. "Brett," I panted.

He winked and covered my core with his mouth.

I moaned, watching him suck at me hard.

He growled, releasing me with a smack. "Watch me fuck your tasty cunt." He thrust his tongue in and out of me before licking up to the hardened nub.

I whimpered, shaking beneath him. "Harder."

He grinned, sucking my clit between his lips.

My body exploded as ecstasy racked my core.

"Simply beautiful." He released my ankles before he thrust two fingers into my pussy. "I want you to smell like me."

I whimpered, taking him as a deep as possible. My leg muscles shook as remnants of my orgasm trembled through me. "Oh God."

He removed his fingers and brought them up to his lips, sucking the juices from my body off of them. His Adam's apple bobbed as he swallowed, his eyes darkening. "So fucking good."

Stroking him hard, I moved my other hand lower and brushed a finger over the base of his sac.

"Hmm…what are you doing, lover?" he asked, licking up the side of my neck.

My heart raced. I didn't know but I knew that I wanted more. I always wanted more. My body craved it. I craved it. I wanted to give him the pleasure he had given me. I wanted...I wanted inside him.

My stomach twisted. Was that wrong of me? Would he object? God, did that make me more of a freak?

Testing my curiosity, I gripped his cock in one hand and reached the other around him. I ran it down his back, lightly scraping my nails into his skin.

He shivered and placed small bites on my neck and jaw. "Harder."

Oh it would be harder in a moment. He didn't have to worry about that. He had every piece of me and now I wanted the same from him.

I switched hands but not before coating my finger with my juices.

Bracing myself, I reached between us and brushed my finger to the tight opening at his rear.

His body tensed, his hot breath scorching my skin.

I ran my finger over the puckered opening in tune with my strokes on his cock.

"Fuck, Evvie," he whispered. "*More.*"

My eyes widened at the pleading in his voice and I did as he said. Tightening my hold on his length, I pushed my finger into him all the while surprised at how swollen his dick became.

"Shit. God. Fuck that feels good," he moaned, moving his hips in sync with my hand. "Harder. Please, Evvie."

My thrusts and strokes picked up speed, my arm muscles burning at the awkward position.

Brett released his hold on my neck and slapped his hand down beside my head. He gripped the sheet, his knuckles turning white. His deep breathing picked up. "I want to come on you."

"Yes. Please. Come all over me, Brett."

He growled and crashed his lips to mine at the same time as he thrust two fingers into me.

I whimpered, pushing my tongue against his. I squeezed my hand around the base of him and pushed my finger deeper at the same time causing him to shudder.

"Evvie." He came hard on a snarl, my name leaving his lips as his semen coated my lower belly, my mound and our hands. His body shook above me as I released my grip on him. I loved watching him have an orgasm. It was simply beautiful and erotic.

The warmth of his release ran down my center and before he could say anything, I grabbed hold of his hand.

Pushing it from between my legs, I brought it up to my lips and sucked my juices off of his fingers.

His heated gaze followed my movement. "My little vixen," he breathed.

I smiled and looked up at him. "Are you—"

He licked his way between my lips and I gasped when he sank back into me. It had always amazed me at how quickly he could get hard after an orgasm.

He must have enjoyed that every bit as I did but I wasn't sure. My stomach tied into knots when he sat back and lifted me into his arms.

"Ride me. God, I want you fucking hard, lover."

The pleading mixed with the deep husk of his voice just about did me in. I gave him what he wanted. What I wanted. What we both needed and more.

***

"WHAT'S WRONG?" Brett asked softly against my neck.

I sighed and snuggled into him. "I thought you were upset with me."

"Why?" He grazed his chin along my shoulder, the stubble of his jaw scratching at my skin.

My cheeks heated. "Well…I…"

"Are you embarrassed for making me come hard, lover?" he purred, brushing his nose along the side of my neck.

My stomach flipped. "No, I—"

"Are you ashamed of making your boyfriend come so hard, I think you'll smell like me for days?" he asked, rolling me onto my stomach.

Revealed by You

And I did smell like him. God, I wanted his scent on me for the rest of my life. "No, I just didn't—"

His teeth bit into my shoulder making me gasp and my core clench. "Did you think that I would be upset for you trying to take control?"

"I didn't take control." I frowned and stretched my arms out under the pillow.

Brett spread my legs and knelt between them. "Maybe not but you did try to."

"I was trying to show you the pleasure you have given me, that's all. I don't want…"

"What, Evvie?" he asked, running a hand down the side of my body.

"I don't want your control," I whispered.

"But you did want to see how far you could take me. How long it would take for me to lose it."

I rolled over onto my side and looked up at him. Was he right? Is that what I wanted? "Are you mad?"

The corners of his lips twitched. "Do I look mad?"

My gaze searched his face. His strong jaw clenched and his eyes were dark. His brown hair had grown a little longer in the past month and I brushed a couple of strands off his forehead. *Was* he mad? I couldn't tell. God, the guy should play fucking poker.

I sighed. "I have no idea."

Brett smirked. "If I wanted you to stop, I would have told you. You should know by now, that I always say what I want. I told you to keep going."

"I know that," I huffed.

"So now that we've touched each other completely…" He rolled on top of me and snarled against my neck

I giggled and wrapped my arms around his shoulders before cupping his face. Staring intently into his eyes, I saw the old Brett slowly coming back. The one that had possessed me from the very beginning. The one that took control. The one that loved me.

His eyes twinkled. "I love you deep."

182

Eighteen

"SHE'S SUCH a bitch, Evvie. God, I can't stand her," Kane complained.

I rolled my eyes as we headed down the long hallway to Brett's apartment several days later. "You are such a liar. You're so in love with Tatiana, it's sickening."

He feigned shock and gripped his chest when a huge grin spread on his face. "Yeah I am, but she's still a bitch and I still can't stand her."

I shook my head. And here I thought my relationship had its issues. I would never understand the thing my best friend had going on with my other friend. Tatiana, a punk rocker type lesbian turned straight who was sleeping with my best friend. I loved them both but it was still odd if you asked me.

"Where's Brett?" Kane asked as we neared the door.

Brett had said something about needing to go home because he forgot some important paperwork but I hadn't heard from him since. And that was a couple of hours ago. "He was supposed to meet me here…" I frowned. Loud heavy bass boomed from behind the door. I looked up at Kane and he shrugged.

Unlocking the door, my heart raced and I took a breath. Anxiety gripped at my core after each step I took.

Kane nudged his way in front of me and opened the door.

We were greeted with the onslaught of screaming metal music. It was so loud, it made my ears ring.

Kane hurried to the speaker holding the small music player and shut it off. "Call him."

I pulled my phone out of my bag and dialed Brett's number. Kane and I exchanged glances when we heard his phone go off in the bedroom.

Heading down the hall, my heart thumped hard. I didn't know what to expect. I didn't know what I would walk in on. I just prayed that everything was alright. That Brett was fine.

Taking a breath, I pushed open the door.

"Evvie," Kane whispered.

I turned on the light and gasped.

"Holy shit."

My gaze travelled down a completely naked Brett lying in the middle of his bed. His wrists and ankles bound to the bedposts. Dark purple bruises covered his body, scratches, scrapes and cuts ate at his skin. My body froze. My brain was screaming for me to go to him but I couldn't move. I couldn't...*do* anything.

"Evvie."

I jumped and spun on Kane. "G-go...c-call the police."

He nodded, his eyes saddening.

A hard lump burned my throat and I took a tentative step towards Brett. "Brett?" My voice came out as a croak.

Who did this to him? Why? Why would anyone do this to him?

I moved around the bed and undid the restraints when Brett started thrashing on the bed. My heart sped up, the blood pounding in my ears as I couldn't get the restraints undone fast enough. "Brett, stop. I can't..."

He pulled hard on the black leather bonds. He groaned, his body tense.

"Stop. Please. Brett." I yanked on the last restraint, finally getting him loose when he shot off the bed and tackled me to the ground. The wind was knocked out of me as my back hit the floor. "Brett," I said, gasping for air. My lungs burned as I took deep breaths.

Rough, needy hands roamed up my body before he pulled me under him. "I..." He cleared his throat and brushed his nose along the side of my neck. "I need to smell you," he croaked. "Make sure you're real." He inhaled, his tense body relaxing.

"I'm real." I ran my hands down his sweat soaked back, biting my lip from crying out when my fingers grazed over rough ridges. Raised jagged flesh covered his skin. My body shook. I saw red. Bile rose to my throat.

Brett's chest rose and fell, his big body shaking in my arms. "Don't leave me. Please don't leave me."

184

He repeated those words over and over in my ear, his throat going raw.

Tears rolled down my cheeks as I held him, his heavy body relaxing as he passed out in my arms. "Never," I whispered, holding onto him. "I'm here. I'm yours."

***

"WHO DID this to you?" My voice shook as I tried holding back the tears that threatened to escape. I brushed a hand down Brett's cheek, his stubble scratching my skin. Running my fingers through his hair, I looked down at his still form covered by a hospital gown and a blanket.

His chest rose and fell, his hand gripping my inner thigh tight. Even passed out from medication, he still knew where I was.

After he tackled me in his bedroom once I got him free, Kane and the EMTs had arrived moments later. Kane didn't seem surprised that Brett was in my arms. When I had asked him why, he told me that Brett's love for me was deeper than anything he had ever seen. Apparently there was a layer of Brett's love for me that I didn't realize.

They carried him out on a stretcher but wouldn't tell me a thing. I begged, pleaded for them to tell me…something.

"Ma'am, visiting hours are over."

Thoughts interrupted, I glared at a nurse as she lifted Brett's hand to check his vitals.

"I'm his family," I croaked. My throat was raw from the anger and pain I felt for Brett.

"Wife?"

"Yes," I lied.

Her brown eyes searched my face before she nodded once and left.

That's what I thought. They would have to pry my cold lifeless body from him before they would be able to get me to leave Brett's side.

The doctors and medical staff that had worked on Brett determined that he had a broken rib, minor cuts and bruises and that he was drugged. *Drugged.* With what, I wasn't sure.

It had been three hours since Kane and I had walked in on Brett. Kane never asked me if I thought Brett had cheated on me but I remembered the accusatory glint in his eyes. Under different circumstances it could have looked like he had cheated on me but I knew different. I knew deep down in the recesses of my soul, that I was his. I was enough for him.

My eyes welled with unshed tears. "Brett...my lover, my best friend...my...mine," I sobbed and kissed his head. "Wake up."

The doctor had knocked him out to help with the pain but I needed to hear his voice. For him to say my name. To tell me that it was okay and that everything would be alright. Seeing him so still and innocent left me ready to kill whoever did this to him. I had a feeling I knew already. I knew it was the calm before the storm. Deep down in my gut, I knew something else was going to happen.

"Evvie?"

I jumped at the soft voice coming from the door when I saw Anna peek her head around the corner. I sighed and motioned for her to come closer.

She chewed her bottom lip and took tentative steps towards us. It had been a couple of weeks since I had seen her after our coffee date. I liked her. I did. As much as I didn't want to in the beginning, I now knew she would never do anything to threaten my relationship with Brett. I trusted her. I didn't know how I knew that I could. I just did.

"Is he...is he alright?" she asked standing at the foot of the bed.

My gaze fell on Brett's relaxed face. His eyes fluttered now and again but every so often, a deep sigh would leave his lips like a weight had been lifted. "He will be."

Anna let out a sigh.

"How did you get in?"

Her cheeks reddened. "I snuck—"

"No visitors," the same nurse from before demanded.
I looked between the older woman and Anna. "She's
family."

A soft smile splayed on Anna's full lips. She mouthed *thank
you* as the nurse huffed and left the private room.

Anna pulled up a chair and scrubbed a hand down her face.
"Do you know what happened?"

I shook my head, tears filling my eyes again as memories of
Kane and I finding Brett invaded my mind. I kissed his forehead,
inhaling the scent of leather and sweat. I wanted to shower him.
To wash away the memories of the nightmare he had
experienced and replace them with me. Us. No one else. Just
Brett and Evvie.

"He's strong. He'll make it through this."

Squeezing my eyes shut, I nodded at Anna's words. I
prayed he would. He had been doing so well. He drowned
himself in work stuff. Setting up more parties and benefits,
conventions, anything to get out of his head. Or that's what I had
assumed anyways. He never told me. He didn't tell me much.
Not until we fought and then words poured from our mouths as if
they were forced.

At that point in time, I decided that I would avenge him. My
possession of him came out thick as blood. He was mine. And no
one messed with what I called my own.

Nineteen

"EVVIE."
I groaned.
"Lover. Wake up."
A small smile slowly spread on my face and I sighed, snuggling into the warm hard body that was beside me.
"Evvie."
My eyes popped open. I took a couple of deep breaths. I looked around the room and blinked a couple of times before I remembered what had happened.
Brett. Bound and restrained. Black and blue bruises. Cuts and scratches. Him breaking in front of me and passing out in my arms.
My heart raced before I turned my head to look up into the bluest eyes I had ever seen. Sapphire depths that drew me in from the beginning, captivating me from the start.
A lump formed in my throat. I swallowed repeatedly and shook my head.
Brett's eyebrows narrowed, his full mouth turning down at the corners. His bottom lip was split, a dark purple bruise marring his cheek. But he was awake. He was…God, what he must have gone through.
"Hey. Why the tears?" he asked softly, brushing his thumbs under my eyes. He kissed my forehead and that's when I lost it.
Sobs wracked my body, tears flowing freely down my cheeks. I cried so hard, it gave me hiccups.
"My sweet Evvie," he said, pulling me tight in his arms. "I don't like seeing you cry for me." His voice was soothing as he brushed his nose along my neck.
I gripped him hard, my fingers digging into the hospital gown. I wanted to crawl inside of him. Protect him. Be his armor that would stop the pain. I wanted to save him. From himself.
I didn't know who had hurt him but I wasn't stupid. It had to have been his mother and that monster husband of hers. Then

there was Claire but I didn't think she actually had the balls to set that kind of torture up.

"Evvie," he breathed against the crook of my neck. "Please stop crying." He ran a hand down my back and held me tight.

I swallowed several times.

Brett cupped my cheeks and placed soft kisses on my face. "I love you deeper than ever," his voice cracked.

"I love you hard," I whispered.

A small smile splayed on his lips. "Now tell me, why the tears?"

I let out a deep breath. "When I walked in and found you strapped to your bed…"

"Did you think that I cheated on you, Evvie?" he asked, his eyes searching my face.

"No, actually. I didn't. I was more confused but then I saw…" Fresh tears welled in my eyes. "I saw the bruises. The cuts. What bothered me the most was you lying there, not having any control. Brett…what happened?"

His jaw clenched, his gaze darkening but he didn't answer. He shook his head and looked away.

"Brett, tell me, please," I pleaded, cupping his cheek. My thumb grazed over the dark bruise. "Talk to me," I whispered.

"I felt like a little boy again," he mumbled. "Unable to fight. Unable to do anything because I wasn't strong enough. I was weak. I swore to myself that I would never be weak again," he said, his eyes going cold. "They tried to break me. They tried to destroy me. But Evvie, you put me back together. I…" his breath hitched. "I know it'll take time, but I know as long as I have you, I can get through anything.

With a shaky breath, I placed a soft kiss on his lips.

He leaned his forehead against mine. "I forgot something at home. Something told me…my gut was saying to stay away, to wait for you." His eyes met mine before he pulled me back against him. "I should have waited," he whispered in my ear. "but I thought it was all in my head. When I got home, my mom and her husband were there. I…"

My heart hurt. Anxiety swirled deep in the pit of my belly. I couldn't deal. My chest constricted like someone was sitting on it. My breaths came out in small bursts. I shoved out of Brett's arms and sat up, sitting on the edge of the hospital bed. Trying to take control of the overwhelming emotions that racked through my body, I took deep breaths.

"Evvie?"

I shook my head. "I can't...I..." Tears of rage burned down my cheeks and I angrily wiped them away. "I want to hurt them for doing this to you. I..." A dark feeling came over me. An emotion so strong, it took my breath away. "I want to kill them," I sobbed and covered my face. God, what was wrong with me? My mother would be so disappointed. My stomach clenched.

Heavy arms wrapped around my shoulders. "Stop. Please."

I couldn't. The control of my emotions was no longer there as the sobs shook through my small body.

"Evvie. I'm fine. They won't get me—"

"They could have destroyed you," I mumbled.

He pinched my chin, turning my head to meet his gaze. His blue eyes glistened. "But they didn't."

I shoved my head out of his grip and rose from the bed before spinning on him. "Brett, I want to rip off every piece that touched you. They saw you. *I'm* only meant to see you." Brett reached out for me but I hugged myself instead. "I-I want to hurt them. Break them until they beg me to stop. I want...I want to avenge you."

Brett got up off the bed slowly and closed the distance between us. His shoulders were tense but as he cupped my face and pulled me against him. His breathed hitched but his body relaxed. "I love that you are possessive of me. I love that you want to hurt them for me but Evvie, I will not have you doing anything that would put you in harm's way."

I tried pushing out of his grip but his hold only tightened. "Brett—"

"What they did to me has not set me back. Yes, I may have more nightmares but because of you, I will get through them."

190

He cupped my face and placed a soft kiss on my lips. "I'll get through this. We will get through this."

"They need to get punished—"

"Evvie, stop. The police can deal with it. I will not have you thinking these dark thoughts."

"I want to hurt them for what they did to you," I cried.

"I know. So do I, but you taught me to ask for help when I need it. You," he kissed my nose. "made me realize that I can't do everything by myself."

"Did they…" I swallowed past the bile that had unexpectedly risen in my throat. I couldn't ask. I didn't know if I even wanted to find out what exactly they had done to him.

His mouth was grim as he waited for me to ask my question. "What, lover?"

I took a breath. "Did they r-rape you?"

Brett's jaw ticked. "No."

A breath of relief left my lips, a weight that had rested on my shoulders since finding him restrained a couple of hours before, leaving me. "Oh thank God."

"I think they just wanted to fuck with my head," he said, moving to sit on the edge of the bed and pulling me in his arms.

I brushed the dark strands of hair off his forehead and grazed my fingers over his face. Memorizing him. Pushing the strength from my being into him.

His blue eyes were clear, no longer cloudy from the drugs that had been used on him.

"They touched you though," I stated.

He nodded.

We sat there for what felt like an eternity, holding each other.

A light knock sounded on the door when a uniformed police officer entered the small hospital room.

"Sorry to interrupt, but Brett, I'm Officer Charles. I need to ask you some questions." The older cop pulled out a notepad, his eyes warm as they looked between us.

Brett sighed and nodded.

The cop threw question after question at him but Brett answered open and honestly.

I had also found out that when Brett got to his apartment, it didn't take long for him to get knocked out and dragged to his bed. He said that the rest of the time was foggy but at one point he woke up, naked, bound and restrained with his mother on top of him. He said as far as he knew, it didn't go further but he couldn't be sure.

Hearing those words made me sick to my stomach. What kind of mother would do that to their child? And how could God let that happen?

Not his fault.

My breath caught as those words sounded in my head. I wasn't sure who they were referring to, but my body felt lighter all of a sudden.

"My mom's a psycho bitch. I don't know why she wanted to come after me," Brett mumbled.

My thoughts interrupted, I cupped the back of Brett's neck, running my fingers through his hair.

"When was the last time you saw her before all of this?" the cop asked, scribbling notes on his pad of paper.

"Over ten years."

"What do you think she wants?"

Brett huffed. "Me."

I cringed at the answer.

The cop raised an eyebrow but didn't respond, his eyes going cold. "Thank you. If I need anything else, I will let you know."

"Thank you, officer," I said softly.

Officer Charles reached the doorway and turned back to us. "And Brett, I will do everything in my power to put these people away for you. They won't hurt you again." And with that he left.

A sigh escaped my lips.

"Evvie." Brett cupped my rear and pulled me flush against him. The movement, although usually sexual, wasn't this time.

I brushed my fingers through his hair, over his face, across his lips, giving him the strength that I knew he needed. I didn't feel very strong at the moment but I tried. I would try anything that I could to make him strong again.

"Do you hurt?" I asked softly.

His lips tugged at the corners. "Nothing that can't be taken care of later."

A small smile splayed on my lips at the innuendo in his words. "I can't help but wanting to destroy them," I whispered.

"No," he said, his voice firm. "Take out your rage on me, Evvie."

I frowned. "Why the hell would I do that?"

His grip on my waist tightened. "Because they will hurt you. It will be over my fucking dead body before I let anything happen to you. Use me. Hurt *me*, Evvie but don't you dare try and avenge me."

"You would do it if the situation was reversed, Brett," I cried.

His eyes darkened. "Damn right."

"You and your double standards," I growled.

"My double standards will keep you safe."

I rolled my eyes.

"I can feel you shaking from anger. I can see the pain in your eyes. I get that. I understand it. But don't you dare go after them." His voice was hard, final, as he held me in his strong arms.

I knew it was totally insane of me to think it, but the possession I felt for the man holding me made me want blood. I wanted Diane and her husband to pay for what they did.

"Promise me."

I met Brett's dark gaze. "I will let the police deal with them but that doesn't change the way I feel."

"I don't expect it to."

"Are you okay?" I asked a couple of minutes later.

He released me and pulled off the hospital gown before getting dressed. "I will be."

I leaned against the wall and watched him change into black sweatpants, a white t-shirt and a black zip up hoodie. The outfit, although casual, still screamed domination.

My body heated and I cleared my throat before looking away.

A heavy hand pinched my chin before tilting my head to look up into deep cerulean eyes. "Don't ever stop looking at me."

My heart thumped, my gaze stuck on Brett's handsome face.

"Promise me."

I nodded.

"Say it," he demanded.

I licked my dry lips. "I promise. I will always look at you. I'll never look anywhere else." The words flowed from my lips like they were meant just for him. "You are it. You're mine. Anyone that hurts you, hurts me."

His hand moved to the back of my neck as he pressed me up against the wall. "I like when you look at me. You see me. As much as I like to think that I'm in control, I'm not. Not at all. My emotions are scattered. All over the place as each day passes. God, Evvie. I need you to be mine."

I frowned. Confusion coursed through me. "I am."

He shook his head. "No. Officially."

"What do you mean?"

"Marry me."

Twenty

"WHAT? REALLY?" I asked, clapping a hand over my mouth. It wasn't your typical proposal. It was more of a demand but I wouldn't have expected any less from Brett.

"I love you." He placed a hard kiss on my lips. "I need to make you mine. I want to spend the rest of my life with you. I want to make you my wife."

Hearing those words pour from his lips sent a tingle down my spine.

His eyes heated. "What do you say, lover?"

My heart raced. "Yes. Yes, I'll marry you."

Brett wrapped his arms around my waist and spun me before grunting.

I pulled back and caught the wince on his face. "What's wrong?"

"Just a little sore," he said, smiling.

I closed the distance between us and ran my hands up under his shirt, grazing my fingers over his waist. Marriage. It screamed forever.

He pinched my chin, forcing me to look up at him. "Marry me. Tonight."

I met Brett's gaze and wanted to laugh but the serious look on his face made me realize that he was in no way kidding. "Tonight?"

He had only been in the hospital for a couple of hours so it was early enough to make it to City Hall but what would my family say? I never dreamt of a big wedding but I really wanted to get married in a church. "Brett?"

His blue eyes twinkling, warming with a love so strong for me, it took my breath away. "Yes?"

I wrapped my arms around his waist. "I want to marry you. I do. But I really would like to get married in a church. For my mom."

His thumb grazed over my bottom lip but he didn't respond so I spoke honestly and told him the truth. "My mom was religious. Kept us all in line, including my dad."

Brett smiled.

"I would just like to honor her memory and get married in the church we grew up in." My stomach twisted with nervous butterflies. It had been over ten years since I had been there but I knew, deep down in my heart, that our old Pastor would welcome us with open arms.

Soft full lips covered mine in a passionate yet loving kiss. "Anything for you, Evvie. As long as we get married and soon, I am happy."

My heart swelled. "Thank you."

"No thanks needed. If you're happy, I am happy." Brett wrapped an arm around my shoulders and snarled into my neck.

I giggled at the ticklish feeling.

"Now let's check in with the doctor so we can leave this shit hole. I need some therapy that only my fiancée can provide."

***

"YOU'RE DOING what?" my dad thundered.

Brett's grip in my hand tightened. The next day we showed up at my father's place. We decided that it would be best to tell my daddy in person that Brett and I were going to get married but now, I was thinking I should have just sent him a text.

"I'm asking for your approval to marry your daughter...sir," Brett added on.

"Daddy."

Edward Neal, my boisterous strong man of a father met my gaze. His deep blue eyes framed by long graying lashes, looked between us both. He sat back in his recliner and scrubbed a hand down his face. "You kids are going to be the death of me."

I rose from my spot on the couch and sat at his feet, grabbing hold of his hand. A tattoo of a rose covered the back of it, other intricate designs disappearing under the sleeve of his

196

black sweater. "Daddy, who told me to go after what I wanted? Who told me that Brett loved me?"

My dad grunted. "You've only been together for a couple of months."

"You see that man over there?" I asked, pointing to Brett.

"Sweetpea..."

"Do you see him?" I demanded.

My dad's bright eyes saddened. "You remind me so much of your mother." He sighed. "Yes, I see him."

"I love him. I want to spend the rest of my life with him. I want him to be a part of my...our family." I smiled.

"I don't want you to get hurt," My father mumbled.

"No relationship is perfect but we are strong. We've been through a lot and have been through enough to know that we can handle anything." My heart thumped. I needed my daddy's approval. My brothers? They would accept Brett only if our dad did. It was one thing for us to be dating, they welcomed that, but marriage? That was a whole other thing. Brett was taking away the only woman they had that was a permanent fixture in their lives. "You also told me that he reminded you of you..."

My dad scoffed. "Yeah and my father-in-law hated me."

My stomach clenched. I never met my grandparents on either side. Only my oldest brother, Evan, did as they died when we were really young. We were a family. We didn't need anyone else. And I wanted Brett's added into our bond.

"Sir, I will do anything to make you see that I love your daughter," Brett said from behind me.

My father patted the back of my hand. "Sit beside your man. A woman's place is at her husband's side, not at his feet."

Tears filled my eyes and I threw my arms around my daddy's neck. "Thank you. Thank you so much, daddy."

He returned the embrace, wrapping me in a big bear hug. "You're welcome, my darling daughter, but know this, if Brett hurts you like last time, I will send your brother after him."

I swallowed hard knowing that he wasn't kidding. My brother, Ethan, a year older than my twenty-four, was your typical badass. Being in and out of jail his whole young life, fighting was second nature to him. Always had been. Always will be.

"You won't have to, daddy. Brett won't hurt me." Not unless I asked for it anyways. I almost laughed. My dad would have another heart attack if he found out what Brett and I do or have done.

He released me and rose to his feet.

Brett mirrored his movements and waited.

My dad grabbed Brett's hand before clapping him on the back of the neck. He whispered something into his ear which no doubt involved some sort of threat.

Brett only nodded or grunted in response.

I chewed my bottom lip in anticipation.

Looking between the two men, two of the men that owned a piece of my heart. My brothers owning the rest. But Brett? He owned more. My mind, body, soul. He owned my very being. At that moment a thought popped into my head. My mother. She had told me when I was very young before she died that I would find that one person that I would give my all to. That I would trust completely. I was only ten at the time when she told me this but now I knew that that person was Brett.

He glanced my way like he knew that I was thinking about him. His eyes twinkled.

Didn't he know that I was always thinking about him?

At that moment my dad threw his head back and laughed before turning to me. "Sweetpea, you have yourself a keeper."

I grinned and stepped into Brett's open arms, inhaling the intoxicating scent of leather and man. "I sure do."

He kissed the top of my head. "I'm the lucky one, sir."

"One rule if you want to marry my daughter," my dad said, his voice firm.

Brett stiffened.

"Call me Eddie."

***

MY MOTHER'S childhood church greeted us with warm hello's and big hugs as we walked into the small grey brick building the following Saturday.

It felt strange and a bit surreal walking into the tinier church. Nervous butterflies greeted me and even though everyone had been very welcoming, I couldn't shake the feeling of possible judgment. Not being allowed to marry Brett in a place my mother had once spent most of her time, would break my heart.

"Nervous, Evvie?"

I smiled up at Brett and sighed. "It's been awhile." I looked around the small lobby as we stood off in the corner. "I haven't been here since my mom died."

"I haven't been to church since my dad married my step-mom," Brett said cupping the back of my neck.

It may have been awhile, but I felt drawn to the church as soon as Brett proposed. Or demanded my hand in marriage rather.

"It makes me happy knowing that smile on your face is because of me," he purred in my ear.

I laughed. "How do you know it's because of you?"

Brett pulled me into his arms and brushed his mouth along my ear lobe.

A hot shiver ran down my spine at the contact.

"I know the look you get on your face whenever you think about me," he whispered.

"Yeah and what look is that?"

"The oh-Brett-is-so-hot-I-want-his-body look."

I rolled my eyes at the smug smile on his face. He knew me well. I couldn't hide the look of lust and want for him no matter how hard I had always tried. "Let's go before I get in trouble for the thoughts that I'm thinking right now."

Brett grinned and kissed my cheek.

"Evvie? Evvie Neal?"

We both turned to the deep voice coming up behind us. A young man that looked no older than forty stuck his hand out in greeting. His warm brown eyes met mine. "You don't remember me, do you?"

I frowned and shook my head.

The man smiled and looked at Brett. "I'm Pastor Dan."

"Brett MacLean." He returned the handshake before grabbing mine in a firm grip.

My heart stuttered. Always the jealous one.

"Little Evvie." Pastor Dan smiled, the corners of his eyes crinkling. "My father was Pastor Jones."

My eyes widened as recognition settled in. "Danny?"

Pastor Dan nodded, his warm brown eyes twinkling.

Brett cleared his throat.

"Danny or Pastor Dan now I should say, was best friends with Ethan," I explained.

Brett's eyes narrowed. "You?"

Danny laughed. "I had a moment of rebellion growing up. Got shipped off to CUC and found my calling to follow in my dad's footsteps. Haven't looked back since."

"CUC?" Brett asked.

"It's a Christian College. As much as I hated my father in the beginning for it, I now wish I could thank him." Danny's eyes saddened when he looked down at me. "My father passed away three years ago."

"Oh my gosh. I am so sorry." My heart hurt. I only knew Pastor Jones as a child but I knew how much my mom had loved him.

Brett squeezed my hand reassuringly.

"So, what brings you here?" Danny asked, clapping his hands together.

I looked up at Brett.

He met my gaze and kissed my forehead, letting his lips linger a little longer than deemed necessary. No matter how many times I had told him that he had no reason to be jealous, his Alpha male always reared its ugly head. Especially when another man was around.

"We want to get married and I thought it would be fitting to get married here since this was my mom's church," I said, stepping closer to Brett's side.

Danny smiled. "Your mom was a big part of the church. I think that would be wonderful. I would like to meet with you at least once before the wedding though."

I nodded. "Ok—"

"Why?"

I winced at the harsh tone in Brett's voice.

Danny smiled, not backing down from Brett's confrontational stance. "I just want to meet up with you to see how you are doing."

"So basically it's to see if we're compatible for each other," Brett bit out.

I looked between the two men before turning back to Danny. Was that the reason? We had our issues but there was no way that I was going to let someone else tell me who I could and couldn't marry.

"It's church procedure, Brett. It's not meant to offend but yes," Danny nodded. "it's meant to see if you fit."

"I can tell you, Pastor Dan," I said, stepping between them. "Brett and I are wanting to get married as soon as possible. I'm talking like this coming weekend."

Danny frowned. "That is two days away."

"Evvie." Brett turned me and cupped my cheeks, placing a soft kiss on my lips. "Can you give us five minutes?"

I searched his face for any inclination that he was going to rip off Danny's face but his emotions were locked. "Okay. Be nice."

Brett winked.

I said goodbye to Danny, promising to start attending church again. I couldn't make any commitments but I felt that I needed to. It was like it was meant to be.

Twenty-One

I WATCHED as Brett strode towards me, a huge grin spread on his face. He pulled open the car door and slid in beside me.

"Brett, what—"

He cupped the back of my neck and crashed his mouth to mine.

It must have been a good talk. I opened my mouth, taking his tongue deep inside me as a groan rumbled from his chest.

"Lover," he breathed.

I smiled at the sense of losing control in his voice. "Tell me."

Brett cleared his throat and adjusted his pants. "I will get you back for that."

I giggled and kissed his cheek. "I can't wait."

Brett rolled his eyes. "How can I punish you when you enjoy it?"

I laughed. The passion filled moment was soon replaced as Brett looked at me with love in his eyes.

"Two days, Evvie. You will be my wife."

My heart skipped a beat. "What did you say to Pastor Dan?"

Brett shrugged. "I told him the truth."

My stomach twisted. "How much truth?"

A wicked smile spread on his face. "I told him how you love it when I restrain you."

I playfully punched him in the arm. "Seriously, Brett, what did you say?"

He laughed and rubbed where I had hit him. "I told him how much I love you. How I can't live or be anything without you. How I need you. How I fell in love with you from the first moment you called me an asshole."

I gasped. "You didn't!"

He chuckled and captured my mouth in a tender but demanding kiss. "Are you ready to become Mrs. MacLean?" he whispered in my ear.

I was. More than ever.

***

I WAS happy. Elated as the next day I would be marrying my best friend, my lover. My one. My only. Lying in bed that night, I watched Brett sleep. His chest rising and falling as quiet grunts left his lips. His handsome face was strained, a deep frown settling on his gorgeous features.

My heart started racing. A nightmare. Another one. I thought they would be over since he hadn't seen his mother in a while. We needed to start our marriage fresh. He needed sex like he needed air to breathe, food to live and I was always willing to give him what he needed but tonight, I was going to be in control.

After he fell asleep, I slipped on some clothes and crawled back in bed beside him.

My eyelids grew heavy and just when I was drifting into that moment of peaceful sleep, a hard body covered mine.

I gasped and stared up into Brett's dark heated gaze. Lust and hunger seeped from his pores as he crashed his lips to mine. A moment of hesitation fluttered through me but I bit it back. I needed to be strong. For him. "Brett."

He groaned. "Open for me."

I struggled under his grip and pushed him back. "Brett."

"Lover, please. I need inside...what the fuck?" His hands pulled at my clothes, trying to tear them off of me.

"Stop. Now," I demanded, grabbing his hands.

He pinned me beneath him and licked up the side of my neck.

My body bloomed but I had to stop him. He would be grateful in the end. "Brett. No. Stop."

He growled and sat back, scrubbing a shaky hand down his face. "You're telling me no?"

"Brett, you need this."

He snarled. "I need inside of you. That's what I need, Evvie." He pulled at my pants, attempting to tug them off of me when I pushed him.

Brett fell back on his ass, his chest rising and falling with each shaky breath. "What the hell is your fucking problem?"

I swallowed past the anger and braced myself for his rage but he needed this. I needed this. "We are getting married tomorrow. I'm trying to help you get control of your damn nightmares."

He reached for me and pulled me in his arms. "The only way I have control is when I'm inside you. You know this. I...I...shit."

My stomach clenched at the desperation in his voice. Cupping his cheeks, I placed a soft kiss on his mouth. "I'm sorry. I am. I want to help you in any way I can but I need you to get out of your head."

Brett took a shaky breath and sighed. "God, what would I do without you?"

I smiled. "I also want to wait to have sex until tomorrow night, when we're man and wife. I want it pure...ish."

He sighed, his lips turning up at the corners. "Nothing about tomorrow night will be pure, lover."

I laughed. My heart lifting that he reacted better than I thought he would over not being allowed access to me. "I love you. I'm sorry for tonight."

"I get it. I'm sorry. I just...you make me feel better. Sane."

I swallowed and brushed my fingers down his cheek before running my thumb over his full lips. His strong jaw ticked. "You're not insane."

He looked away.

Pinching his chin, I turned his head to meet my lips. "For the rest of our lives, I will help you deal with this. With your mom. With whatever issues you have. I understand the need for sex."

"I don't think you do. You have no idea how addicted I am to you. To being inside of you." His eyes saddened. "I crave you."

My heart thumped. Was he upset at how he was feeling? Maybe his addiction went further than I thought. "We'll deal with this."

He nodded. "Thank you."

"For what?" I asked, frowning.

"For not telling me that you'll help me get over this."

"I don't want you to get it over it. I love the way you need me. The way you make me feel wanted. But I don't want your addiction taking control. I'm new at this whole thing but I've seen what my dad had gone through with alcohol. I just don't want it to destroy you."

"I love you. Everything about you. Your Skin. Your heart. Your mind and soul. You are perfect. For me. I'm not a religious man, by any means, but I do believe." He linked our fingers and brought our joined hands up to his lips. "I look forward to spending the rest of my life with you. God put you on this earth for me. You, my sweet Evvie, were created...for me."

Tears welled in my eyes and I swallowed past the hard lump in my throat. Brushing his hair out of his eyes, I reined kisses on his face. "My prayers were answered when I met you. We've had our issues and I know we will have more but knowing you are mine and that this is real, makes me believe that we can get through anything."

His deep blue eyes twinkled. "My one."

"My only."

The rest of the night, we lay in each other's arms. Not sleeping. Not talking. Just feeling.

***

AS I stood at the entrance to the sanctuary in the church, I gripped my father's arm in a tight hold. The last two days had flown by as we quickly got everything ready for our wedding. We could have waited, but our Vegas trip was coming up and we were going to use that as our honeymoon.

Earlier that morning we had an unexpected visit from Officer Charles. The older cop had reassured us that he was doing everything in his power to track down Brett's mom. They had a lead that they were looking into and would hopefully have her behind bars and soon. They did find his step dad and brought him in for questioning. The disgusting monster of a man blamed everything on Diane like the pussy that he was.

"You ready for this, sweet pea?"

I jumped, my thoughts interrupted and I looked up at my dad.

He raised an eyebrow. "Distracted?"

"I'm fine." I smiled reassuringly and let out a deep breath. Seeing the hard burly man in a black suit brought tears to my eyes. "I wish mom were here," I whispered.

He nodded once, kissed me on the cheek and didn't say anything else until it was our time to walk down the aisle. The wedding was small as only a few people sat in the audience to celebrate our marriage. We didn't want a huge wedding and only invited a couple of people.

Brett's sister had greeted me while I was in the bathroom and hugged the life out of me. For a small woman, she sure was strong.

I wished Everett was there also but no one had been able to get a hold of my brother. Last night I had gotten a text from an unknown number wishing me good luck on my wedding day. I could only assume it was from him.

The music switched and we started walking down the aisle. The tiny hairs on my body tingled as everyone stared at me but the only one I cared about was Brett. He stood at the end, waiting for me. Kane stood beside him, a huge grin on his face and he clapped a hand on Brett's shoulder like a proud father.

Brett's deep blue eyes drew me in, pulling me forward as I took the small steps towards him. At that moment, I stopped forcing my dad to pause beside me.

Small gasps sounded around me but the look on Brett's face let me know that he knew I wasn't running. Never. But I needed a moment.

"Evvie?"

"I want to walk the rest of the way by myself," I said to my dad without taking my eyes off of Brett.

"Okay." My dad kissed my cheek, walked up to Brett and whispered something in his ear. My father nodded towards me and blew me a kiss.

Brett grinned, his eyes heating with a love so deep, it practically tugged me towards him. I could almost hear him say, *Come to me, lover. Show everyone here how much you love me.*

A giggle escaped my lips and I quickly walked the rest of the way towards him. Towards my husband. My future. *Our* future.

***

"NO WORDS can describe how much I love you. How much you mean to me. Or how much you make me happy. You've taught me to be a better man, to open up, to love. I thank God every day for giving me you. My best friend, my lover, my Angel."

Tears welled in my eyes as I replayed Brett's vows over and over in my head. They came from his heart and I couldn't ask for more.

"From the first moment we met, I knew you were the one. I'm not an easy man to get along with but you, my sweet Evvie, put me in my place. You teach me. You love me. You see me. You're my one. My only."

I looked at the gold double band set on my ring finger. My stomach flipped. Mrs. MacLean. I was now Mrs. Brett MacLean.

"I will spend the rest of my life making you happy. I will make it my mission to keep that smile on your face. God gave me a gift when he brought you into my life. We've had our ups and downs but we're stronger than ever. I love you, Evvie Neal, and I look forward to spending the rest of our lives showing you how much."

A sigh of bliss left my lips as I let the words that came from Brett's heart wash over me.

"I like knowing that I put that smile on your face."

I grinned at the deep voice in my ear.

Brett grabbed my hand and kissed my ring finger before pinching my chin. "I plan on putting more smiles on that beautiful face of yours tonight and the rest of our lives, lover."

I smiled up at him.

As the sounds of the city went by us, the only thing that I could think about was the man sitting beside me. The man I loved. The man I just married. *Mine.*

We drove back to our apartment in silence but I could feel the lust rolling off of Brett. It was stronger than ever since we hadn't had sex in two days. Normal for most but unusual for us. If I didn't want him so bad, I would make him wait just to see how long he could go without it.

After Brett unlocked the door, I stepped into the living room and pulled off the white dress I was wearing. Letting it pool at my feet, I waited. For the feel of his touch, the taste of his breath, the sounds of his groans of passion. My body vibrated, never needing him more than ever. To consummate our love. Our commitment to each other for the rest of our lives.

"How much do you want me?"

I trembled at the deep voice in my ear. "I ache for you. I want you so bad, it hurts."

"Tell me more," he said, his voice firm.

My pussy clenched at the demand. "I want you so deep inside of me, making love to me so I'll feel you for days."

He stepped in front of me. A wicked smirk spread on his face as he wrapped a hand around my throat. "Evvie, it's been two days. The things I do to you tonight will not be making love."

***

THE NEXT morning I woke to a light swat on my ass. I giggled and sighed, stretching my arms out under the pillow before turning to Brett.

"Good morning, my wife," he said, his blue eyes twinkling.

My body stirred and I placed a soft kiss on his lips. "Morning, my husband."

208

He grinned and cupped the back of my neck, deepening the kiss. Pushing me onto my back, he knelt between my legs. "So beautiful."

My gaze roamed down his hard chiseled body. My mouth watered. "You're beautiful, too."

A cheesy grin spread on his face. "You think I'm beautiful?" he asked, kissing my forehead.

"Mmmhmm. Your heart," I said, lazily grazing my fingers down his chest. "You love me for me. Every inch of my skin," I breathed as he trailed kisses down my jaw.

"You've made me who I am. Without you, I am nothing." He gripped my hips, pulling me under him and brushed his mouth along mine.

I couldn't believe that we were now married. Although we knew each other's bodies, last night was like a fresh start. Getting to know one another all over again as husband and wife.

I pushed Brett onto his back and straddled his hips. The sense of power consuming me as I ran my center over his rock hard erection.

He growled against my mouth and threw me off of him, covering my body with his.

I smiled against his lips and pushed him again. Our bodies entwined, our limbs entangled in sheets as our mouths remained locked.

Brett pushed me one last time and we both ended up on the floor. Bubbles of laughter bursting forth from us both. "You alright?"

I smiled and nodded, brushing the strands of hair out of his eyes. "More so now than ever."

A cheesy grin spread on Brett's face. "I love you. My sweet Evvie. My one."

"My only," I finished for him.

"Did you have fun last night?" he asked, nipping my chin.

My body bloomed as memories of the many times we had consummated our marriage during the night reined full force in my mind. "Yes."

"Good. Now spread your legs for me."

I attempted to do as he said although my body was caught in the white sheet.

Brett moved between my legs, his erection resting against my mound.

Lifting my hips, I took him in. A sigh escaped my lips at the sense of familiarity. The only skin touching was our most intimate spots, the rest covered by the sheets.

I could never get enough. Him being inside of me felt like home. Safe. No wonder it calmed him whenever he had a nightmare.

Brett grunted, his hips speeding up, pushing his thick length deep inside of me.

A tingle of pleasure spread through my body and exploded into tiny electrifying amounts of ecstasy.

"Scream my name, lover."

I moaned, his name leaving my lips again and again.

Twenty-Two

BRETT AND I had been married for a week before our trip to Vegas. The Saturday night, I got a call unexpectedly as I walked down the long hallway to our apartment. I glanced at the phone, not recognizing the number. "Hello?"

"How was the wedding?"

Everett. "No hello?"

He grunted. "Hello, Evvie."

I sighed. "The wedding was small but good. Where are you?"

"Don't worry about me."

I huffed. "You sound like Ethan."

"'Bout time he learned something from me."

"What's going on, Ev?" I asked, once reaching the door to my home.

"I just wanted to let you know that I'm fine and see how you are doing."

"We haven't talked since daddy's heart attack, Everett."

There was a pause. "Evvie, be safe. I love you." And with that, he hung up.

I frowned and walked into the apartment. Throwing my phone and keys onto the table by the wall, I let out a heavy sigh.

"What's wrong, lover?"

My gaze landed on Brett sitting on the black leather couch in the living room. He held a small tumbler with dark amber liquid and took a sip as I neared him.

"Everett called me. It was the weirdest conversation ever," I explained, sitting at Brett's feet.

"Where is he?" Brett asked, curling his hand around the base of my throat.

I shrugged. "He's safe. That's all I know." My stomach clenched. I tried not to worry for my family but the men in my life didn't always make the smartest decisions.

I leaned my head back and looked up at Brett.

His jaw clenched and unclenched.

"Are you okay?" I asked, turning towards him.

His blue gaze met mine and he smiled. "Long day."

"Ready for Vegas, lover boy?" I started unbuckling his belt and pulled his shirt out of his pants.

"I am ready for our honeymoon. Being in Vegas with my wife is just an added bonus."

I smiled. "Getting to meet Mathis' wife will be interesting." I had no idea what she was like but once he told me that he got married, I ended up seeing their names in the paper. Something about her being a high paid call girl. I liked the guy. If he was happy, then I was happy for him.

Brett grunted in response and placed his glass on the counter. "What are you doing?"

"My husband is stressed. I'm going to make him feel better." I lifted his shirt, pushing it to his waist and kissed just above his belly button.

"How are you going to do that?" he asked, his voice lowering.

I smiled and nipped along his waist, biting my teeth into the hard muscles just above his hip bone. "I'm going to suck your cock and then you're going to fuck me."

"Hmm...no making love?" he asked, fisting my hair in his hand.

"Not right now. I want you to give me all of you." I bit into his flesh, making him jump.

"You will pay for that," he growled, pulling back my head.

My heart stuttered at the heat in his eyes. Reaching into his pants, I pulled out his thick length and wrapped my hand around the base of him.

He groaned and sat back, tightening his hold in my hair.

"What do you want my husband?" I crooned licking my tongue over the tip of his cock.

His nostrils flared. "I want to fuck your mouth."

My core clenched with desire for him. "Guide me."

I covered the head with my mouth, closing my lips around the tip and took him as deep as possible.

A soft groan escaped him as he held my hair in his hand. "Your greedy mouth is hungry for me."

I moaned and nodded, releasing him with a pop. "Always hungry for you." Our eyes locked. Pushing his shaft against his stomach, I licked up the length. Grazing my teeth lightly over him, I kissed and sucked, devouring him completely. The smell of him, salty yet sweet, just about did me in.

I grabbed hold of his pants and boxers and pulled them off of him. His thick erection, hard and wet from my saliva made my breathing pick up.

Reaching under my dress, I pulled off my panties and dipped a finger through the soaked folds of my pussy.

He grinned. "You wet for me?"

I nodded and gripped him tight in my hand, stroking him from base to tip.

"I want you inside me," he husked.

My heart thumped. "You sure?"

Brett nodded and moved his ass to the edge of the couch.

I covered the tip of his cock with my mouth. Inserting a finger inside of me, I coated it with the juices of my body.

Picking up speed with the strokes of my hand and mouth, I brushed my soaked finger from the heavy sac to between his ass cheeks.

"Evvie," he breathed, bucking against my mouth.

My body buzzed with adrenaline knowing I was giving him the pleasure he had always given me. I rubbed my finger over the rim, lubricating it before pushing it past the tight barrier.

"Oh fuck." His hold on my hair tightened as he started thrusting his cock between my lips.

Matching the thrusts of my middle finger with the movements of my hand and mouth, a thrill ran down my spine at the moment of control.

"Deeper," he demanded.

Lowering my mouth to the base of his cock, it hit the back of my throat at the same time I pushed my finger into him as far as his body would allow.

His dick swelled, pulsing in my mouth before his release shot down the back of my throat. He came on a growl, my name leaving his lips.

I moaned swallowing him completely, thrusting my finger in and out of him as hard as possible.

All too soon, Brett pushed me back onto my knees. Wiping a finger along my mouth, he smirked and inserted it between my lips. "Suck."

I licked his finger, swallowing the taste of his essence. "Did you enjoy that?"

His mouth brushed over mine. "Your warm mouth wrapped around my cock is something I will always enjoy."

"Yeah?" I smiled and cupped the back of his neck.

"Hmm...stop teasing me and bend over."

I laughed and did as he said.

Hiking my dress to my hips, he thrust his cock into my waiting heat.

I whimpered, my body stretching to meet the size of him.

His hips sped up, his pelvis hitting my ass after each deep impact.

"Oh God, Brett. Harder. Please," I begged, meeting him thrust for thrust.

He gripped my hair and slammed his cock into me.

The rough movements mixed with the tight hold he had on my hair, brought me over the edge. I screamed, trembling around him, his name leaving my lips until my throat turned raw.

"You like my dick deep inside you, lover?" he growled, pushing into me as far as possible.

"Yes, harder." I didn't know why or what had come over me, but it felt like I needed him under my skin. I needed him more than ever, giving us both the ecstasy we craved.

"How hard?"

"Rip me open," I blurted. My eyes widened at the dark words leaving my lips.

Brett grunted and gripped my hips with both hands. "Hold on."

I braced myself, my fingers digging into the carpet as he impaled me so hard, my knees lifted off the floor. "Oh yes," I screamed, coming undone around him.

He pulled my core open with his thumbs, pounding into me. "Your hungry cunt is nice and wet for me."

"I need...you deeper," I panted.

He snarled and brushed a finger over the hole of my rear before pushing it between the tight barrier.

I gasped at the wonderful feeling of erotic pain as his fingers spread me open.

"You want me rough?"

I nodded. "Break me."

His fingers pulled at my ass as he thrust his middle finger deep inside of me. His cock powered into me, hitting the sweet spot that was made just for him. "Like that?"

"Oh yes. More. Please, give me more." The words leaving my lips were new for me and for him but I needed him to consume me. To reveal the dark urges he had slowly brought to light. To possess me. To control my aching body.

He replaced his finger with two, thrusting them inside of me hard.

The deep delicious roughness of his cock mixed with the movements of his fingers pounding into me at a frantic rate, made us come at once. We collapsed a moment later with him lying on top of me.

He spread kisses on my upper back, nipping lightly and grabbed hold of both my hands. "Thank you for that."

I sighed. "No, thank you." I think we both needed it. The feeling of losing control as we gave each other what we needed and took what we wanted, sent a thrill down my spine.

Brett moved to get up when I squirmed.

"No. I want to fall asleep with you inside me," I said, grabbing hold of his hand.

He pulled down the blanket from the back of the couch and wrapped it around us.

We curled up on the floor and I fell asleep to the beating of his heart and his length still semi-hard inside of me.

***

I WOKE the next morning in our bed, sore and stiff but happy and elated. The spot beside me was empty with a white piece of paper on Brett's pillow.

> *Gone to the club.*
> *Be back soon.*
> *Love, your husband*

I smiled and stretched before rising from the bed.

I trudged to the kitchen, made some coffee and yawned, waiting for the warmth of the caffeine to finish brewing.

As I was about to pour myself a cup of the heavenly goodness, a knock sounded. Frowning, I walked to the door and opened it. At that moment, I felt like an idiot for not checking the peephole.

"Claire," I gasped as the tall red head stood before me.

She chewed her bottom lip, not meeting my gaze as a woman stepped from around the corner.

My eyes widened. Brett's mother sneered at me. "Diane, what the hell are you doing here?"

She smirked. "Why, we came to see you, of course."

Twenty-Three

"WHAT THE hell do you want?" I asked gripping the door handle tight in my hand.

Claire looked away, her gaze not meeting mine as Diane pushed her way past me. "We came to chat."

Claire scoffed. "No, we didn't. You want to ruin her."

"Get the hell out of my apartment," I screamed, my body vibrating from the rage over what that woman had done to my husband.

Diane sneered, her brown eyes darkening as she looked at Claire. A woman I thought I would never see again. A woman I thought I would hate for the rest of my life. But as I looked at her, something was off. Her hair was pulled into a tight messy bun. Her skin paler than usual. And her high cheek bones, sunken in like she hadn't eaten in days.

"I want to talk to you about Brett," Diane said crossing her arms under her chest.

"Don't you think you've done enough damage?" I asked through gritted teeth. I wanted to rip her hair out, punch the smirk off of her ugly-assed face and wipe the floor with her. My brother, Ethan, taught me to fight and at that point, I had to force myself not to dive at the woman.

Watching his mother take a seat at our kitchen island did something to me. My stomach clenched. I felt dirty like just the mere presence of her tainted our home.

Diane laughed. "I didn't do enough apparently, since he married you," she said, indicating the wedding set on my ring finger.

I crossed my arms under my chest and glared as Claire gasped.

"You guys are married?" she asked, her eyebrows narrowing.

I ignored her. "What do you want, Diane?"

Diane grinned. "I want to offer you—"

"No."

Both of us turned to Claire.

"I don't want any part of this now that they are married," Claire said and took a step past me.

"You wait just a second." Diane ran a hand through her brown curly hair.

"Either you leave or I will call the police." I held my stance, firm and stiff while I waited for Brett to show up.

"Diane, we should leave," Claire said, heading towards the door.

"No. Tell her why we are here."

I frowned and waited.

Claire huffed but looked me in the eyes and sighed. Her gaze softened. "I am so sorry."

"What do you mean?" Never in my life would I have thought that Claire would apologize for anything, let alone to me.

"Tell her," Diane commanded.

"I am pregnant," Claire said, opening her sweater.

My gaze landed on the bump protruding from her belly. My heart raced. "Who..." I swallowed.

She shook her head. "I don't know."

A hard lump formed in my throat. I couldn't imagine it being Brett's. My husband's. What would we do if it was? What would *I* do if the baby was his? Could I love it like it was mine?

Diane smirked. "Now we got her attention."

"I swear, none of this was my idea." Claire closed the distance between us and tentatively grabbed my hands. "I wasn't ready for children..."

"Then why?" I cried, pulling from her grip. "Why would you try and have Brett's baby?"

"To trap him, of course."

I looked at Diane as the words left her lips and swallowed past the hurtful things I wanted to yell and scream at her. Not like it would do any good. How could she be so evil? "You want his money. That's why you want to trap him. What if it's not his?"

218

Diane frowned and looked at Claire. "Who else did you fuck?"

Claire looked between me and Diane. "It's not important."

Diane grabbed her arm. "Like hell it's not. Tell me. Who else could be the father?"

"My brother," I mumbled.

Diane huffed. "I told you we needed to trap Brett. Have his baby and then we would get his money."

I couldn't believe my ears. "You are a sick woman. Don't you think enough has happened since you've come back?"

Diane sneered. "Not enough has happened. Brett is mine and will always be mine."

I growled. "I don't think so. I married him. I am his wife. I am his and only his. I don't care if you're his mother, you disgusting bitch. He's your fucking son!"

"You think so, do you?" she asked stepping towards me.

I rolled my eyes and headed towards my phone. "Leave, before I call—"

A moment later, everything went black.

***

"EVVIE, WAKE up."

I groaned at the deep voice in my ear. Opening my eyes, I met Brett's dark blue gaze before noticing Claire sitting in the corner of our bedroom. A police officer stood off to the side. What the hell happened? My head pounded, a shot of pain screaming through my mind as I turned back to my husband.

"You okay?" Brett asked his eyes narrowing.

I nodded, pinching the bridge of my nose. "What happened?"

He sighed and kissed my forehead. "Claire told me everything. My mother slammed your head against the wall."

I frowned. That explained the headache. I sat up and cringed as my stomach rolled. Taking a couple of deep breaths, I swallowed past the onset of nausea.

"You feeling up to some questions, Evvie?" the policeman asked me.

I nodded and winced as a sharp pain stabbed me between the eyes. "Yeah."

He asked me what had caused Diane to knock me out. What did she want? Did she threaten me? I answered the questions that were thrown at me, not believing my own ears when the words left my lips. *Trap Brett. Money. Baby*. I couldn't believe it.

Brett told the officer about Stefan wanting a million dollars for Claire not paying him. At that point, Claire gasped and a silent sob shook through her. I didn't know what her deal was. A part of me felt sorry for her but then the other part reminded me that she brought this on herself.

We also mentioned Diane and Brett's stepdad attacking him a couple of weeks prior.

"Looks like you folks have been to hell and back. If you need anything else, here's my card," Officer Jones said, handing me a small rectangular business card. "I will make Diane pay for this."

Brett walked the cop out.

I couldn't face the reality of the woman sitting in our bedroom possibly carrying my husband's child.

As Brett joined me back on the bed a couple of minutes later, I looked at Claire. Really taking her in this time as Brett smoothed a hand in circles over my back. Her cheeks were gaunt, her eyes darker than usual. Was she telling the truth? "Was this whole thing a bunch of lies?"

Claire met my gaze. "I..." She sighed. "No."

"You convinced my husband that he was the father of your baby. You convinced him that you had a miscarriage. He left me because of you. You—"

She shook her head. "I don't know if...if Brett is the father."

"That doesn't fucking matter!"

"Evvie," Brett whispered in my ear.

"No, she needs to hear this," I said, looking up at him.

220

"I am sorry for everything. I know you don't believe me."
Claire wrung her hands in her lap. "If this baby is Brett's or
Ethan's, it will be your family either way, Evvie."

My heart thumped, my body shaking at the mere thought of
her carrying something that belonged to me. Call me selfish but I
wanted to carry Brett's baby. I wanted to give him the children
that he so deserves.

"Claire, get out," Brett demanded.

She looked at me. "I—"

"I said, get out," he snapped.

She nodded and left the room, the sound of the front door
shutting a moment later.

My body shook and I moved to the edge of bed. "What if
this baby is yours, Brett?"

Brett rose to his feet and walked around the bed before
grabbing my hand. He kissed my ring finger and then my
forehead. "Bath."

I huffed. "This is not the time." I wasn't in the mood for our
nightly rituals. I wanted to rip off every ounce of Claire that had
touched him. I knew the situation with her was before me but I
couldn't help but blame her. For everything. A part of me felt
sorry for the woman as well. Whether she was telling the truth
and it was all Diane's idea, either Claire was a really good
actress, had some screws loose or in fact loved Brett, I didn't
care. I was sick of these women coming in and destroying the
very thing we had worked so hard to take control of.

"Bath," he said, his voice firm.

I rose to my feet and stomped past him before turning on the
bath. "Happy—"

Heavy arms spun me before soft lips crashed to mine in a
demanding kiss.

My lips parted, taking his tongue deep inside my mouth as
his hands roamed over my body.

Brett released me and placed a soft peck on my forehead.
Undressing me, he kissed every inch of skin that was revealed to
him. It was so sensual, it felt like he was kissing my soul.

By the time he put me in the bathtub, I was a pile of mush. Relaxed and no longer rattled from Claire and Diane showing up not too long ago.

He grabbed a washcloth and ran it over my back. "It scares the shit out of me, knowing that this baby could be mine." His breath caught. "I worry that if it is, you'll leave me."

My eyes widened. "I would never."

"You say that now, Evvie, but I can't expect you to be okay with this." Brett wrapped his arm around my shoulder and pulled me against him.

Tears welled in my eyes. "I feel guilty because I don't want this baby to be yours. I want to give you a child. Me. Not some other woman."

"I know," he whispered against my neck. "As much as I want children with you, right now I want you all to myself. I'm selfish. I couldn't deal with you giving your love to someone else right now."

I turned in his arms and sat in his lap, wrapping my legs around his waist. "Listen to me when I tell you that the love I feel for you could never be shared."

His eyes narrowed. "We're strong. We will deal with this."

I nodded and rested my head against his shoulder. Grazing my thumb over his nipple, I sighed. We sat in silence for what felt like an eternity. At that moment, I wished I could have been inside his head. I wanted to know what he was thinking. How he was feeling.

The muscles of his strong jaw ticked, his full lips set in a grim line. The dark scruff of his five o'clock shadow made the tips of my fingers tingle.

A realization came to me, one that I couldn't believe I never noticed before. "You haven't had a nightmare since the night before we got married."

Brett met my gaze and quickly looked away.

I frowned. "You have had one haven't you?"

He nodded.

"Why didn't you tell me?" I asked, rising to my knees.

"I'm trying to deal with them."

I grabbed his chin and forced him to look at me. "Not on your own."

His jaw clenched. "I don't want to hurt you. You telling me no...Evvie, for a moment I thought you were scared of me...again."

Didn't he know me at all? "Never. God, Brett, I was trying to help you. To help us. I'm no expert but I know if you keep letting your nightmares win, they will take control of you."

He shook his head. "I don't fucking think so."

I huffed and rose to my feet, stepping out of the tub.

"Evvie."

I shook my head and walked to the bedroom, the cool air caressing my soaked skin. "I don't want you dealing with this on your own. You need me."

Brett scrubbed a hand down his face, the droplets of water running down his hard body that I tried so hard to ignore at that moment. "I'm trying to take control of them. I'm trying to deal with them without having to be inside you. Without needing to control you."

I spun on him. "I need you to control me. You won't hurt me, Brett."

"Evvie, I could—"

"No!" I cried.

He raised an eyebrow, momentarily surprised by my outburst.

I took a couple cleansing breaths before I explained. "I don't want you getting stuck inside your head."

Brett frowned and closed the distance between us. "You're worried for me?"

Grazing my fingers down his chest, I brushed them over the soft skin just above his length. "Of course I am. You've been doing so well. I don't want you having a setback."

He pinched my chin, tilting my head to meet his mouth. "I love you."

"Promise me," I breathed.

He curled a hand around the back of my neck. "I promise, but if it gets to be too much, please let me know."

"What do you mean?" I asked, turning in his arms.

"If I get too rough, tell me." He kissed my shoulder and met my gaze in the mirror.

I nodded. "I will. I promise you that, my husband."

***

"I SEE you two got married," Dr. Santos said, indicating the rings on our hands.

We both nodded, entwining our fingers.

"How are things?"

I gripped Brett's hand tight in mine as we sat across from Dr. Santos. His small office smelled of sandalwood and leather, the two scents mixing as one making my body relax.

"We've had some minor setbacks," Brett mumbled.

Dr. Santos raised an eyebrow. "Like what?"

Brett told him about Claire and the possible baby. His mother and stepfather and what they did to him. Hearing about me walking into him being strapped to the bed, made my stomach clench. I never wanted to experience something like ever that again.

"Evvie?"

"Hmm?" I looked at Dr. Santos, not realizing he was speaking to me.

"Are you alright?" The doctors warm brown eyes softened.

I let out a deep breath, my eyes welling with unexpected tears. Brett cupped the back of my neck.

"Tell him everything," he whispered in my ear.

I nodded and I did. I told him exactly how I felt. "I'm scared that Claire's baby is Brett's."

"Why?"

I chewed my bottom lip. "If this baby is Brett's, Claire will have her claws in my husband forever. I..." A possessive surge of hatred burst forth, making my heart stutter. I told Dr. Santos about Diane's plan to trap him, to take his money. But that backfired when she found out about Claire sleeping with my brother.

The doctor nodded. "I can't imagine that this is easy for you. For either of you."

Brett grunted in response and brushed his thumb under the sleeve of my sweater. "I don't want Claire's baby. I actually never even wanted kids until I met Evvie."

My heart swelled. "If we're never blessed with children, as long as I have Brett, I am happy."

Dr. Santos nodded. "Have you contacted your lawyer, just in case?"

"Yes," Brett said, cupping my inner thigh. The move, although small, reminded me of our first date. If I knew then what I know now, would I have still agreed to go out with him? I'd like to think I would.

"Now, back to you two."

I was thankful for the change in subject. "What about us?"

"Still getting nightmares?"

"Yes," Brett replied, brushing his thumb back and forth against my thigh.

"But he's not waking me up," I quickly added.

"What do you do after waking up from the nightmare?" Dr. Santos crossed his ankle over the opposite knee and sat back in his chair.

"I take a cold shower," Brett mumbled.

"Do you give yourself the release your body needs?"

I couldn't help it. A prickle of pleasure ran over my skin at the mere thought of Brett touching himself. *So inappropriate, Evvie.*

"No."

Dr. Santos nodded once. "I get why you don't want to wake Evvie. I honestly do. But if you don't give yourself the release your body craves, it'll build and build until you explode. And then you won't be able to control yourself at all."

"I get releases later on. Our sex life is healthy. It's not like I'm deprived or anything."

My cheeks heated. Hearing them talk so casually about sex made me feel like a prude and I was anything but.

"That moment when you wake up from your nightmare, you need the peace and calm of your wife's body. Use it. Embrace it. As long as it's safe, sane and consensual, there is nothing wrong with waking her up to appease your ache."

"I told him no the night before our wedding," I said and explained what had happened.

"Evvie is right actually, Brett." Dr. Santos nodded, his chocolate gaze warming and looking at me proudly. "An addiction is an addiction. Doesn't matter if it's to alcohol, drugs or sex. You're still addicted. Now in your case, it's not overtly a problem because you are only having sex with your wife."

"She's enough for me," Brett said, kissing the back of my hand.

"Good. Now, I know it's hard and I can say this from experience, giving up control is difficult but sometimes you need to."

Brett looked away, his gaze lowering to our joined hands. "What if I can't?"

"Take things slow. This doesn't need to be dealt with right away, Brett."

"That's what I tried telling him," I said, brushing my thumb over the back of Brett's hand. "He's terrified of hurting me, which I appreciate, but I want to help him anyway that I can."

"Clearly, your wife is not fragile."

Brett grunted. "Not at all. But I know I can be rough and even though she," he cleared his throat. "likes it, I don't want to hurt her."

Dr. Santos nodded in my direction. "Are you worried, Evvie?"

I chewed my bottom lip and looked between the two men.

"Tell him, Evvie," Brett whispered in my ear. "Tell him how much you like the sting of my palm and the bite of my belt."

A slow grin spread on my face. "I don't want to scare the poor guy."

Brett chuckled. "Somehow, I doubt that'll happen."

"It would take a lot to scare me, Evvie," Dr. Santos replied, his mouth turning up into a smile.

"I have a question," I said, my heart racing against my ribs. I didn't know how he would react but I needed to get it off my chest.

"Ask away."

"I..." I cleared my throat. Maybe it was a bad idea. "Never mind."

"Ask him," Brett said, cupping the back of my neck.

"What if he thinks I'm a freak?" I asked, playing with Brett's gold wedding band.

"Dr. Santos, I've had the urge to mix pain with pleasure for as long as I can remember."

My eyes widened at Brett's admission.

"The need to have a woman whimpering beneath me as I slap her ass or grip her throat, excites and satisfies me," Brett said, looking down at our joined hands. "When I realized Evvie liked what I gave her, I think I fell in love with her more."

I smiled as he gave me the courage to talk about my desires. "Thank you."

Brett placed a hard kiss on my lips before nipping my ear. "You owe me."

And I knew exactly how he would make me repay him.

"I don't care what anyone says, you are not a freak, Evvie."

I frowned at the harsh tone of Dr. Santos' voice but my body felt like a weight had been lifted off of it. Knowing that there was nothing wrong with me, made me feel better.

"A masochist can be in many forms. Some need pain to get off. Some turn into masochists because they were abused as children. Some turn into Sadists," Dr. Santos said, looking at Brett. "I'm not a sex therapist by any means but from experience, I can tell you that what you crave is completely normal."

I let out a heavy sigh. "I never experienced any of this until Brett. I've begged for him to...to hurt me."

He nodded. "That's normal, and as your husband, Brett should be willing to help quench your dark thirst."

"And I am. Very willing." Brett grabbed my hand and kissed my ring finger. "As your husband, your best friend, your lover...I am willing to do anything to make you happy, Evvie. I will curb those cravings. I will please those desires."

"Thank you. Both of you." I wiped the tear under my eye.

"Now, Brett. I want you back in after your honeymoon."

We said goodbye to Dr. Santos and walked hand in hand to Brett's car. There was a lift in my step and although everything wasn't fine and well, we had each other. And with that, we could get through anything that life threw at us.

***

"EVVIE, WAKE up."

I frowned at the deep voice in my ear and rolled onto my back. Warm liquid ran between my legs, coating my inner thighs. At first I thought it was Brett's semen but the sharp cramp in my lower abdomen let me know it was something different. Something was wrong. Very very wrong.

I met Brett's gaze and frowned.

His brows were furrowed, his eyes dark with concern. "You're bleeding."

Twenty-Four

BRETT HELD my hand as I laid in the hospital bed and waited. I had no idea what was going on or why I would be bleeding the way I was. I tried convincing Brett that I was fine but he was adamant that I get checked out. The mess I made of our bed was embarrassing but also concerning.

"You're in good hands, Evvie. Don't be scared," Brett whispered in my ear.

But I was. My mother died of ovarian cancer when I was a child. I had every right to be terrified. "Brett, what if it's something horrible?"

He brushed his hand up and down my arm. "Whatever it is, we'll deal with it."

I nodded.

A moment later a tall man in white walked into the room. His green eyes were warm and a small smile splayed on his older face. "Hello Mr. and Mrs. MacLean. I'm Dr. Boe."

We both shook his hand and waited as he sat at the foot of the bed. "You were bleeding, Evvie?"

"Yes, my husband woke me up because it was so much," I responded, gripping Brett's hand tight in my own.

He nodded and lifted the blanket. "Let's find out what's going on." He asked me about my family history while he examined me and I told him about my mom. I had never been concerned before when it came to anything health related but now, I made a mental note to make yearly appointments with my doctor for a physical.

"When was your last period?"

I thought a moment and looked at Brett before turning back to the doctor. I couldn't remember. "I...I don't know."

Dr. Boe nodded again. "Are you on the pill?"

"Yes."

"Have you ever been checked for endometriosis?"

I frowned. "No. Is that what I have?"

"We'll run some more tests to confirm." He pulled off the white hospital gloves and sat back. His eyes saddened when he looked at me.

Brett's grip in my hand tightened. "What is it?"

My heart raced. I knew it. Something was bad. All these thoughts raced through my mind. Was it cancer? Did I have what my mom did?

"You're having a miscarriage."

A laugh escaped my lips. "Excuse me?"

"I'm so sorry."

Tears welled in my eyes. My neck heated. I could feel Brett staring at me but all I could do was gape at the doctor. "I'm on the pill. How...how is that possible?" my voice cracked.

"The pill isn't 100%, Evvie."

My chest constricted and I took deep breaths. I was pregnant and I didn't even know it. My baby. "Our baby." A sob left me on a wail. I cried so hard, my body shook. My muscles tightened as I gripped my lower belly.

"I'll give you some time. Brett, come get me when she's ready," the doctor said between my cries.

Tears flowed down my cheeks. I couldn't believe I was pregnant and losing the baby. Finding out I was carrying Brett's child and losing it all at once made gut wrenching sobs shake through me.

"I'm here, Evvie. Let it out," Brett whispered into my ear, his voice cracking.

"Brett, I can't...oh Brett. Our baby." I curled into a ball, wrapping the blanket up and around me. I couldn't deal.

Warm arms wrapped me. "You're strong. We'll get through this."

I sniffed and wiped under my eyes before sitting up. "I'm so sorry."

His brows furrowed. "Don't you dare apologize for this."

I looked away when a heavy hand grabbed my chin.

"Look at me."

Tears filled my eyes but I couldn't meet his gaze. I was losing his baby when another woman who he couldn't stand was possibly carrying his.

"Look at me, damn it."

I bristled at Brett's harsh one but met his gaze.

He cupped my cheeks. "You're going to listen to me and you're going to listen to me good. Do you understand me?"

I sighed. "Brett."

"Do you understand me?"

My jaw clenched. "Yes. I understand you."

"Good. Now, Evvie." He cleared his throat. "My sweet darling beautiful wife. You are fucking amazing. The strongest person I know. We will get through this. *You* will get through this." His eyes filled with unshed tears. "I know this is hard. I can't even begin to understand what you are going through right now but I am here. For you."

A hard lump formed in my throat. "But the baby."

"A half an hour ago we didn't even know we were pregnant. I'm sorry for being a dick and for putting it harshly but, Evvie—"

"I want your baby. It makes me sick to my stomach that Claire could be carrying yours. If I have this endometriosis thing, who knows if I can even have babies," I cried, shoving out of his grip.

He frowned. "You are my wife. My wife is not a quitter. I love you and I am sorry that this happening. If we can't have babies naturally, we'll adopt. I will give you a baby. Do not fucking doubt me. Either way, I will make it my life mission to make it so you can be a mother."

At that moment, I burst into tears. "I..." I hiccupped.

"Shhh..." Brett brushed a hand over my hair, holding me tight against him. His body shook, letting out his own silent cries.

I squeezed my eyes shut and gripped his shirt tight in my hands.

"If Claire's baby is mine, which I doubt it is..."

I looked up at him and angrily wiped my cheeks.
"You...you don't think it's yours?"

He shook his head. "I don't want to get your hopes up but I have a feeling it's not." His cheeks reddened. "I had a dream that it wasn't. Something told me that the only baby I would have, would be with you."

I sniffed and let out a heavy sigh. "To have this gift and then it be ripped from us...it's breaking my heart."

"I know, Evvie." Brett cupped the back of my neck and placed a tender kiss on my forehead, letting his lips linger.

"I just...people every day take advantage of this. Your mom was giving the greatest gift a woman could receive and look at what she did." Fresh tears rolled down my cheeks, dripping off my chin.

"My mother is a monster. That's why I never wanted children. I thought it was genetic and I didn't want my children to be raised like I was."

I looked up at him. "You would never abuse your children."

The corners of his lips tugged into a small smile. "I know that now. I always thought my temper would control me but when I met you...when I fell in love with you and realized that I wanted to spend the rest of my life with you, I was damn determined to never be like my mother. I would be like my step mother and my father. The love they had for my sister and I was how parents should be with their children." His voice became thick, his eyes welling over. That time, he didn't seem angry that he was emotional. He let the tears flow.

We held each other for what seemed like an eternity. Softly crying as one.

Wiping the tears from under my eyes, I placed a soft peck on his lips. If the baby wasn't his, then it would be my brother's. Either way, I would love it. I would have to.

"You ready for the doctor now?" he asked, his voice softening.

I nodded.

Brett let the doctor in and joined me back on the bed.

"We offer counseling if you need to speak with anyone."

I shook my head, telling him about Dr. Santos. Dr. Boe explained to us what it was and also gave us hope. He had heard of many women getting pregnant while having the disease and giving birth to healthy beautiful babies. My heart lifted at that but I was still hurt that God would give me a gift and take it away so suddenly. I couldn't help but think that I was being punished. I was a good girl growing up. I graduated high-school, worked full time and was polite to everyone. Yes, I stopped going to church but that was only because it was too hard without my mom there. Having such a commitment to the church, everywhere in the small building reminded me of her. Was God punishing me for my lack of attendance?

"Lover."

I wasn't a virgin when I got married. Did God take away our baby because of that?

"Evvie. Stop."

I shook my head, tears flowing down my face as silent sobs tore through my body.

"Stop blaming yourself, my sweet Evvie."

I stared out the window as Brett and the doctor talked. I could feel them looking at me every so often.

"Will you please check her to make sure she's fine?" Brett asked as he rubbed a hand over my back in small circles.

"I'm fine," I mumbled. Several emotions rattled through me, knocking the breath out of me every chance they could. Pain, sadness, guilt…my body felt heavy but I couldn't shake the moment of depression as it settled deep inside of me.

"Check her."

I huffed. "Brett."

"No. We need to make sure that you are healthy," he argued.

"I don't care about me," I snapped.

"Well I do." Brett pinched my chin. "We can always make new babies. We can't make a new Evvie. What would I do without you? I'll tell you. Nothing. Wanna fucking know why? Because I would die if something happened to you."

My eyes burned. "But—"

233

"No," he growled. "I told you before and I'll say it again. Without you, I am nothing. I don't exist."

He held me tight against him as I cried, again. Help me. Help us. Help us get through this. Help us be strong. Help me be strong for Brett.

The doctor did one final exam on me, giving me the go ahead to leave. "One last thing, did you have a head trauma recently or a fall of some sort?"

Brett and I looked at each other.

"Yes, a head trauma," Brett said, squeezing my hand.

"That could be a reason for the loss as well."

I gasped. Diane. She did this. She made me lose our baby. Because of her, the greatest gift that could ever have been given to me was ripped from my very being.

Her sick twisted mind that wanted a grip on my husband caused him to lose a piece of himself.

"We'll deal with this," was all Brett said.

We thanked the doctor for the information as Brett pulled me to my feet. The doctor said his goodbyes and gave his sympathies. I nodded and allowed Brett to help me get dressed. I was in a daze, a trance like state. One moment I was happy after spending the night making love to my husband and then now, it was all ripped from me. From us.

***

OVER THE next couple of weeks, I had the nagging feeling that I would fall into a deep depression since losing Brett's baby. We cancelled our honeymoon, pushing it back a month. Mathis was a good man and understood. He ended up telling Brett that he would chop off his balls if he saw us in Vegas before then.

Since the miscarriage, Brett hadn't even attempted to make love to me. Not until I was ready. I could sense the control vibrating through him and the need for me but I hadn't wanted sex...not until now. Finally. At first, I thought I was broken. Dr. Santos told me that my body went through a trauma. It was protecting itself.

234

"You sleeping, lover?"

I smiled as soft kisses trailed over my shoulder blades. "Not anymore." *Yes, please. I am so ready for you now, my husband.* I could have said those words out loud but I knew he would rather me show him with my body so I just waited.

"Good."

I looked back at Brett. "What are you doing?"

He grinned and turned me onto my back. "I'm showing you how much I love you. It's been a couple of weeks, my sweet Evvie."

My skin flushed. "I'm sorry."

He kissed my forehead. "Never apologize. I understand. I was going to wait awhile longer but you..." His gaze heated. "You were moaning my name in your sleep."

My breath caught in my throat. "Really?"

He brushed a hand down the length of my body. "I want to make love to your body. I want to be tender and give you what I know you want and need from me."

"You do?" I asked, frowning.

He chuckled. "Surprised?"

"Yes, I am actually," I said and watched as he knelt between my legs.

"Why?"

"Because..." I chewed my bottom lip. I didn't know how to respond without offending him.

"I'm always rough?" he asked, grabbing hold of my hand and placing a soft kiss on my knuckles.

"Yes."

His deep sapphire eyes twinkled. "Complaining?"

"No, never. I just—"

"I'm teasing." He laughed. "I knew what you meant, Evvie."

I let out a breath of relief. What had gotten into him? Since everything that had happened over the past couple of weeks, I couldn't help but feel like our relationship would never be normal.

"As much as I enjoy seeing my marks on your beautiful skin after I take you rough, right now…" He licked his bottom lip.

My insides melted at that small movement.

He winked. "I'm going to savour you."

"How are you going to do that?" I asked, wrapping my legs around his waist.

"Sweet Evvie. I'm going to give you something you've been wanting for a while now. Something I know you crave and need from me."

My heart thudded. "What?"

He gripped my hips and pulled me under him. "Do you want me to tell you or show you?"

I smiled and grabbed hold of his wrists. "Both."

He leaned down and placed another kiss on my forehead, letting his lips linger as he inhaled deep. "If you're not ready—"

"No. I am. Please."

"That's what I was hoping you would say. Now where was I?" He leaned down to my ear and nipped the side of my neck. "I'm going to make love to you," he purred. "I'm going to kiss and lick every inch of your skin. After I'm done, if I feel the need to do it again, you won't stop me, will you, Evvie?"

I shook my head, words lost on my tongue at the deep husk of his voice.

Brett kissed my jaw, trailing light touches down to my ear while his hands roamed down the sides of my hips. "I'm going to love your body how it deserves to be loved."

"But…"

"But what?"

I wrapped my hands around his neck. "I like the rough side of you."

"I know," he breathed against my ear. "But I'm going to show you a side that has lain dormant until I met you. A side that is meant for only you."

I nuzzled my nose against his neck, breathing in the scent of man and soap. My body quivered, building with pent up desire for him. "What's changed?"

236

"Me. You've changed me."

My eyes widened and I cupped his cheeks. "I have?"

A smug grin spread on his face. "Lover, you have no idea what you have done for me, do you?"

"No, I guess I don't."

He brushed strands of hair off my forehead, his eyes warming. "You've loved me. That's what you have done." He trailed kisses over my collarbone.

I tilted my head back, giving him the access I knew he desired.

"After what you've been through, your body needs a little tenderness from the man that loves it most."

My heart jumped. "Tell me."

He raised an eyebrow. "What?"

"Tell me again what you were thinking during our first time together."

He smirked and brushed a finger down the side of my cheek. "When I saw you standing by the patio doors, the way the moonlight caressed your skin, you were like an angel," he kissed my lips. "sent from Heaven. Just for me. I remember the way your blonde curls touched your shoulders. I was jealous of them," his voice lowered. "Your hair was touching you and I wasn't. When you stripped…God, Evvie. You have no idea how hard it was for me to control myself."

My stomach flipped.

"At that moment, I knew that I would never get enough of you."

A small smile splayed on my face.

"You're beautiful. Passionate. You see me for me even when I'm being a dick. You're patient, kind and you love hard."

"I think you're the one that loves hard, Brett," I said, running my hands up and down his strong thick arms.

His eyes darkened. "I fuck hard. Big difference."

This was true and I wasn't complaining in the least.

"I'm possessive and jealous. I can be an asshole and yet, here you are…with me. In our home."

I frowned. "Brett—"

"I don't deserve your love but I welcome it with my mind, body and soul. You keep me grounded." He shook his head. "I…I don't…"

A lump formed in my throat and I captured his mouth with mine.

He licked between my lips, his hands caressing my body, gentle yet firm.

I didn't expect him to not give me at least some of his roughness. I craved it. It was familiar. I didn't want him to change for me but gentleness was warranted sometimes. Shock still fluttered through my belly at the mere mention of him making love to me.

"Let *me* make love to you, Evvie," he whispered against my mouth.

My hands grazed down his back to his hips, our kiss deepening.

In a slow even stroke, he lowered into me.

A hot shiver travelled through my body and I moaned as he filled me completely.

Our hips met thrust for thrust. It was gentle but passionate, tender yet filled with so much love, tears welled in my eyes.

Brett lifted his head. "Why the tears?" he asked, brushing his thumbs under my eyes.

"I…don't…"

"Is my love making that bad, Evvie?" he teased.

My cheeks heated. "No."

He chuckled and brushed his nose along the side of my neck, inhaling deep. His thrusts deepened but still he remained sensual.

The control it took for him to not ravish me and fuck the shit out of me made me fall in love with him even more. "I love you," I whispered, grazing my fingers through the hair at the back of his neck.

"Hmm…I'll never get used to those words coming from your mouth."

I smiled and wrapped my legs tighter around his body. "I love you," I repeated and placed soft kisses on his shoulder.

"Again," he demanded.

"I. Love. You."

His mouth covered mine in a hard bruising kiss as he pushed into me as deep as he could go.

I gasped, my body exploding as a cry of ecstasy left my lips.

Brett groaned and sat back before lifting me into his arms. The warmth in his eyes was soon replaced by lust.

My breath caught. I knew that look. That look of aching and an all-consuming need. He was no longer in control. Our time for love making was over and I couldn't wait for the things he had in store for me.

"Thank you," I said before he became rough like I knew he wanted and needed.

His eyes softened, his jaw ticking. He cleared his throat a couple of times and he took a deep breath. "No. Thank *you*."

I brushed my thumb over his bottom lip. "Good now?"

"Yes, but I really need back inside of you," he said, wrapping a hand around his length.

My body buzzed and I gripped his shoulders.

A wicked grin spread on his face. "Put me in you, lover. I want to watch your face as your body slides down my cock."

I wrapped my fingers around his rigid erection, my hand sliding from base to tip over the slick length.

Our eyes locked.

Small breaths left my lips as I stroked his cock through the folds of my center before slowly impaling myself on him.

"Beautiful."

I smiled and placed a soft kiss on his lips before he pushed me back on the bed. For the rest of the night, Brett gave me what I needed from him. What I craved.

Through these months of being with him, I had learned so much. His feelings revealed, his past laid out before him, his true desires on display. For me.

His passion, his love, his dark possession consumed me. I was drowning in him and as each day past, I fell further and further into his depths. Not wanting to come up for air in the least.

He gave me him. *All* of him. Revealing a part of himself that he never shared with anyone. The once broken boy that grew up into a strong and powerful man was mine. It would take a while for him to heal, to get over what had been done to him but I would be by his side every step of the way.

Only *I* knew the *real* Brett MacLean.

Epilogue

Brett

Mine,

I've been told that writing out your feelings helps. Whether it's good or bad, it helps you deal with the onslaught of the emotions that soar through you. You've told me this, my doctor has told me this. I'm not sure if that's really the case or not but I'll try.

I've learned that whenever I write out my feelings for you, it's like they get stronger, more intense. Real.

No words can describe what I actually feel for you but I'll do my best and at least give you an idea. I'd rather show you but for once I'll listen to your sweet words of encouragement. So here I am, writing you this letter.

From the first moment you kissed me, I've been in love with you. You revealed a part of myself I never let anyone see. Ever. You didn't judge when you found out my dark secrets. You stood by me when most people would rather destroy me. For that, I fell in love with you all over again.

I thank God every day for giving me you. For putting you on this planet, for creating you. I'd like to think that he brought you into this world for me. The selfish part of myself believes that anyway. But I know that you were put on this Earth for others as well.

You brighten up the sky when it's stormy. You are the air I breathe. The life that flows through me. You ground me when I feel like I'm going to float away. You keep me sane when I'm ready to lose it. You love me for me even though I'm sure I frustrate you.

You're my center. That piece of myself that I've been missing my whole entire life. You make me feel alive when all I've felt is cold and dead inside.

Evvie, my best friend, my lover. You put up with my possessive ways. When I get jealous and ready to attack, you calm me. You make me be a better man. Without you, I wouldn't be where I am today.
  You are my everything. My rock, my anchor. Mine.
  I love you. More than life itself.
  Evvie MacLean. We are one. Together. Permanent.
  You're my forever.
  I love you deep. Always have. Always will.

Yours
Xx

I slid the letter into the leather bound journal for later. I wouldn't give it to Evvie just yet. It wasn't the right time. I didn't know when the right time would be but I did know that when it happened, it would be fucking perfect.

My eyes burned, straining with working away on my computer for the past several hours. I didn't know how call center people did it. I worked at my laptop for a couple of hours and I was ready to lose my ever loving mind.

"Brett?"

I looked up at the sound of Evvie standing at the doorway to my office. She wore my white dress shirt and nothing else, the cotton falling over her full hips. Her curly blonde hair was piled high on her head with ringlets framing her face. God, she was beautiful and she was all mine.

I sat back in the leather chair and crooked my finger, motioning for her to come towards me.

She grinned and sauntered my way. The white cotton brushing her thighs.

I loved when Evvie wore my shirts. They always smelled like her, giving me a piece of herself as I went about my day.

"Come to bed," she demanded softly, standing about a foot away from me.

My dick stirred, lengthening in my pants. "Sorry."

She raised an eyebrow. "You're sorry? What for?"

I grinned and in a quick move, had her in my lap.

Evvie gasped, her nipples peaking to sharp points beneath the cool cotton that was caressing her skin.

My mouth watered, itching to taste the hard buds. "You woke up."

"I came to see what you were doing," she said, attempting to struggle out of my grip."

"I think you wanted to play."

Her lips parted. "I always want to play."

Before she could protest, I had her up and bent over the desk, pinning her beneath me. "Get ready, my little vixen."

"For what?" she whispered.

I licked up the side of her neck and undid my belt, pulling it from the loops.

Her eyes dilated when I snapped the leather in the air.

I whispered in her ear the many things I was going to do to her for the rest of the night, letting her hear how much I wanted her. Letting her feel my body against hers as I took what I wanted and gave her what she needed.

Hours later, I watched her sleep. Half her body lying on top of mine as she snuggled into my side.

A sense of satisfaction washed over me. Her body I had control of, but that was it. Nothing more. Nothing less. She controlled my heart. She was my one. My only.

~ THE END ~

Revealed by You

A Note From the Author

Well now that that's done, what's next for Brett and Evvie? One more story, of course. This next part of their world will be told in Brett's POV. I'm sad to say that it will be the final book in the Torn trilogy but everything that has happened, will get resolved. All questions will get answered. I promise you, it won't be pretty. It won't be easy. But you will see just how deep Brett's love for Evvie goes.

***

Turn the page for a snip it into Perfected by You (Torn, #3), the final part in Evvie and Brett's story.

Revealed by You

Perfected by You

Releasing 2014

Mine

My dear sweet Evvie. My wife. My lover. My one. My only.

I'm writing this as a way for you to get to know me further. Deeper.

You know parts. Pieces. But do you really know all? I'm not a man of many words as you know. I'd prefer to show you how I feel through the use of our bodies. Loving every inch of you, every curve, every freckle, as we move as one.

The first time that I met with Dr. Santos without you, he told me to start writing in a journal. He said it was a way for me to get out of my head. I told him he was a contradicting asshole. He laughed. I'm not a nice person when you're not around, my sweet Evvie. I don't take well with being told what to do. This is why I own my clubs. Why I'm the boss. Why I'm in control. I need it. I can't have it any other way or else my life would be fucking miserable. The only good thing in it, is you. You are my strength. My light.

After I left Matteo's office, his words bounced around in my head and I found myself at a book store. A black leather bound book filled with blank pages called to me. I remember my fingers tingling as it drew me in with each step I took towards it. The need to have the small 5x8 book took control. It was thrilling really. It was the same feeling I got when I first met you months ago.

I never told you how I felt. That moment when I walked in on you hugging Kane, a deep seeded need to rip his face off surfaced. It shocked me to the core, taking my breath away. I had never felt that way about anyone. I told you that I have an ex, someone who ripped my heart out when her boyfriend came back. Well with her, I never felt how I feel with you. I never had the urge to mark her as mine. To control her. With you? Evvie, I have to be in control of you. In the bedroom at least. Other times? You are your own woman. I know it. You know it. But I love you more every day that you submit to me when we play. I thank you for giving that piece of yourself to me. I know it's hard to lose control. Trust me.

Now, this book is for my thoughts but I think it will be filled with so much more. This will be my gift to you, my little vixen. I can't tell you how happy my words will be. You know my past. My history. But all you know is what I've told you. Let me show you what has really happened. Allow me to suck you in with my words. The only thing I ask in advance is for your forgiveness.

With this book, I'm giving you a piece of myself. It's like a puzzle. Each journal entry a piece fitting into place. Some you may have to force until you find the right one that fits. But just know that this puzzle will reveal the real me. The whole me.

About the Author

When J.M. isn't working her Monday-Friday 9-5 job, she's spending her time reading, writing and with the love of her life.

She's an all-around Canadian girl. Born and raised in a small city.

If you don't see J.M. writing, you'll find her with her nose in a book. Whether it's her words or someone else's, she's drawn to it.

J.M. loves stories with Alpha broken males and that need to be ripped apart and put back together again. Men that fall to their knees over a wink or a giggle from their females.

Two things you will never find J.M. without; her cell phone and lip gloss. If she has both of those items, you have a happy girl.

Since starting her writing adventure in 2013, J.M. has met many people, real life, online, in her head and she loves every single one of them. Without the support from others, none of this would be possible and she's grateful for all that has been given to her.

Other books by me:

Shattered Series (Erotic Romance with suspense elements):
Break Me
Always Me
Remember Me
See Me (coming soon)

Torn Trilogy (Erotic Romance):
Possessed by You
Revealed by You
Perfected by You

A Heart Story (New Adult)
In the Heart of Forever

***

Co-Authoring with Dawn Robertson
A Vegas Girls Tale (Erotic Romance):
Uncomplicated
Pursuit (coming soon)

Revealed by You

Find me:

Please don't hesitate in contacting me. I love to hear from everyone.

Facebook: https://www.facebook.com/jm.walker.author
Twitter: https://twitter.com/jmwlkr
Blog: http://www.authorjmwalker.com

Turn the page for a sneak peek into a book that's due out in Summer 2014 from one of my favorite authors and very good friend, Dawn Robertson.

Also, check out my favorite, the Hers series:
Hers
Finding Willow
Kink the Halls
This Girl Stripped
His (coming soon)

Be sure to drop her a hello.

Revealed by You

Statistic
Coming 2014

Prologue

What makes a person tick? Is it the way they are raised? Perhaps it is a genetic predisposition. Our DNA coded from the moment of conception to write out the entire way our life will play out. Of course some things will be left to chance; fate better yet. But I can tell you from personal experience, some people are just born bad.

I always did my best, despite having the genetic odds stacked against me. Saying I didn't win the parental lottery would have been one of the understatements of the century. Yet, I was always able to skate by in life. Trying not to become a statistic. Little did I know other people would take my choices away from me.

I guess most of my problems started when I got married. I was such a naïve twenty year old. I thought the world was all sunshine and roses. He was my world, my reason for living. That was until he lost interest in me. A high risk pregnancy, bed rest, sex restrictions, and a colicky baby will kill intimacy for anyone. Breastfeeding isn't sexy. Neither are the stretch marks Liam left me with. I didn't care, and I still don't. But *he* did, and that is why I caught him in bed with my eighteen year old babysitter when my son was barely three.

I know, my life is starting to sound like a soap opera. I wish these were the darkest days. Back then, I thought they were. I thought going through a divorce with a four year old son was the end of the world. Ha. I wish I would have known what my future would hold. What damage could be done at the hands of a stranger I *thought* I knew.

Does anyone truly ever *know* another person? My answer to that question would be no. Even the most open and honest people have dark secrets. Shit they would never reveal to anyone. You know you have those types of secrets, we all do. Hell, I do. I typically would never tell anyone. Except since the world knows most of them now, it is my turn to tell my own story.

The true story of Aurora Alexander. The real dangers of picking up strange men on the internet under the guise of dating, and new beginnings. It all began as a game. A way to spread my wings, and learn the dating game after being out of it for a decade. It ended in a violent attempt on my life.

I am a fighter. I have lived to tell my story. No one can silence me.

Author Dawn Robertson:
http://eroticadawn.com
http://facebook.com/authordawnrobertson
http://twitter.com/eroticadawn
http://goodreads.com/Dawnrobertson

13767620R10143

Printed in Great Britain
by Amazon.co.uk, Ltd.,
Marston Gate.